Red Missiles in Cuba

Posse Series, Volume 2

Dennis J. Dunn

Published by Global Connections, Inc., 2024.

This is a work of fiction. Similarities to real people, places, or events are entirely coincidental.

RED MISSILES IN CUBA

First edition. February 1, 2024.

ISBN: 978-1735810096

Written by Dennis J. Dunn.

Also by Dennis J. Dunn

Posse Series
Red Missiles in Cuba

Watch for more at https://dennisjdunn.com.

Table of Contents

Chapter 1 | The Puzzle 1

Chapter 2 | Volkhov's Gambit 11

Chapter 3 | Khrushchev's Blunder.................................20

Chapter 4 | Teen Spies...25

Chapter 5 | Intelligence Gathering 36

Chapter 6 | Volkhov Stops a Leak..................................44

Chapter 7 | The Escape Plan...52

Chapter 8 | The Escape 59

Chapter 9 | Some Evidence...69

Chapter 10 | Bienvenido a Cuba 74

Chapter 11 | El Toro 85

Chapter 12 | Answers 94

Chapter 13 | The Lion 101

Chapter 14 | Who Is Miller?... 109

Chapter 15 | Another Lesson.. 115

Chapter 16 | Volkhov's Response 122

Chapter 17 | Hard Facts 132

Chapter 18 | Peacemaker's Role.................................... 140

Chapter 19 | Saint Grig.. 148

Chapter 20 | The Sniper 160

Chapter 21 | The Sword of St. Michael........................ 167

Chapter 22 | Il Buono Papa 174

Chapter 23 | Volkhov's Move.. 183

Chapter 24 | A Solution... 190

Chapter 25 | Volkhov's Two Reprisals 199

Chapter 26 | Volkhov's Third Blow.............................. 207

Chapter 27 | Commander Vasili Arkhipov................... 214

Chapter 28 | The Aftermath.. 222

Chapter 29 | The Posse Celebrates................................ 227

To all the men and women who showed uncommon courage in standing up for the rule of law and the advance and evolution of representative government.

1.

The cover design by the author depicts the Russian plan to disguise their missiles in Cuba as palm trees. The CCCP labeling is a Cyrillic abbreviation for what transliterates in Latin letters as SSSR (Soyuz Sovetskikh Sotsialisticheskikh Respublik), which translates into English as Union of Soviet Socialist Republics or USSR.

The photos showing the deployment and range of the Soviet nuclear missiles in Cuba are in the public domain and the citation for both is: Theodore Sorensen Personal Papers, Box 49, "Cuba: Subjects: Standing committee, 1962: September-October and undated." John F. Kennedy Presidential Library. Cropped by author to fit the space.

Cuba Map (TCSPP-049-006-p0064)
Missile range map 9TCSPP-049-006-p0063)

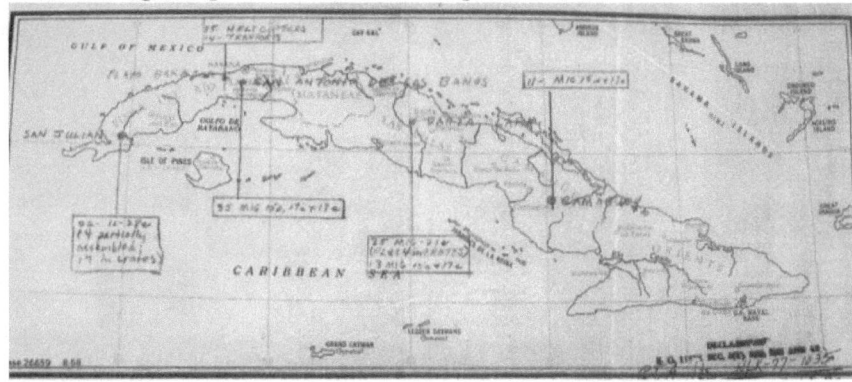

Chapter 1
The Puzzle

Comfort, Texas, Morning, October 2, 1962

A **SOFT LEMON** light spread across the Texas Hill Country and shone on the enlarged photos pinned to a corkboard wall. Edgar Kelly stood in the Sanctuary's conference room, frowning. Some photos showed Soviet freighters being loaded at docks in western ports of the Soviet Union. Tied down tarps covered the cargo and black tents shielded the loading docks from view. Other photos displayed Soviet tankers sailing from Leningrad, Odessa, Kaliningrad, Kronstadt, Murmansk, and Archangel without an obvious destination. Still others revealed an unusual number of Soviet warships and submarines moored near the ports or embarking for destinations unknown.

Kelly was America's top undercover agent but he didn't consider himself a spy. He thought of himself as a guardian of constitutional democracy, the first line of defense for the US and its partners in the greatest experiment in history—the ability of men to live in peace and freedom across the globe. He was motivated by the belief that representative democracy, as manifested in certain nations influenced by Western values, was the evolutionary fruit of God's political plan for human beings. Under such governments, and only such governments, citizens found and lived in peace, justice, freedom, and the rule of law, where they could grow their talents and follow the journey that had been set for each of them. Kelly's goal was to protect and spread such democracies and thwart the growth of dictators, tyrants, ideologues, narcissists, and authoritarians who oppressed, confused, and divided people, and waged incessant, cruel war not only against democratic governments, but also against the values and beliefs that gave life to these governments.

The greatest external enemy of the world's constitutional democracies in the post-World War II period was communist Russia and its allies, from Mao's China to Fidel Castro's Cuba. Kelly was their nemesis and worst nightmare. He was forceful but principled. He'd try to open the eyes of an oppressor to a better way, but if the tyrant had been found guilty of violating basic human rights by an independent and respected court on the basis of direct and irrefutable proof, he'd send him on to his maker for final judgment. He was the unlikely mastermind behind the demise of Stalin and his brutal regime in 1953. When Stalin's successors tried to expand communism, Kelly largely contained them. They could feel his presence but neither knew nor saw him. He was like a thick fog, moving in among them, impossible to grab or hold, blinding them, upending their latest ploy against democracy, and then disappearing. He outsmarted them with finesse, subterfuge, internecine strife, and, if necessary, a sledgehammer. In Stalin's case, he arranged for Stalin's own secret police to assassinate him and was delighted when they covered up their error by announcing that Stalin had died of a cerebral hemorrhage and then lost power to Khrushchev who used their mistake to outmaneuver them and launch the policy of de-Stalinization.

Kelly's codename was the Sheriff. He spoke several languages and held a PhD in Russian history. He served as an intelligence officer in the US Army and ended up in Texas after World War II. In the field, he used many aliases. He held an endowed position at Central Texas State University in San Marcos for his public cover, occasionally directing graduate students who were writing theses and dissertations and sometimes offering for US government agents a seminar on cryptology, intelligence, and encryption.

In the years following the war, Kelly had put together a skilled team known as the Posse. It included former and current military officers, security agents,, intelligence operatives, diplomatic personnel, and concerned citizens of every nationality and nation. It was connected by a network of leaderships cells in major cities that answered to the Sheriff and helped him build subgroups for missions. Many of the cells had close ties to the defense and intelligence agencies in countries that supported the postwar democratic order and assisted the Posse when asked. Kelly and the Posse operated from a secure location called the Sanctuary in Comfort, Texas. It was a rural location but strategically located between major research universities and military bases in the San Antonio-Austin corridor. Few outside the Posse knew who or where Kelly was. The Sheriff and the Posse only became involved in a crisis when there was a serious threat to democracy, but once involved, it meant no one would rest, least of all the badmen.

The Sheriff had teams of agents keeping a close eye on Soviet seaports, airports, military installations, missile launch sites, and satellite countries. The Russians, master chess players, moved their pieces on the international board of geopolitics with long-term goals. A minor gambit one day might have a major impact years later.

The photos on the Sanctuary's wall showed that something unusual was taking place in the western part of the USSR at the end of September and beginning of October 1962. Ordinarily, Kelly had to study Soviet activities carefully for hints of an impending development. But by October 2 there was no way to miss the moving vessels and the Soviets' extraordinary efforts to hide what was going on. He was a rational man and what he saw made no sense. His gut told him the Soviets appeared to be maneuvering to gain an advantage against the West, perhaps attempting the unthinkable—gaining a first strike nuclear capability against the US—but his mind told him that Nikita Khrushchev, the Soviet leader, whom he knew, would never risk threatening the US with nuclear war. He believed the communists were totalitarians who wanted to snuff out democracy, not destroy the world.

Earlier, he'd called an emergency meeting of five nearby Posse members to help him figure out what the Russians were up to: his wife Margo, Ana Cortez, her husband Ed Byrnes, and Russian emigres Samuel Oliver and Willie Taylor. They were all key leaders in the Posse's global effort to block communist expansion, and the Sheriff counted upon them as a sort of privy council.

The five arrived at the Sanctuary's conference room promptly at nine a.m. By then, the sun had warmed the room and the air conditioner had clicked on. A choir of cardinals, warblers, painted buntings, and mourning doves could be heard through the windows of the conference room. Autumn sage in large wooden planters mingled with the smell of coffee and fresh pastries. Kelly warmly greeted the Posse members and asked them to examine the photos. He sat back and watched them closely. They moved swiftly but deliberately, intensively eying the photos. He listened for reactions. He heard gasps and shallow breaths. He listened again and thought he heard blood pounding through veins. He swallowed hard. Then he saw their clenched jaws and furrowed brows and felt anew the fear and panic that had engulfed him when he first scrutinized the images.

After several minutes, Kelly urged the Posse leaders to take seats around the table. Some poured fresh coffee, but no one grabbed a pastry. They had lost their appetite.

"I want your insights," he said firmly, spreading his hands to invite comments.

"Are they preparing an attack?" Ana blurted out in a shaky voice, unintentionally spilling her coffee on the table. After Margo, the Sheriff turned to Ana Cortez for advice. She understood Russian political culture better than anyone he knew. She was also adept at using her beauty and brains to trap barbarians—including Stalin, who had murdered her parents and then asked her to marry him.

Kelly winced. "It looks ominous."

"It looks like the D-Day invasion," Margo shouted, jerking a hand toward the photo display. She was Kelly's alter ego and anchor. She managed the Posse when he was away and kept him young with her wit, spiritedness, and sensuality. She was also a superb chef who believed the Iron Skillet was stronger than the Iron Curtain.

"It's threatening," Kelly said, clenching his fists.

"When did the pictures come in?" Ana inquired sharply, soaking up the spilled coffee with a napkin.

The Sheriff rubbed his eyes and placed his muscular forearms on the table. "They have been dribbling in since the end of September, but most were taken last night and the day before by a U-2."

"When did the tents and tarps appear?"

Kelly sat back in his chair and sipped his coffee. He said the tents had started covering the dockyards last week and were now in place across the major western ports of the Soviet Union. The freighters with cargo on deck wrapped in black tarp had popped up for the first-time last night.

"What don't they want us to see?" Margo asked in an edgy voice.

Kelly grimaced. What he was about to say deeply disturbed him. "They might be transporting or planning to transport offensive weapons. Perhaps even nuclear weapons."

The room went quiet. No one spoke or moved for a moment or two, showing their shock and disbelief over such a potential escalation.

"That might prompt a nuclear confrontation." Ana voiced the group's consternation. The others nodded, their faces tight with concern.

"Could the whole thing be a training exercise?" Ed Byrnes offered another potential explanation for the Soviet actions. Byrnes, Ana's husband, was a close friend of the Sheriff. The Air Force veteran held a degree in Russian history and oversaw the State Department's Russian desk. He had come to Central Texas State University as a graduate student to study with Kelly. Ed ended up working with the Posse and meeting Ana. The couple had two children, nineteen-year-old Jesse and sixteen-year-old Meg. He respected Kelly but didn't like his overbearing manner and thought the Sheriff should pay more attention to him than Ana.

Kelly shook his head. "It's not a dress rehearsal. It's opening night. The Soviets are working furiously on many fronts in secret. If the material being loaded isn't offensive weapons—say, economic aid or, as you suggest, a drill—why the haste and stealth? The only logical explanation is that the cargo would be harmful to US interests if it can reach its destination without being identified and stopped. The warships and submarines are for protection of the freighters and their tankers. Some of the meandering ships are decoys to cloak the destination of the cargo ships. That's my take."

"Then the key questions are what is the cargo and where is it headed," Margo said emphatically.

Samuel Oliver and Willie Taylor nodded in unison. Born in the Soviet Union, they'd emigrated to the US after the Bolshevik Revolution. They taught with their wives at a university in Austin. Valued members of the Posse, they'd played pivotal roles in bringing Stalin to justice.

Kelly leaned forward in his chair and eyed Oliver and Taylor. They regularly read and analyzed Soviet newspapers and journals and listened to Soviet broadcasts. "Has any information appeared in Soviet media about what we're seeing in the photos?"

Oliver shook his head. "Nothing on upcoming military operations during the past twelve months in Soviet newspapers or Radio Moscow broadcasts."

Taylor added that the Soviet Ministry of Defense's publications, including *Red Star*, contained no hints of any planned naval operation. Both men said there were articles criticizing China and a series of stories about Soviet aid to expand communism in Southeast Asia and

Africa and a barely visible thread of a story on Soviet aid to Cuba and Latin America.

Ana pushed away her half empty coffee cup. "What did the Soviet media say about Cuba and Latin America?"

Taylor leaned an elbow on the table. "The newspapers indicated that the USSR is proud of its new ally and had increased military aid to Cuba." He added that the few articles on military aid to Cuba stressed that the aid was modest and defensive in nature.

Margo looked at Kelly. "Is that in line with US intelligence?"

Kelly sat back. He said US intelligence had reported that about thirty-five hundred Soviet "agricultural and irrigation specialists" had constructed eight defensive Surface-to-Air Missile (SAM) batteries in Cuba with a slant range of twenty-five miles. The so-called specialists, he said, were military personnel, a transparent example of *maskirovka*, the Soviet doctrine of deception and denial. US intelligence had also indicated that Cuba was sending small-caliber weapons to rebels in Venezuela and other countries in Latin America.

"Is there any evidence that the activity in the photos is connected to Cuba?" Ana pushed her black hair back.

Kelly shrugged. "No evidence, but it's a strong possibility. Castro is an ardent communist who rashly pushes the communist campaign against democracy and demands Soviet weapons to defend his government against a rerun of the Bay of Pigs. Cuba is only ninety miles from Florida. Nuclear weapons in Cuba would be an existential threat not only to the US, but to the world itself."

Kelly went on to say that the US was concerned about the Soviet Union's policy in Cuba. President Kennedy had specifically apprised Moscow that any offensive military aid would be blocked and would result in dire consequences. Congress had also passed a resolution to thwart any attempt by Moscow to establish a military base in Cuba. With the executive branch, it was investigating possible Soviet violation of the Monroe Doctrine and the Rio Treaty.

"Is there any reason to suggest that Cuba is not in play?" Ed said, leaning forward in his chair.

Kelly nodded. "The distance from Russia to Cuba is huge, over eight thousand miles, and it'd take weeks for Russian ships to reach the Caribbean, particularly given their present pace and evasive maneuvers. We've time to take preventative action. Second, given Russian deviousness, Cuba could be a decoy for a move somewhere else."

"We need to know what the Soviets are hiding under those tarps," Margo said, folding her hands.

Kelly nodded. "We have caught the Soviets in a major initiative and it probably involves Cuba, but it could involve more than Cuba. We don't know what they're planning. They must know we're watching because of the extraordinary efforts to hide the freighters' cargo and its destination."

Ana turned to face him. "We know Khrushchev is boorish but not stupid. Certainly, he'd never listen to a hothead like Castro. What could lead him to try something as rash as moving offensive weapons, perhaps, nuclear missiles, to places where there are none?"

Kelly appreciated Ana's push. She was a strategic thinker. He looked at her and then the other Posse members. "I'm concerned about Yuri Volkhov. Acting director of the KGB, he leads the Kobaists, a neo-Stalinist faction. They're fanatical communists. I think Volkhov and the Kobaists have goaded Khrushchev into doing something reckless in the belief that the US would make concessions in the face of an impetuous, malevolent threat."

"By opening the Pandora's box of nuclear war?" Ana groaned, shaking her head in disbelief. "It's always the authoritarian states that deliberately jeopardize peace and prosperity to push their repressive, hubristic ideology."

Kelly and the other Posse members nodded. They knew democracy and freedom were fragile, but now for the first time in history the zealots had the power to eviscerate in a flash not only democratic states but the entire world. The Sheriff and Posse leaders agreed they had to move against the USSR's threatening behavior, but a permanent solution required removing the communists and developing a long-term effort to grow democracy in Russia.

"So, what's the plan?" Margo said abruptly, sitting back in her chair.

The Sheriff took a deep breath. The photos showed that the Soviets had launched a massive, secret naval operation that was both brazen and hurried. It was a mounting, unprecedented danger. He was uneasy and sensed the Posse leaders were shaken too, but he had to get proof of the full nature and extent of the menace.

He told the Posse that President Kennedy had set a deadline of mid-October to gather hard evidence of the Soviet scheme. He said the president realized that a timebomb was ticking, but it was a powder keg with a long fuse, so there was time to find out what the Soviets were up to and then to develop and execute a counterplan.

Kelly ordered the Posse to track and analyze all Soviet ships on the high seas to get a sense of their likely destination. He said he'd slip a spy or two into the Leningrad dockyards to find out what kind of cargo was being loaded on the freighters. "Once we have answers, especially about what the cargo is and where it's going," he said, "I will brief the president and then we will set a trap for the Russian ships, much like the English did to the Nazi battleship *Graf Spree* in 1939. We will gather in Washington on October 12 and assess and organize the evidence before we deliver it to JFK."

The Sheriff's plan was deliberately restrained. It reflected his agreement with JFK that there was a window to gather evidence and design a countermove to neutralize the Soviet menace. But it also revealed a lingering skepticism. He couldn't quite believe what appeared to be happening. Although he knew there were fanatics in Soviet Russia, he was confident that they could be controlled by Khrushchev. He misunderstood Khrushchev's desperation and

Volkhov's utter dogmatism. Armageddon knocked on the door, and he and the world were not prepared for it.

Chapter 2
Volkhov's Gambit

Moscow, Morning, October 3, 1962

VOLKHOV STOOD LOOKING through the tall window of his fifth-floor apartment in the House of the Embankment across the glistening Moscow River to the crenellated red brick walls of the Kremlin. The outdoor temperature was warming, portending a rare summerlike October day. His flat was hot and stuffy. There was no air conditioning, and the windows were stuck shut. The sun flashed through drifting clouds that looked like layered white cannon balls.

A silver-plated samovar of steaming black tea flavored with cinnamon, cloves, and orange peels rested on a sideboard against the back wall of the flat. The smell of freshly baked *ponchiki* pastries dusted with powdered sugar and made with farmer's cheese mingled with the spicy tea to fill the room with a sweet, tangy aroma.

The ten men and one woman sitting on red vinyl padded chairs around the oval walnut table wanted, like him, to be in the Kremlin. Instead, Nikita Khrushchev sat there. When Stalin died, Khrushchev had outmaneuvered them and their allies. He became the general secretary of the Soviet Communist Party and pursued liberalizing policies that modified Stalin's autocratic and violent ways and personality cult.

Volkhov led the Kobaists, a group of neo-Stalinists who were determined to rebuild the Stalinist dictatorship. He preferred to stay in the shadows and pull the strings of power. He was brilliant,

11

unscrupulous, capricious, and a communist through and through. Lavrenti Beria, Stalin's watchdog, had trained him. Many top leaders on the Presidium, the highest governing body that surrounded Khrushchev, supported him. Some did so openly, others clandestinely. A big man, he liked violence and street fighting. Rumor had it that he had killed a dozen men with his bare hands.

Volkhov's base of power was the KGB—*Komitet Gosudarstvennoy Beozopasnosti*, or Committee for State Security, commonly called the secret police.. His men dominated the KGB. He had dossiers on every Presidium member, which gave him enormous leverage in the event of a showdown with Khrushchev and his supporters. He also maintained a secret file on all the bastards whom Stalin had sired. He thought one or more of these children would someday lead a resurrected authoritarian state.

The Kobaists wanted to restart the global revolution and to push the Americans out of their leadership position. They wanted Khrushchev, whom they detested, to do their bidding or to get out of the way. They worked to spread authoritarianism around the globe, much like Stalin had before, during, and after World War II.

Volkhov's eleven colleagues were the deputy leaders of various government agencies and the worker bees of the Kobaist movement. He believed that most of them would follow him blindly. The bigwigs on the Presidium, powerbrokers like Leonid Brezhnev and Alexei Kosygin, would listen to the Kobaists when the chips were down, but they played a waiting game to see if Khrushchev would stumble.

Volkhov considered Khrushchev weak, but he had to be careful. The general secretary had allies. He sensed, however, that the balance of power was shifting.

Massive problems loomed from Berlin to Beijing. Khrushchev, nimble and always one step ahead of the Kobaists, was frustrated by the intractability of the issues. Increasingly, he turned to the Kobaists for advice and action. Volkhov knew Khrushchev's outreach was temporary and desperate, but he had a plan to box Khrushchev in, win the day for communism's advance, and perhaps unseat the man.

Volkhov poured himself a cup of hot tea and sat down at the head of the table. "Comrades," he said in a deep, loud voice, "it is time to act." Everyone came to attention, anticipating what he would say. They likely hoped he would deliver a careful plan to kneecap Khrushchev and give them power.

He had a plan, but it wasn't careful. It was more dangerous and frightening than any of them could imagine. He was eager to share it so that they too could thrill to this daring gambit. He yearned to explain what it meant to be on fire for communism.

"We have waited patiently for Khrushchev to push the revolution," Volkhov said. "Instead, he has weakened the revolution. He has diluted the Stalinist movement."

Volkhov sat back. He extended his open hands to the group and waited for his conspirators, some of whom he had rehearsed for this moment, to reinforce the verdict and set the stage for his dramatic announcement.

"Khrushchev is an embarrassment," Iosif Grigulevich declared in a deep, gravelly voice that sounded like a croaking frog. He poured himself a cup of tea. Grigulevich was Volkhov's assistant, forceful and scary—and the most experienced secret agent in Soviet history. Under Stalin, he was the USSR's top spy. He spoke a dozen languages, had managed Trotsky's assassination in Mexico in 1940, and had finagled his way into the confidence of the Costa Rican government, using the alias Teodoro B. Castro. Costa Rica had named him ambassador to Italy and Yugoslavia with residency in Rome in 1952.

In Rome, he became a favorite of Italian politicians who welcomed him into their social circle. He also befriended bishops and cardinals in Vatican City and was astute on Vatican politics. He'd been working on a Tito hit when Stalin died unexpectedly in 1953.

To his surprise, Khrushchev recalled him to Moscow and forced him into retirement. Many diplomats in Italy never knew that he was a Soviet spy. When he suddenly disappeared, rumors flew that the mafia had kidnapped and killed him, his wife, and two daughters.

The Vatican and Costa Rican officials found out who and where he was after the Sheriff ran his fingerprints in 1953. Embarrassed to admit that they had been taken in by Teodoro B. Castro, they never dismissed the rumors.

Volkhov brought Grigulevich out of retirement and made him his top hatchet man. He valued Grigulevich's psychopathic personality. The cold-blooded killer had a suave and charming personality. But the acting KGB head saw Grigulevich for what he was: an insincere toady who could turn on him. Volkhov regularly reminded Grigulevich that he was in charge and could have him shot.

Grigulevich moved with the prevailing wind. He used his charm to ingratiate himself with the powerful. His job today was to stress that the Soviets' advantage in any contest with the United States was that history was on their side, that the future belonged to them. And that the way to reignite the revolution was to replace Khrushchev's weak and timid leadership with Volkhov's decisiveness and competence.

He started by arguing that Khrushchev had brought the USSR to the brink of disaster by fumbling the Suez Crisis, mismanaging the Hungarian Revolution, botching relations with Mao and Tito, and mishandling West Germany, the United States, and NATO. With a fawning bow to Volkhov, which made Volkhov smile and the others frown with envy, he declared that Volkhov had saved the day in each of these calamities by forcing Khrushchev to act with force and resolution. He ended by declaring that Volkhov "is a genius who will lead us to victory."

Deputy defense minister Dmitri Ulitsky placed his empty teacup on the table. Volkhov admired Ulitsky's zeal and toughness. He was no slouch went it came to lauding Volkhov, but today he was reserved.

He wanted to hear Volkhov's plan. He followed Grigulevich's lead and charged, angrily, that under Khrushchev the USSR had lost its fire and swagger and now faced challenges from Chinese parvenues and Eastern European nationalists.

Sophie Ustinova, another stalwart Stalinist, stood up. Volkhov appreciated her doggedness and visceral love of communism. She was the deputy director of Komsomol, the communist youth league. She laid down a blistering attack on Khrushchev, saying he had divided the communist movement by attacking Stalinism, preaching peaceful coexistence, and pussyfooting around with religious believers and intellectual dissidents. She said it was time to push the revolution forward, not retreat into peacemaking with capitalists, backsliders, and dissidents.

Ustinova would have continued, but Volkhov nodded and gestured to her chair. She sat and waited for Volkhov's revelation.

"Comrades," Volkhov said excitedly, hitting the table with his fist and rattling nearby teacups. "It's all true! But now we are going to corner Khrushchev and compel him to face down the United States and push the international revolution. The Americans have strengths, but they're declining with age."

"It's time to slam them!" Ulitsky said, leaning forward.

Volkhov nodded and sipped his tea. He then stood up and set the stage for what he had in mind. He said the USSR would soon be able to force the Americans to abandon West Berlin, give Taiwan to Mao, and shut down the Russian-language radio broadcasts from Munich—Radio Free Europe and Radio Liberty. He also said that the Soviets would have the power to make the Americans leave Guantanamo naval base in Cuba, give up efforts to contain communism's expansion in Latin America and Africa, and remove their Jupiter missiles from Turkey. Volkhov sat down and bit his lip in anticipation, watching the excitement in his comrades' eyes grow.

"What is it?" Ulitsky shouted in a shrill voice. "What's the plan that will give us the upper hand?"

Volkhov placed his teacup on the table. "Its success depends on utter secrecy." He stopped and took a deep breath. "We're installing nuclear ballistic missiles in nine clandestine sites in Cuba. From there, they can reach most major cities in the United States!"

There was silence in the room as the temerity of the move and its attendant risk sank in. The United States was a superpower with the most formidable military in the world. It had ICBMs, intercontinental ballistic missiles whose range pushed to ninety-three hundred miles. It had nuclear submarines armed with Polaris missiles with a range of twenty-five hundred nautical miles. It also had Jupiter missiles in Turkey and Italy. Its nuclear arsenal was superior to the Soviet Union's in range and strategic positioning.

Ulitsky's eyes bulged. "Oh, nyet, Yuri, what are you thinking?" he blurted out in a shocked, choppy voice, choking on his half-eaten pastry. "Have our allies on the Presidium signed off on this plan—Brezhnev, Kosygin, and the others? Has Khrushchev accepted it?"

"Da!" Volkhov exclaimed, jumping to his feet. "Everyone, including Khrushchev, has endorsed it on the condition that the missiles not be fired but used to bluff the Americans to make concessions."

Volkhov must have startled Oleg Donovsky, the deputy minister of foreign affairs. He openly defied Volkhov. "Why would they make concessions?" Donovsky demanded. "Tolstoy said the two most powerful warriors are patience and time."

"Tolstoy was a novelist, not a general," Volkhov said dryly, noting Donovsky's caution. He believed his plan was failsafe, so there was no need for prudence. "If we're careful, the US will make concessions for three solid reasons. We have sophisticated rocket and thrust technology, our nuclear weapons have greater yield than those of the

US, and John F. Kennedy is in the White House. Kennedy is a weak, inexperienced leader whose father bought him the presidency."

No one spoke at first. The idea of secretly placing nuclear missiles in the shadow of the United States had left most of the group aghast. Volkhov's troika of reasons for why Washington would not react didn't square with the reality that the United States was by far the most powerful nation in the world. Volkhov would have to provide more information to bring his comrades along.

Grigulevich, leaning back against his chair, broke the somber mood by asking a logistical question. "How are we getting the missiles into Cuba?"

Volkhov was grateful for the opening. In the eyes of his comrades, he saw excitement but also trepidation. To reassure them, he answered Grigulevich's question in some detail. He told them that the missiles were being loaded onto freighters and would soon be transported to Cuba. Once there, they'd be armed with nuclear warheads, stockpiled in Cuba since late summer, and then deployed to look like palm trees. They'd be protected by SAMs and operated and maintained by nearly forty-two thousand Soviet military personnel, disguised as civilians, who were already in Cuba.

He told them about Migs-21 jetfighters and Il-28 light bombers capable of carrying nuclear weapons, both already deployed in Cuba. He added that when the missiles were near operational status, submarines from Kronstadt and a naval flotilla from Kaliningrad and Murmansk would arrive in Cuban waters to provide more firepower for defense. Other naval forces were being deployed to the Mediterranean, Baltic, North Atlantic, and South Atlantic to distract the Americans.

"How are you keeping this secret from the Americans whose U-2s are flying over our ports?" Donovsky asked.

Volkhov was ready for this objection. He said that there was a multipart plan to distract the Americans and reduce their suspicion. He quickly explained the tents, tarps, and decoy ships. He added that the Russians were continuing with and enhancing friendly activities with the Americans, including an Intourist-sponsored American student tour, the disarmament and European security talks in Geneva and Vienna, United Nations meetings, and a new initiative led by Viktor Petrov at the TASS news agency in Washington to pay American writers to boost the image of the USSR in the Western press. He also said that he and Khrushchev had agreed to send Russian Orthodox and Catholic clerical delegations from the Soviet Union and its satellite countries to the Second Vatican II Council that opened on October 11. The move burnished the reputation of the communist states as peaceful, respectful members of the international community that wished to engage in dialogue with people who had different cultural values. He added, with a smirk, that he had slipped five KGB agents, including a sniper, among the delegates to keep the delegates in line and to muddy up discreetly the reputation of the Pope John XXIII and the Catholic Church.

Finally, he told them about one last trick to distract the Americans from Cuba. He said the Soviets and the Americans had been meeting in Washington to enhance the ALSIB commemoration, the annual celebration of the Alaskan-Siberian air route that brought Lend-Lease aid to the Soviet Union during the Second World War. The meetings would continue and be expanded to build a spirit of amity. "The Americans will be blindsided when the missiles are displayed," he said with a wicked laugh.

Volkhov sat back in his chair with an air of confidence and waited for a reaction.

"What's the timetable?" Ulitsky asked. His excited voice showed that he relished being part of a scheme to turn the Cold War in Russia's favor.

Volkhov beamed. Ulitsky had caught fire. He told the group that the missile sites were being built now and should be fully operational by the end of October or beginning of November.

"I can't believe Khrushchev is endorsing this course of action," Ustinova said, inadvertently challenging Volkhov.

Volkhov said the Soviet leader was on board because nothing else had worked. His mind opened to the strategy of aggression after the Vienna Summit. There, he saw Kennedy wilt in the face of his verbal attacks and the building of the Berlin Wall. Volkhov repeated Khrushchev's quip: "Why not throw a hedgehog at Uncle Sam's pants?"

The group smiled in unison. He had everything covered. They liked what they had heard. Donovsky confirmed his perception.

"Yuri, you are the master," Donovsky said. "You will go down in history as the new Lenin and the new Stalin. The revolution is on the brink of victory!"

"When the missiles are unveiled," Volkhov shouted in a thunderous voice, "the surprise will be total, and the dividends huge."

"What if the Americans discover what we're doing before it's set?" Ulitsky asked.

Volkhov's smile disappeared. Grigulevich smirked. But Volkhov was ready for the objection. He shrugged. "We may be able to exact some concessions or, if Kennedy grows a pair of balls, we may be forced to back down. We blame Khrushchev for the fiasco and get rid of him. Then we take power, so we still win."

The group nodded and grinned, but Volkhov sensed some uncertainty, especially from Grigulevich. But he didn't care if they had reservations. He planned to light the spark of revolution even if the Americans discovered what was afoot. He didn't inform his comrades or anyone else of secret measures that he held in reserve and thought would guarantee war. He was convinced that the future belonged to communism. All that was needed was a little push. He stood up, walked to the large window, and looked out at the Kremlin. The revolution was about to ignite. He was certain he could outfox Khrushchev and the Americans. Then a Kremlin window opened.

Chapter 3
Khrushchev's Blunder

Moscow, October 3, 1962

KHRUSHCHEV RUBBED HIS bald head. He had decided to partner temporarily with Volkhov and the Kobaists to challenge the United States. The gamble of secretly installing missiles in Cuba hinged on trusting the Kobaists, American inattentiveness, and Kennedy's inexperience.

Khrushchev wanted reassurance that Kennedy would understand his plight and make concessions or, at least be reasonable and provide a safety net. He sat restlessly on a stiff Biedermeier oak chair behind a small, brown wooden desk in his first-floor office in the Kremlin's Grand Palace. Although it was unseasonably warm outside and the needles of the large blue pines in the courtyard of the Kremlin were wilting from the heat, the room was cold. Khrushchev, overweight and sweaty, had the air conditioner set to frigid.

Signed pictures of Mickey and Minnie Mouse and Marilyn Monroe hung on a wall adjacent to the desk. They were gifts from Dr. Robert Miller, an American who had guided Khrushchev on his visit to the United States in 1959. Miller had arranged the gifts to temper Khrushchev's angry disappointment after he was blocked for security reasons from visiting Disneyland, a lifelong dream. Large pots of imported Russian sage with its blue flowers, silvery stems, and upright shapes filled the office with a lavender, sage-like fragrance.

Alexei Adzhubei rested on a cushioned white birch chair in front of Khrushchev's desk. He wore a white and gray wool turtleneck sweater. Khrushchev's son-in-law, Adzhubei also served as the editor-in-chief of *Izvestia*, the USSR's mass daily newspaper. Khrushchev had invited him for a working breakfast. He liked to talk over major issues with Adzhubei to get his perspective. This morning he had something important to say over breakfast—hot cheese pancakes topped with a dollop of sour cream and a spoonful of cherry preserves along with hot mint tea.

"I'm in a precarious situation." Khrushchev sipped his tea. "I need Kennedy to make concessions."

"What do you mean?" Adzhubei asked.

"The United States," Khrushchev said, "must recognize that communism is expanding. It's time for America to stand aside, enjoy an indolent retirement before being buried, and make concessions to make our advance easier. I want the US to turn over Berlin, guarantee Germany never touches a nuclear weapon, give Taiwan to China, stop anticommunist broadcasts from Munich, promise not to invade Cuba, and remove its Jupiter missiles from Turkey."

Adzhubei took off his thick, dark-rimmed glasses and put them on the desk. He rubbed his nose and sat back in his chair. A crow with a solitary white feather on one of its wings flew by the window.

"When I interviewed Kennedy at his home in Hyannis Port on November 25 last year," Adzhubei said, "he struck me as a reasonable man. He leads a superpower as well as the NATO alliance. He says he wants peace. He is interested in disarmament talks. He is naïve but not a fool. He will not make those concessions."

"I know," Khrushchev said softly. "That is why I am sneaking nuclear ballistic missiles into Cuba. It gives me leverage to negotiate with Kennedy."

Khrushchev's revelation must have shocked Adzhubei. He challenged his father-in-law. "That is a dangerous move. Kennedy might see it as an escalation and hardly peaceful coexistence. The US might misinterpret the purpose of the missiles and assume we are threatening an attack."

"Da," Khrushchev said, "but I will prove that it is not. I will be in the United States at the UN when the missiles are unveiled. I will announce them and tell the US and the world that the missiles are not a threat. My physical presence will prove that the missiles are solely defensive and will not be fired at the United States."

"Perhaps they aren't a threat as long as you are there," Adzhubei said, shaking his head. "If the US does not concede, you will eventually leave. The missiles will still be there constituting a threat."

"It will never come to that," Khrushchev said. "I will work something out with Kennedy, and I have given strict orders not to fire the missiles. They are there only to provide leverage for negotiations."

"I hope you are right, Nikita." Adzhubei's eyes showed worry. "Keep in mind that JFK is not alone. The United States, when aroused, is unpredictable and unstoppable. It might appear weak because of its divided leadership and slow decision-making process, but it'd be foolish to mistake democratic debate for paralysis. When it is threatened—and our missiles in Cuba would be an unacceptable provocation—the Americans will act as if one person.

"The Japanese tried to exploit the American vulnerability of consultation and debate in 1941 and were shocked at American decisiveness. The Americans also flattened the Italians and the Germans on the western front and supplied Lend-Lease equipment for our war on the eastern front. The plan would have to be foolproof with no loose ends and include an escape hatch for us if all hell breaks out."

"I appreciate your candid assessment," Khrushchev replied, "but you are wrong. It might have been true during the war, but not today. The American people are not committed to democracy and shared sacrifice but divided by race and class. Congress reflects the division. JFK is weak and supine. He showed his naivete at the Vienna Summit and the building of the Berlin Wall. Some saber-rattling does not hurt. Besides, I'm going to give him something."

"What?" Adzhubei raised his voice.

Khrushchev knew his son-in-law meant no disrespect and was only reflecting his genuine shock at the thought of missiles in Cuba. "If Kennedy gives me what I need, at least a nuclear-free Germany along with Berlin and Taiwan, I can then give him a nuclear-free China and an end to the constant crises that we stir up in the Middle East, Southeast Asia, Africa, and now Latin America in our effort to advance the international revolution. I will remove the missiles. The crisis will be over. I will persist with the policy of de-Stalinization. The revolution will have the wind at its back and sail onward across the globe, transforming the world into a communist paradise, with people united and happy and no longer divided by resources, religion, or nationalism. And I will undercut the Kobaists. That could be seen as victory for the Americans as well as for me. The Cold War will be over."

"You are forgetting that the US is a superpower and pushes different values than we do." Adzhubei scratched his chin. "This clash is behind the Cold War. Mao is a problem, but the US did not create him."

"All my problems, domestic or foreign, involve the United States," Khrushchev stressed. "It must work with me to live in peace."

"I think you underestimate the Americans' reaction to missiles in Cuba," Adzhubei said. "What would you do if the US discovered the missiles before they were operational and demanded immediate dismantling and removal?"

"It won't. Our people are being very careful."

"If you mean the Kobaists, we're in trouble."

A soft breeze stirred the branches of a huge blue pine in the Kremlin's courtyard. Some of the wilting needles fell to the ground. Adzhubei's words lingered in the cold, still air of Khrushchev's office.

"Nonsense," Khrushchev said, irritably. "I'm in charge." He stood up and opened a window near his desk. Looking across the glittering Moscow River to the House on the Embankment, he imagined Volkhov looking back and smiling. At that moment, Khrushchev realized that there was no safety valve. He turned around and saw the pictures on the wall that Dr. Miller had given him. In his hand he held a telegram from Miller offering to guide him if he should decide, as was being reported, to come to New York in late October or early November and address the UN general assembly. He wondered, if worst came to worst, if Miller whom he liked and trusted could help.

Chapter 4
Teen Spies

San Marcos, Texas, Afternoon, October 3, 1962

THE RAIN CAME down in sheets, a late afternoon thunderstorm that Texans called a gully-washer or toad choker. Kelly grabbed his umbrella and strode from his car to his campus office in San Marcos. The wind was blowing, and some drops of cool rain hit the back of his neck and sent shivers down his spine.

Key members of the Posse were already on the trail of the massive Soviet naval operation. But he'd run into a brick wall trying to recruit a spy from the NATO consulates or from Posse assets in the USSR. Soviet security had tightened around Leningrad Harbor, and no one could penetrate the dockyards. KGB agents were all over NATO consular officials and had closed the port facilities to all visitors, including Soviet citizens.

With his plan to get a spy quickly into the port of Leningrad blocked, Kelly turned to Soviet submarine Commander Vasili Arkhipov, who was among the Soviet Union's elite naval commanders. He knew him because Margo and he, at Margo's insistence and using aliases, had attended a cooking seminar at Julia Child's summer home in southern France in 1961 where they had met Arkhipov and his wife. The couples hit it off not only because Russian was their common language. They also shared an understanding of the intimacy, universality, and generosity of food and feeding. They stayed in contact and occasionally exchanged recipes and holiday greetings.

Kelly knew Arkhipov was a professional military officer and a Russian patriot but skeptical of ardent communists and warmongers. He held that the purpose of a strong army was to prevent war and believed, with the Kellys, that war was the last option. Kelly called him on a direct line at the Leningrad Naval Base and was told by an operator that he was not available. He then sent a telegram asking Arkhipov to call him on a secure line to talk about the possibility of sharing a Thanksgiving dinner in Paris. A response came back saying Commander Arkhipov was unavailable.

Frustrated and running out of options, Kelly decided to contact Khrushchev directly. He had been Khrushchev's guide, using the pseudonym of Dr. Robert Miller, when the Soviet dictator had visited the US in 1959. He had seen recent reports from various news agencies that Khrushchev was thinking about coming to New York to address the United Nations. Kelly sent him a telegram offering to guide him if he were to come to New York. He thought the proposal would prompt Khrushchev to respond, opening a backchannel where he'd be able to draw him out and discover whether the USSR was attempting to ambush the US with nuclear weapons. Ominously, Khrushchev didn't answer.

By the afternoon of October 4, Kelly was desperate. He had an office hour scheduled for doctoral students at the university, but he didn't plan on seeing anyone. He was going to find out, one way or another, what the Soviets were up to with those freighters around Leningrad Harbor. He was considering dangerous measures such as staging an "accident" on the high seas that'd permit "rescuers" to board a Soviet freighter and check its cargo under pretense of rendering aid.

In his office corridor, he glimpsed Jesse Byrnes, the son of Ana and Ed Byrnes and a freshman at CTSU. Jesse stood with one foot against the wall of the corridor, reading over some notes. An overachiever like his parents, Jesse was a double major and enrolled in the ROTC program to boot.

"Jesse." Kelly greeted him. "What are you doing here? Don't you have class?"

Lean and six feet tall, Jesse wore jeans and a white polo shirt. "Dr. Kelly. I'm skipping one class to study for a test in another. Can you talk?"

Kelly nodded and invited Jesse into his office. He shook his umbrella and sat down in front of the framed copies of the American Constitution, Bill of Rights, and the Declaration of Independence that hung behind his desk. A Christmas cactus with shiny, smooth leaves and a few red flowers sat near the window next to a rosemary plant. The air conditioning blew cold but refreshing on that wet and muggy afternoon.

"What can I do for you, Jesse?" Kelly said, sitting back in his chair.

"I want to volunteer Meg and me to be reporters of Soviet life," Jesse said, his hands folded on his lap.

"What do you mean?" Kelly frowned.

Jesse grinned. His blue eyes were bright. "Meg and I will be in the Soviet Union on a whirlwind tour from October 6 to October 14."

Kelly took a deep breath. "I hadn't heard about your trip. What about school?"

Jesse explained that the schools had approved the trip, an educational tour organized by Intourist. American students were selected to promote friendship, tourism, cultural enrichment, and student exchanges. Thirty students from across the United States were going. Meg and Jesse wanted to go because the itinerary included a side trip to Mongolia, where they had friends.

"Mongolia?" Kelly said. "Who do you know there?"

"A few summers ago," Jesse said, "Batu Khulan and his two teenage children, his son Altan and daughter Dureen, stayed for three months at our horse ranch."

Kelly stroked his chin. He'd often visited the Byrnes ranch, outside San Marcos. And he knew Khulan. "Right," he said. "I was in

Washington that summer and missed their visit. Khulan would be a
CEO or prime minister if not for communism."

Jesse nodded. "Dureen and Altan are the same age as Meg and me.
We're good friends. They plan to show us the Gobi Desert, something
called Yurt City, and Lake Khövsgöl in the mountains. It's supposed to
be over a million years old! Mom and Dad agreed to the trip because of
Khulan's family."

Kelly sat back in his chair. "That is an unusual destination for
Intourist. It's a KGB front, but every division has a different agenda. It's
practically a state-sponsored organized crime conglomerate, but some
elements want trade and tourism. Others want isolation and control.
Tell me more about the itinerary."

Kelly took notes while Jesse told him. They'd be in Leningrad on
October 6–7; in Moscow and Vladimir a day later; then fly to Irkutsk
with a side bus trip to Lake Baikal; and end up traveling on a spur of
the Trans-Siberian to Ulaanbaatar, the capital of Mongolia, arriving on
October 10 and returning via Aeroflot and Finnair on October 14.

Someone knocked, but the Sheriff didn't look away from Jesse.
"Come back in thirty minutes," he yelled. He leaned forward. "What
does the tour in Leningrad include?"

Jesse unfolded his hands and said it was one of the best parts of the
trip. "It's basically a zippy boat ride. On October 6, we take a hydrofoil
from Lake Ladoga down the Neva River. It gives us a view of the city.
We'll speed past Leningrad Harbor and into the Gulf of Finland. From
there we'll pass Kronstadt naval base and visit Peterhof Palace with its
magnificent fountains, Catherine's Palace, and the glittering town of
Pushkin. Intourist wants to showcase the city's restoration after World
War II to increase tourism. The next day is a free day when we can
explore Leningrad on our own."

"Fascinating," Kelly said.

"Once we get to Moscow," Jesse continued, "we spend a day looking
at the Kremlin, the Armoury Museum, and Red Square, then pop

out to Vladimir and fly that night to Irkutsk. The highlight for us is Ulaanbaatar."

"Yes," the Sheriff said. "The Soviets are trying to build up investment and tourism in Mongolia, their first satellite. And, of course, you have friends there."

Jesse beamed. "Would you like Meg and me to write our impressions of Soviet life?"

The Sheriff smiled broadly. "Not only that, I want you to spy for the Posse."

"Spy?" Jesse said with excitement. "What will we do?"

"It's a delicate assignment," the Sheriff said," and I don't want to put you in danger, but it would help to have eyes on the ground around Leningrad Harbor. The Soviets have shrouded the docks in tents and covered the cargo being loaded onto freighters with tarps. You two might be able to see what's going on."

"We'd love to do that—be Posse members and do full reports on what we see. We have good cameras, great memories, and Meg is a master sketch artist. If she sees it, she can reproduce it on paper."

"You're both observant, personable, and fluent in Russian," the Sheriff said. "You hold diplomatic passports because of your dad's position in the State Department. Because you know a lot about Russian culture and history, people will feel comfortable around you. You might hear something revealing."

"I think mom and dad will be excited about us working for the Posse," Jesse said.

Kelly shook his head gently. "It's better not to mention it to them. They'll worry. You're not doing anything that you wouldn't have done on this trip except paying more attention to the Leningrad Harbor area. Let's keep it quiet."

"Right." Jesse looked thoughtful. "They would worry."

"Exactly," the Sheriff said. "It should be safe. You'll be in Leningrad during the day when the docks are busy, but if Intourist is running the show, there should be no problems. Just rely on your natural observation skills, tourist cameras, and whatever you pick up in conversation about what's going on around Leningrad port or other Soviet ports. Don't do anything silly or take any risks."

Then Kelly warned Jesse about two secret police agents, Oleg Smirnov and Sergei Brodsky. Kelly had knocked them out in a bar in Texas in 1953. Released from a Siberian forced labor camp, they were now running the KGB's Leningrad office. "They are dangerous," he said, "but not likely involved in an Intourist student tour group."

The Sheriff went on to say that if Jesse and Meg saw offensive missiles, they should immediately send him a telegram addressed to Papi, saying "the matryoshka dolls are full of surprises." He showed him pictures of Russian long-range ballistic missiles but didn't tell him anything about the missile crisis. If they found themselves in danger, they should use their initials JB and MB in any communication to "Papi"—phone call, telegram, note at US embassy or consulate—and the Posse would extract them. Kelly gave Jesse a list of State Department contact numbers and accounts. "The Posse will have your back."

Kelly saw Jesse to the door. He asked if Meg would go along with keeping their parents in the dark, and Jesse assured him that she'd be skeptical but would follow his lead. Kelly wished the kids a fruitful journey, and said he looked forward to their report. Jesse had a question. His parents would expect them to write. Kelly told him to send postcards with touristy information to them at their home address with nothing about the Leningrad Harbor area. Jesse nodded and left.

The Sheriff closed the door, put on a tape of Louis Armstrong's "La vie en rose," and returned to his desk. He didn't like placing Meg and Jesse in danger without their parents' approval. But he was simply taking advantage of an opportunity to advance national security and to augment the teens' tour. He really should talk to Ana and Ed, especially since those two goons now oversaw the KGB in Leningrad. But the spying assignment was safe. Why worry his closest friends? And what if they refused? And why had they not mentioned the student tour?

Kelly was wrong about the danger to Jesse and Meg. And wrong about keeping their parents in the dark. He had not factored in the paranoid mind of Yuri Volkhov, the acting director of the KGB.

§

VIKTOR PETROV ARRIVED in San Marcos around noon on October 3 in a car rented at the Austin airport. An undercover KGB agent masquerading as a journalist for the TASS news agency in Washington, he had close ties to the Volkhov wing of the Communist Party and was a close friend of Iosif Grigulevich. He was in San Marcos to try to recruit Kelly as a Soviet propagandist.

The KGB's interest in Kelly was accidental. It had no idea that he was a super spy. His name had been forwarded to the Soviet embassy by a female Russian sleeper agent who met the Kellys at a cocktail party, a scholarship fundraiser held by her millionaire husband's sister. The sleeper agent, who lived in Dallas, thought Kelly would be a great recruit for the KGB.

Petrov was not thrilled about the assignment because the sleeper agent often produced bogus leads. He wanted to get back to Washington for a reception and dinner that night at the embassy to plan a celebration of ALSIB, the Alaskan-Siberian Lend-Lease airlift during World War II. Petrov hoped to meet with Kelly early but saw that his office hours started at two-thirty.

Petrov didn't know what Kelly looked like but figured that was not a problem because Kelly would be in his office. When the rain started, he was surprised by the sullen gray curtain of steel that enveloped his car. He couldn't see anything, and he didn't have a raincoat or umbrella. He waited a few minutes for the rain to taper off, but it never slackened. He didn't want to miss his chance at Kelly, so he jumped out of the car and made a run for it.

In the hallway, he could see the light in Kelly's office through the transom window above the door. He knocked hard. A man shouted at him to come back in thirty minutes. Angry and frustrated, he paced the hall. He found a restroom, cleaned his spectacles, and tried to dry off his clothes. A few minutes later, a young man with a wide grin came out of the office.

§

SOMEONE POUNDED ON Kelly's door. "Come in," he shouted, thinking it was one of his graduate students. The door opened to reveal a man in a damp dark suit.

"Professor Kelly, I'm Viktor Petrov, a journalist with the TASS news agency in Washington."

Kelly examined Petrov. The Russian was short with broad shoulders and had a wrinkled, inscrutable face like an old bulldog. He wore wire-rimmed glasses. The Sheriff wondered if his cover had been compromised.

Kelly came around to the front of his desk to greet the Russian. "Was that you knocking on the door earlier? I'm sorry I was rude. I was advising a student."

"No problem," Petrov said, smiling. "Students are the priority."

Kelly invited the Russian to sit down and returned to his seat behind his desk. Louis Armstrong played softly in the background. "Would you like a towel?"

"Yes, please," Petrov said, "and is it possible to turn down the air conditioning? I have a chill."

Kelly went to a closet, found a clean workout towel, and handed it to the Russian. The air conditioning was on a master thermostat and couldn't be adjusted. He returned to his desk chair. "What can I do for you, Mr. Petrov?"

"The question," Petrov said, grimacing as he draped the towel around his shoulders for warmth, "is what can I do for you?"

Kelly scratched his forehead. "I don't understand."

Petrov said that the Soviet Union was interested in improving its image abroad and wanted to hire sophisticated analysts and reporters who would write articles on Soviet international programs.

"You came from Washington to see me about that?" the Sheriff asked skeptically.

"Yes, but I had difficulty finding you," Petrov said in a querulous tone that Kelly surmised was borne of his irritation about being wet and cold.

Kelly countered the implied complaint. "Why have you gone to so much trouble to see me?"

"You were highly recommended," Petrov said, changing to a cheerful voice.

The Sheriff shot a quizzical glance at the Russian. He sat back in his chair. "By whom?"

"We do research on Russian specialists," Petrov muttered vaguely. "Your name came up."

Kelly smiled broadly. "I'm flattered, but I don't publish much. And I'm in Central Texas, where Russian studies are not a major focus. There are much more prominent scholars on the coasts." He raised his eyebrows, waiting.

"It's not important," Petrov said, sitting back and crossing his legs. "Suffice it to say, we like you and someone we trust recommended you."

The Sheriff decided not to push it. Who had brought Petrov to his door? The only person in recent memory who'd expressed interest in his background was that woman at the benefit party for a CTSU scholarship. Probably a sleeper agent for Soviet Russia. He leaned forward in his chair. "You're right. It's not important. I'm flattered that someone thinks I merit a visit by someone from TASS."

"All right." Petrov uncrossed his legs and leaned toward Kelly. "Let's cut to the chase. We're offering you a well-paid side job as a public relations representative for Soviet interests."

The Sheriff sat up straight. "Why would you think that I have such competence?"

"You teach and have contacts with many students," Petrov said, slowly.

Kelly nodded. "But I'm no PR person. Besides, I'm dedicated to teaching and research."

"It pays very well." Petrov grinned. "Perhaps up to $30,000 a year."

"That's a king's ransom! More than double my salary." Kelly made a show of being impressed, to convince Petrov that he was corruptible.

Petrov's grin widened.

"But is that illegal? Would I have to inform the US government?" Kelly lowered his voice to a whisper.

"No!" Petrov said. "We'll pay you in cash. There will be no record and no tax due, and you will not be a lobbyist, so no need to register. It'll be between you and me."

Kelly took a deep breath and sat back, as if reflecting on the offer. He decided to explore the proposal to see if it would lead to any insight about the mysterious goings-on in the western ports of the Soviet Union. "Are you asking me to spy for the USSR?"

"No," Petrov said, shaking his head and laughing. "Spying is obsolete. It's old school. We're looking for fair and balanced reporting on our achievements."

The Sheriff grinned. He wondered if Petrov sized him up as naïve or clever. He thought he could find out. "Can you give me an example of what you mean?"

Petrov took his glasses off dramatically and placed them on Kelly's desk. "I can give you many examples. The Soviet Union is building a better world. Our engineers are constructing hydroelectric dams in Africa. Our medical personnel are training physicians in Cuba. Our educators are training teachers in Vietnam and Indonesia. We desire articles about these activities in Western newspapers and journals."

The rain had stopped, but droplets from trees streaked the windowpane. Kelly looked intently at the Russian agent.

"The Soviet Union is a superpower. It helps its allies in many ways. Let's take Cuba as a concrete example. How could I describe Soviet Russia's effort to help the Cubans improve their lives?"

Petrov glanced at Kelly with a suspicious look. "Why do you mention Cuba?"

"You gave it as an example," Kelly said softly. He realized he had aroused Petrov's suspicions. Cuba might be connected to the Russian naval activities after all, seeing as how uncomfortable Petrov was about Cuba. Kelly decided to drop the subject. But Petrov could be useful for information. Perhaps he could even be turned.

"Well, let's say I'm interested in your proposal. I will draft a story about Soviet aid in different parts of the world and send it to you for review. What do you think?"

Petrov sneezed and searched for a handkerchief in his pockets. Kelly extended a box of Kleenex. "Thank you, Professor Kelly." He blew his nose loudly. "Your idea is wonderful. I look forward to reading your draft. Now, I have a plane to catch." He stood up and handed Kelly his business card.

After the Soviet agent left, Kelly decided his cover was still intact. Petrov could be squeezed for information. He asked the FBI to check on the background of the woman he figured was a sleeper agent. He turned his attention to finding out what the Soviets were doing in Leningrad and other Soviet port cities. For reasons he could not explain, he was suddenly anxious about Yuri Volkhov and the safety of Jesse and Meg.

Chapter 5
Intelligence Gathering

Leningrad, October 6, 1962

J ESSE STOOD ON the outdoor platform of Finland Station in Leningrad with his sister Meg. They had come on a train from Helsinki with their tour group early on the morning of October 6. He read aloud a corroded green bronze plaque that proclaimed Lenin had arrived at the station in April 1917 to lead the Bolshevik Revolution against the Romanov dynasty. Excited about being a spy, he had told Meg they had arrived to undo the communist movement. She chortled and shook her head, which irritated him. He had filled her in on their snooping work before they had left Texas, and she had agreed to go along but thought they should have informed their parents and be more alert to the dangers of the assignment. He knew she was thrilled to be in Russia but thought she was too cautious and a mite too captious.

A committee welcomed them at the station. A banner proclaimed that the welcome committee consisted of a uniformed band of World War II veterans playing "There Are So Many Golden Nights," a troop of young Pioneers wearing red neckerchiefs and waving communist propaganda posters, and a party of smiling Intourist workers, who wanted this tour to be a resounding success. Students in the tour group smiled and applauded.

Cold glasses of lemony-smelling kvass sat on a foldout metal table on the railway platform with a sign: Help yourself. Jesse and Meg passed on the kvass. It was too early in the day. Besides, it might have been made with Leningrad's tap water, notoriously contaminated with giardia and lead. Two vases of red and pink freesia sat on the table on the railway platform, giving off a sweet fragrance.

Anatoli Putin gave a welcome speech. Jesse recalled that the young man was one of several that Professor Kelly had briefed him on. Putin happened to be both their Intourist guide and a KGB agent in charge of spying on Western visitors in Leningrad.

After the speech, the group took an Intourist LAZ-698 bus down historic Nevsky Prospect to the Astoria Hotel on St. Isaac's Square, an elegant prerevolutionary hotel that the communists preserved for foreigners. On the way, Putin gave a brief overview of the hydrofoil tour, recounted some of Leningrad's history, and described its resplendent sites and monuments. He said the city had been called St. Petersburg. It was the capital of the Russian empire from the time of Peter the Great until 1918, when the communists named Moscow the new capital. They renamed the city to honor Lenin when he died in 1924.

The tour group made a brief stop at the Museum of the History of Religion and Atheism, formerly Kazan Cathedral, because the hotel rooms were not ready. The museum was filled with antireligious exhibitions and propaganda. Meg told Jesse she had seen a workman press down a stake at the "burnt at the stake" Inquisition exhibition that opened a maintenance trap door in the floor.

Jesse was excited to be in Leningrad. He could feel Meg's excitement too. She kept exclaiming on the history of the city and its creative geniuses before the communists came to power. People like Alexander Pushkin, Dmitri Mendeleev, Fyodor Dostoevsky, Leo Tolstoy, Piotr Tchaikovsky, and Anton Chekhov.

When the group finally reached the Astoria Hotel, Jesse was impressed with its ongoing renovation. The lobby sparkled with white tiles, crystal chandeliers, overstuffed leather armchairs, and piano music. The perfume-like aroma of potted, white-petaled gardenia shrubs filled the air. Despite the remodeling, the hotel lacked vibrancy. It felt like a decorated tomb.

Standing in line with Meg and the other students to register, Jesse saw Putin approaching with a bashful, handsome Russian teenager in tow.

"Your parents were in the Soviet Union in 1953," Putin said. "I never met them, but I know your dad is a diplomat specializing in the Soviet Union."

"Yes, Jesse said. "That is one of the reasons we're here. Our parents are great admirers of the Russian people, and their interest naturally filtered down to us."

"You're not spies, are you?" Putin said half-jokingly. Jesse eyed Meg. He knew she'd have something witty to say.

"Nyet!" Meg said teasingly. "We're travelers, much like your name indicates. Think of us as sputniks in search of truth."

"Khorosho!" Putin said laughing. "Both of you speak Russian beautifully. It is a pleasure to have you here, and I hope you will give a positive report to your parents about your trip."

"Of course," Jesse said. "We are overwhelmed with the warm welcome."

"I want to introduce Ivan Bobkin, my assistant in training. He's a first-year college student studying English and comparative literature at Leningrad State University. He'll be around to iron out any problems for you."

"Glad to meet you," Meg and Jesse said.

"My pleasure," Bobkin said, looking intently at Meg. "How old are you?"

"She's sixteen," Jesse said, eyeing Bobkin. He knew the communists had no moral standards when it came to sex. He wanted to make sure Bobkin realized that Meg was off limits. She was five-seven, intelligent, and attractive. She could handle herself, but he felt compelled to protect her.

"Are you a spy, Ivan?" Meg asked with a smile.

Jesse watched Bobkin's jaw drop. He was tongue-tied. Jesse knew Bobkin had not expected to be outed so quickly, especially by a beautiful girl and in front of his boss.

Jesse watched Putin clean up the awkward moment. "She's joking, Bobkin," Putin said. "Don't be so serious." He then turned to Meg and Jesse.

"Please go in and enjoy your breakfast. We will take care of the registration and put your luggage in your rooms. We will depart by bus in front of the hotel for Lake Ladoga in ninety minutes or so for the ride on our new hydrofoil boat called *Rocket*." Looking at Jesse, he continued, "your roommate is the guy from California and Meg's is the gal from New York, right?" Jesse and Meg nodded.

After a delicious breakfast of blinis with caviar and salmon, cheese cuts, egg dishes, and hot coffee at the Astoria's French dining room, the tour group, escorted by Putin and Bobkin, made their way by bus to the *Rocket* anchored at Lake Ladoga. The hydrofoil had a large cabin with draped panoramic windows and seating capacity for sixty-eight passengers. It was sleek, white with black trim, and fast, capable of flying over the water, Bobkin told them breathlessly, at nearly sixty kilometers per hour.

Jesse and Meg were the first aboard. They chose aluminum bench seats in the front of the cabin with an unobstructed view. They had cameras and notepads to record everything they saw. Other students filled in the rows behind them, but everyone had a good view of the scenery and could move around the half-empty boat.

Wisps of white clouds floated in the distance. It was warm, a respite from winter's onset. When everyone was seated, the pilot started the engine and opened the throttle. The engine roared to life, and soon they were skimming across Lake Ladoga. A flock of northern fulmars squeaked, objecting to the motor's high-pitched whistle, then flew away.

Putin gave a brief commentary on Lake Ladoga. He said it was the major source of Leningrad's water supply and served as the city's lifeline during the Nazi siege in World War II. It enabled the Soviets to resupply the city in summer by barge and in winter by trucks across its frozen surface.

Jesse told Putin and Bobkin that he admired the Russians' tenacity and ingenuity in using the lake to save the city, a symbol of heroic resistance that inspired the Russian people. Meg said that she thought every family in Leningrad had lost someone in the war and that the shared sacrifice had created an unbreakable bond. Putin and Bobkin beamed with pride.

Jesse thought the *Rocket* would slow down when it reached the town of Shlisselburg, where Lake Ladoga emptied into the Neva River as it flowed west to the Gulf of Finland in the Baltic Sea, but it didn't. It flew until it reached the outskirts of Leningrad, which appeared miraculously as a fairyland city amid marshes and swamps. When the hydrofoil finally slowed, the true beauty of the city was clearly visible. On each side of the Neva, Leningrad unfolded its charms—Baroque and neoclassical buildings, churches, palaces, canals, romantic bridges, and hideaways made famous by Dostoevsky.

For most of the afternoon boat ride on the Neva, the drapes remained open to reveal the grandeur of the city. Jesse and Meg took many pictures and wrote out copious notes. Like the rest of the students, they were awed at the sites and the reconstruction of a city that had been under siege for almost nine hundred days during World War II.

As the *Rocket* neared the Leningrad shipyard and Kronstadt naval base at the mouth of the Neva, Putin and Bobkin closed the drapes. The *Rocket* resumed its speed. Jesse and Meg knew that was a sign that the guides wanted no photos. They discarded their cameras, smiled, stood up, and just looked out through slight openings in the drapes.

Jesse sensed that Putin and Bobkin didn't object because they clearly liked Meg and him. They apparently thought that the *Rocket's* speed and water spray blurred the outside scenery. Jesse was careful not to arouse suspicion by staring. He kept looking from side to side, taking in what he could while nodding and smiling at the Russians' achievements.

Once the hydrofoil cleared the dock and naval base and entered the Gulf of Finland, the drapes were opened again. Jesse picked up his camera and started taking pictures of the shoreline. Meg sketched what she had seen. The ride ended at the grand palaces of Peterhof on the shore of the Gulf of Finland.

"See anything interesting?" Bobkin asked Meg.

Jesse had concluded that Bobkin's job was to befriend the foreign students to find out if any of them might be recruited to spy for the KGB or were Western spies. He watched Meg wrap Bobkin around her little finger.

"Interesting?" Meg repeated. "Leningrad is magical, with its web of canals, romantic bridges, and breathtaking architecture. I love it."

Jesse saw that Bobkin was taken aback. He looked moved by her admiration and perhaps the sparkle in her eyes.

Bobkin stood there for a minute, nodding in silent agreement. He then tried to draw Jesse and Meg out on what they had observed at the mouth of the river. They responded by expressing enthusiasm at the beauty of Leningrad, the courage of its people, and the engineering expertise of the Russians in controlling flooding in the city which was only four or five meters above sea level.

Jesse went on to talk about the Peter and Paul fortress, the Admiralty, the gold-gilded Hermitage Museum, and the white and green façade of the Winter Palace. Meg waxed eloquently about St.

Isaac's Cathedral, Falconet's amazing *Bronze Horseman*, and furtive glimpses of Dostoevsky's mysterious walkways.

Bobkin seemed impressed. He told them that they knew and appreciated more about his hometown than he did. He rubbed his chin, thanked them for sharing, but didn't move.

Jesse sensed that he liked Meg but lacked confidence to talk to her. Meg smiled at Bobkin, which seemed to embarrass him. The young Russian didn't say anything but didn't seem to want to leave.

"You're an interesting guy," Jesse said.

"I think so too," Meg said. "Ivan, would you like to join us for dinner?"

Bobkin blushed. "Yes, I'd like that very much. I'll meet you in the hotel restaurant at six o'clock when the tour group is scheduled for dinner. I must clean up. And please, call me Bobkin. Everyone does."

Jesse and Meg had a nice time with Bobkin at dinner, bland and overcooked coriander chicken. Three other students joined them. The talk mainly revolved around the beautiful sights of Leningrad. Bobkin told them about the city's postwar reconstruction. Meg brought up Boris Pasternak's *Doctor Zhivago*, which had been published in Russian in the West in 1957. It was banned in Russia. Bobkin said he had not heard of the book but would like to read it. Meg said she'd send him a copy. He asked Meg about her gold cross necklace. She said it was a symbol of love, which seemed to puzzle him. He said his grandmother had a similar one, but it was lost.

Jesse noticed that Bobkin hardly took his eyes from Meg. He appreciated that Bobkin treated her with respect. Jesse overheard him ask Meg what she was going to do the next day since it was a free day. She said that she and Jesse planned to hire a boat to try fishing in the Neva while looking again at the wonders of Leningrad. He wished her good luck with the fishing and told her that the Neva teemed with sturgeon, salmon, and smelt.

After dinner Meg and Jesse said goodbye to Bobkin and the other students and went to their rooms. They met fifteen minutes later in a private seating area on the mezzanine of the Astoria to compare notes on their impressions of the dockyards and the cargo on the freighters. Meg had sketches of what she had observed but not been able to photograph. They both saw offensive missiles, but Jesse said he thought that they had to get closer to the ships and dockyards to confirm their findings. He dismissed Meg's fear that the fishing ploy, which he had conceived, would place them in danger. He said that the Russians were busy, and no one would be paying attention to them. He was oblivious to Volkhov's paranoia.

Chapter 6
Volkhov Stops a Leak

Soviet Union, October 7-8, 1962

THE NEXT MORNING, with the rising sun shooing away lazy white clouds, Jesse and Meg chartered a cuddy cabin boat to explore the Neva Delta and Gulf of Finland. The captain provided fishing poles and bait and stopped the boat not far from the Leningrad docks. He stayed in the cabin and turned his attention to an old *Playboy* magazine that some American tourist had left behind years ago. The air smelled fishy.

Jesse and Meg sat next to one another in bolted chairs at the back of the boat near the fishing pole holders. They had cameras and sketchbooks close by. They cast their lines with unbaited hooks and proceeded to carefully observe, photograph, and sketch the Leningrad shipyards and cruising cargo ships. Jesse put on sunglasses in a turtle frame and watched Meg use a pair of opera glasses disguised as a lady's handheld fan, a gift from Professor Kelly, to get a better view. They saw missiles again. Jesse readily agreed to Meg's suggestion that they use symbols and shorthand, rather than literal descriptions, to reference their findings. He also liked her idea to bury the photographs of the missiles in rolls of touristy photographs. That way, on the odd chance that Soviet agents were to see them, they could be explained away as innocent pictures. "You are a better spy than me," Jesse told Meg.

After an hour or so of pretending to fish, Jesse wanted to move, but Meg told him that they had better catch a couple of fish to burnish their reason for being around Leningrad harbor. Jesse appreciated her strategic thinking—she was just like their mom—and immediately baited their fishing lines and caught five fish. He then asked the captain to cruise out to the Baltic Sea where fishing might be different. The captain said he would do it for $20. Jesse offered $10. They settled on $15 plus the fish.

The sea passage to the Baltic led directly by Kronstadt naval base. Soon a naval patrol vessel came in their direction and warned the captain to return to port because he was in restricted waters. The captain told Jesse he would get in trouble if he didn't go back but said he wanted to keep the $15 and the fish.

Jesse and Meg had seen enough. Jesse agreed to turn around, and he and Meg were back in the Astoria by late afternoon. They again compared impressions, which they copied in shorthand in notepads and travel diaries. Jesse smiled and said the fishing was good. Over dinner he told her that the hotel's telegraph office was closed and that they had to get ready for the night flight to Moscow, so he would wait until morning before alerting Washington, which was eight hours behind Moscow, that the matryoshka dolls were full of surprises.

§

BOBKIN'S ASSIGNMENT ON October 7 was to coordinate the transfer of luggage for the student tour group from the hotel to the airport. Instead, when he stopped by the office late on October 6, Putin told him that the higher-ups in the KGB office in Leningrad wanted Meg and Jesse Byrnes monitored on October 7.

"Why?" Bobkin asked, wondering if something was wrong.

"I don't know," Putin said. "Oleg Smirnov, the director, and Sergei Brodsky, the assistant director, called me separately and said it was important they had a report on the Byrnes kids. I was going to do it but have paperwork to catch up on before we depart tomorrow for Moscow. Sorry for the late notice. I'll take care of the luggage."

"No problem," Bobkin said with a smile. "I like Meg and Jesse. They're so bright and have a deep love of the Russian people."

"I agree," Putin said. "I think monitoring them will be good training for you. I look forward to your findings. I will use them in my report to the local honchos."

Bobkin knew Meg and Jesse planned to fish and look at scenery. On October 7 he was at the boat rental quay out of sight and saw them arrive. The weather was perfect for fishing and sightseeing.

When Meg and Jesse rented a fishing boat, Bobkin arranged to follow them in another boat. He didn't expect anything out of the ordinary.

Watching them from a distance with binoculars, he saw nothing amiss, but he wondered why Jesse and Meg appeared so interested in the activities around Leningrad's docks and the ships moving back and forth from the warehouses to the Baltic Sea, and why they had caught no fish. He decided they were amateurs and didn't know how to fish. He was tempted to show them how but knew his job was to monitor. He was relieved when they finally caught a few fish. He couldn't take his eyes off Meg.

Late in the afternoon, as a red sun set over the city, Meg and Jesse returned to the hotel. Bobkin went to Putin's office and told him about his day following the Byrnes kids. Putin invited Bobkin to go with him to the main KGB office. He could meet Smirnov and Brodsky and gain experience by making a formal report.

The top KGB officers in Leningrad were big—bigger than Bobkin had expected—and strong men. Smirnov wore a T-shirt of the Soviet Olympic wrestling team years ago. Brodsky's card-table desk held a statue of a boxer. The plaque had Brodsky's name and noted he was a heavyweight champ on a Kazakh collective farm. The office was painted in drab olive green and had bars on the window. A dying yellow dandelion drooped over the edge of an empty glass vase on a windowsill. Bobkin wondered why someone had not watered it.

After introductions, Bobkin asked them how they came up the chain of command. They told him their path was checkered. They had been on the fast track until 1953 when they failed to capture a young lady called Ana Cortez whom Stalin wanted to marry. Then they had their asses kicked by some lowdown cowboy in San Marcos, Texas.

Bobkin was incredulous. "One cowboy beat both of you?"

"He had help," Smirnov said defensively.

Smirnov and Brodsky continued with their story. They said Stalin sent them to a Siberian work camp where they had time to think about their mistakes. They got out in 1958 and again moved up the ranks and now led the Leningrad office. Then Smirnov turned to Bobkin. "Putin told us you have a report."

Bobkin beamed. He was grateful that Putin gave him this chance. He told them what he had relayed to Putin and gave them a written copy that simply stated that Jesse and Meg had rented a boat, caught a few fish in the waters around Leningrad and Kronstadt, and were turned back by a naval patrol.

Smirnov and Brodsky told Bobkin that they didn't think the activity suspicious. They said they knew there was much activity at the docks, along the Neva, and at Kronstadt, but that was not unusual and would attract the attention of tourists. They told him KGB Acting Director Volkhov had requested the report. They were simply going to put their names on his report and send it to Moscow.

Bobkin smiled. His future in the KGB looked bright. "Did Volkhov indicate why he wanted the Byrnes kids followed?"

"No," Smirnov said, shaking his head. "Sometimes it's a training exercise to find future KGB managers. You did a great job." He gave Bobkin his phone number and told him to call if he needed a reference.

§

AT SEVEN P.M. THE report landed on Volkhov's desk at Lubyanka Prison, KGB headquarters, in Moscow. Volkhov had set up the Intourist tour to distract the American government from focusing on Cuba and what the Russians were doing in the western ports of the Soviet Union. He had not anticipated that the children of the State Department's Russian desk chief would be on the tour. Meg and Jesse Byrnes had diplomatic passports, knew Russian culture, and were fluent in Russian. At first, he didn't think their presence would be a problem. But given the necessity for secrecy, he ordered the KGB office in Leningrad, who knew nothing about the missiles, to monitor the teens. He needed to make certain they did not see anything revealing about the cargo at Leningrad Harbor. He didn't know Ana Cortez was their mother.

Volkhov wasn't alarmed when he read the report. He'd have Smirnov and Brodsky interview the students, push them on whether they took photos or drew sketches, and report back to him directly. He wanted to take no chance with anyone, knowingly or unknowingly, uncovering the missile gambit.

Late that evening, Volkhov heard back from the Leningrad pair. They told him they went to the Astoria and took Putin and Bobkin with them to make the teens feel comfortable. They found Meg and Jesse sitting in hotel reception with their luggage, waiting with the other students for a bus to the airport where they were scheduled to depart on a flight to Moscow.

The KGB officers said Jesse and Meg were polite and full of praise for the wonders of Leningrad. When pressed on why they rented a fishing boat, they said they enjoyed fishing, and wanted to see the awesome engineering challenges that the Russians had overcome to build the beautiful city of Leningrad. They added that they hoped to understand the communist revolution's aversion to the aristocratic class, whom Chekhov depicted as lazy and floating around aimlessly in the Gulf of Finland. When asked if they had taken pictures or made sketches of what they had observed, they affirmed that they had. They wanted mementos of their trip.

In summary, Smirnov and Brodsky reported that the teens seemed to be awestruck tourists who appreciated the bravery and beauty of Leningrad and had admitted to taking pictures and making sketches. They added that Jesse and Meg were delightful and that Bobkin never took his eyes off Meg, who seemed to like Bobkin's attention. They thought something might be made of that puppy love down the road.

Volkhov decided it was not a major issue, but he wanted to make sure that nothing accidentally leaked about the missiles. When Jesse and Meg arrived in Moscow and toured its sites, he ordered the KGB to monitor and prevent them from contacting any American official or journalist.

He was relieved to hear at the end of their time in Moscow that they had made no effort to reach out to anyone. They had purchased some colorful matryoshka dolls after they arrived in Moscow and sent an innocuous telegram to "Papi," who he assumed was their father, at the State Department. "The matryoshka dolls are mysterious and full of surprises." Meg had also given Bobkin, who followed the teens everywhere they went in Moscow, a copy of the Broadway play called *The Sound of Music*, which she had translated into Russian. Volkhov looked at a photocopy of the script but dismissed it as frivolous.

Nonetheless, Volkhov was anxious. On the afternoon of October 8, when the students boarded a train at Yaroslavsky railway station for a trip to nearby Vladimir, he ordered the KGB to break into the luggage car and steal Jesse and Meg's film, sketches, and notebooks. He then had Putin inform them that hooligans had broken into their luggage and had taken some of their possessions but that Intourist, by way of an apology, had bought new film, notebooks, sketch pads, and pictures and drawing of Leningrad's famous sites, which were now in their luggage.

Volkhov was not surprised that Jesse and Meg went to the luggage car and inspected their luggage. He was surprised when Jesse thanked Putin for the replacements and sent a telegram from the railway station to "Papi" from JB and MB, saying the trip was marred by a theft, but Intourist had replaced the stolen items and had given them pictures and drawings of Leningrad's magnificent sites, and they were grateful and having a great time. Volkhov wondered about "JB" and "MB" but concluded they were initials.

After the train departed, Volkhov carefully looked over the developed pictures and sketches. He thought the sketches showed evidence of missiles and missile parts on ships. There were photographs of missiles, but they were buried among hundreds of pictures. He didn't know for sure if the teens knew what they had, but he ordered the KGB to keep Jesse and Meg in Mongolia at the end of their trip to make sure they gave no reports to anyone, especially their father, until the missiles were unveiled. He thought two weeks or so would be sufficient.

To reduce the concern and suspicion of the American government and distract it from Cuba, he decided, with Khrushchev's agreement, to approve a new American request that was sent by the Soviet embassy in Washington to strengthen the ALSIB celebration by allowing an unarmed B-52 to fly nonstop from Anchorage to Irkutsk and carry replicas of Lend-Lease aid for a new ALSIB museum as well as over one hundred diverse American veterans of the ALSIB program. These men and women of all races and nationalities would be dressed in World War II military fatigues from all branches of the US armed forces. The plane would arrive on October 9 and depart the next day for a direct flight to Washington, DC, where the American veterans and representatives from the Soviet embassy would be honored. Volkhov thought the ALSIB party would persuade the US, even if it the US was concerned about what the Russians were doing in their ports and Cuba, to give the Soviets the benefit of doubt.

At the same time, he knew Jesse and Meg's parents would be concerned by an extended stay in Mongolia. He had an agent meet Jesse and Meg in Vladimir before their plane departed for Irkutsk and inform them of good news—the Mongolian government had invited them to extend their time in Mongolia at its expense for up to two weeks. He asked them to sign a postcard describing the adventure and their desire to undertake it and said Intourist would deliver the postcards to the State Department to inform their parents.

Jesse and Meg filled out the postcards per the agent's direction and signed with their initials, JB and MB. The agent was back in Moscow, at Volkhov's desk one hour later. Volkhov was pleased. He had an Intourist agent deliver the postcards to Spaso House and stress that the Soviet and Mongolian governments would make sure the teens remained safe and had a glorious time. He believed he had stopped any potential leak.

Chapter 7
The Escape Plan

Washington, October 8, 1962

THE SHERIFF TORE at his hair. He stood in a conference room on the seventh floor of the State Department, looking out a large, open casement window at the silvery brown Potomac. The fast-flowing water shimmered under the rising yellow sun. The cool wind coming in from outside hinted that fall was here but winter was coming.

The river passed Arlington National Cemetery's fall foliage. Kelly imagined it saluting the heroes, marked by solemn white marble tombstones and monuments, who had defended American democracy. For him, the Potomac, which flowed by Mount Vernon and Monticello where George Washington and Thomas Jefferson were buried, connected the past and the present of the great American experiment in democracy. It symbolized the American people's enduring commitment to the values of freedom and constitutional government.

The Soviet Union was maneuvering to deliver a body blow to the United States. It increasingly appeared that Khrushchev had knuckled under to Volkhov and the hardline Kobaists and was going to confront the United States and the West with an act of staggering aggression. Kelly believed that Jesse and Meg had time-sensitive information on the USSR's plans that could shed light on Moscow's game plan.

He also worried that the teens were in danger. He held the telegrams and postcards that they had sent. They had information on Soviet activities around Leningrad Harbor and Kronstadt naval base.

That was the only explanation for their being held in Mongolia for two weeks after their trip ended on October 14. He had the unpleasant job of informing their parents of the danger and his role in it.

A knock on the door indicated that Ana and Ed had arrived. The Sheriff greeted them warmly and invited them to come in, grab a coffee, and sit down on a soft blue-and-gray striped sofa near the window. He sat opposite them in a matching armchair. He left his coffee cup on the conference table. He knew by the worry in their eyes that they could tell he was stressed. He forced himself to unclench his fists.

"What's wrong?" Ana said cautiously, sipping her coffee.

"Meg and Jesse are in trouble and I'm responsible," Kelly wanted to get the bad news over as soon as possible. He was ready to be punished and get on with constructing a plan to save the kids.

"What did you say?" Ana splashed coffee on the tile floor. She and Ed leaned forward and put their cups down. Kelly knew they had heard him but had difficulty digesting his words.

"I asked Jesse and Meg to spy on Leningrad Harbor for the Posse," the Sheriff said. "The KGB confiscated their photos, notes, and sketches. It's keeping them incommunicado in Mongolia for two weeks beyond their original return date. Likely to prevent them reporting on what they saw."

Ana stood and swung her fist at Kelly's face. He made no attempt to protect himself, but Ed restrained her.

"You jeopardized our kids." Ed's face colored. "Ana's parents were murdered in the Soviet Union. You had our kids send pablum postcards to us to keep us pacified. What's wrong with you?"

Kelly shook his head. He watched his friends, disconsolate, collapse on the sofa. He saw the sorrow, disbelief, and betrayal in Ana's eyes. Despair and anger in Ed's. In that moment, he realized that his scheming was damaging his family, friends, and loved ones. He felt vulnerable and knew he had hurt and disappointed beautiful souls and undermined his purpose.

"I'm so sorry." Tears streamed down his cheeks. "I love you and I love Meg and Jesse. You're my closest friends, at the heart of the Posse family. I should have told you."

Ana and Ed sat before him in silence. Finally, Ana spoke in a clear voice. "Do you think anything worthwhile came of it? Did they uncovered time-sensitive, critical information relevant to the security of the United States?"

"It was not worth it." The Sheriff shook his head. "I put their lives at risk, and they are still in jeopardy. I should have informed you and worked with you and the Posse. I promise to in the future. You are right to condemn me."

"What did they discover?" Ana pushed.

The Sheriff uttered a plaintive sigh and then spoke in a soft voice. "I think that they identified the cargo at the Leningrad Harbor and on the freighters as long-range missiles. Even though the KGB stole their notes, their memories are excellent and Meg is an extraordinary sketch artist. Volkhov would not hold them if he didn't think they had something."

Ana pursed her lips. "We don't condemn you. We condemn what you did. We didn't inform you of the trip to preempt scheming. Now show us what you're doing to get our children home safely."

"I won't defend what I did," Kelly said tensely, "but I promise I will get them back safely and soon if you will help me."

"What's the plan?" Ana and Ed said together.

Kelly knew he had to perform to regain their trust. He moved directly to the plan and its backup that he had been working on as soon as he had received the messages from Meg and Jesse. It would take the Posse, the State Department, the CIA, the Defense Department, and perhaps the Canadian Department of Foreign Affairs and International Trade to get them home immediately. He spoke quickly and confidently.

"On October 9 and 10 Jesse and Meg will be near Irkutsk and Lake Baikal, where the annual ALSIB celebration is scheduled to commemorate the Alaskan-Siberian airlift during the Great Patriotic War. The ALSIB program had American planes, piloted by Soviets and Americans, fly Lend-Lease supplies from Alaska to Siberia.

"The celebration involves American pilots flying C-47s, T-6s, and B-29s, all workhorses of the ALSIB mission, to various Siberian cities with fuel stops along the way. Ultimately, most of the planes will reach Irkutsk where the main commemoration of the ALSIB will take place. These planes lack the fuel capacity to fly out of Soviet airspace and across the Bering Strait and Arctic Ocean without many time-consuming stops. We need a long-range plane like the B-52 bomber."

"A Trojan Horse?" Ed said, smiling and shaking his head. "I love the audacity of the move, but Moscow would never allow a B-52 to fly in and out of Irkutsk."

"I think we can entice the Soviets to accept the B-52," Kelly said, looking into Ana's hopeful eyes, "by explaining that the US wants to enhance the ALSIB celebration by including an unarmed B-52 that will carry replicas of Lend-Lease aid for a new ALSIB museum in Irkutsk and over one hundred US uniformed veterans of the ALSIB project. We will embed Posse members among the veterans to make sure that Jesse and Meg are on that flight. A delegation from the Soviet embassy will meet today for a noon lunch at the State Department to continue discussions on the ALSIB celebration. I'll have State present the proposal at that meeting."

"I like the idea," Ana said. "I think Moscow will endorse it not only to gain publicity, but also to distract us from whatever it's doing in Leningrad and other ports. How will you get Meg and Jesse off the tour?"

The Sheriff nodded. "When they are at Irkutsk on October 9, Posse members from the B-52 will swarm the student tour group, pretend to be gauche tourists, spirit the kids away in the ensuing confusion, and hide them on the B-52 until departure on October 10."

"It's a good start," Ana said in a reassuring voice, "but it alerts the Soviets and gives them too much time to find them. If the KGB doesn't find them, Volkhov will never allow the B-52 to depart."

"What are you thinking?" Kelly said respectfully, knowing Ana was a brilliant strategic thinker.

"I suggest allowing Meg and Jesse to ride the train into Mongolia. If we get them off in Mongolia, it has no connection to the Irkutsk events, including the Americans on the B-52, and is totally on the Soviets and their Mongolian allies. The KGB will be searching the Gobi Desert while Meg and Jesse are transported back to Irkutsk."

"How would you take them from the train?" Kelly said.

"I will call Batu Khulan," Ana replied. "When he was at our ranch, he showed us what he could do with a yurt. He will have a plan to get them off the train without the watchers' knowledge."

"A yurt?" Kelly said with a quizzical look on his face. Kelly knew Khulan had a huge yurt manufacturing company and a thriving horse racing business. But he didn't understand how a yurt could be used to get the kids off the train without the knowledge of the KGB.

"Yurt production is no small operation," Ed said. "Khulan is a master yurt designer. When he was in Texas, he showed us yurts with trapdoors, hidden rooms, Buddhist temples, and second stories. He could hide a small army in a yurt. If anyone can get Meg and Jesse away from the KGB, it'll be Khulan."

"The problem," Ana said, "will be to quickly transport them back to Irkutsk."

"I've got that covered," Kelly said, happy to augment Ana's idea. "It was in my backup plan in case the Posse failed to retrieve Meg and Jesse in Irkutsk. I just couldn't figure how to get them off the train once they were in Mongolia and under the control of the KGB."

Ana and Ed leaned forward.

"The Canadian government has a trade delegation in Mongolia to promote the versatility of the de Havilland Beaver, the all-purpose bush plane that connects Canada's remote northern regions. It is scheduled to fly the trade delegation from Mongolia to Lake Baikal on October 10 for a promotional sales pitch to the regional Siberian government. I had the US State Department ask Ottawa to allow the Canadians to take part in the ALSIB celebration in Irkutsk. They could drop Jesse and Meg off at Lake Baikal, where our friends would get them to Irkutsk. Moscow has approved of the Canadians' participation because Canada helped with ALSIB during World War II."

"That will work. I'll fill Khulan in on the details, so that he can get Jesse and Meg to wherever the Beaver will be parked."

Kelly noticed Ed frowning. "What's the matter, Ed?"

"The KGB will have a large presence at Irkutsk because of the ALSIB festivities," Ed said. "Is there a way to dilute their numbers to give Meg and Jesse a better shot at slipping on the B-52 undetected?"

Kelly sat back in his chair, closed his eyes, and tilted his head up toward the ceiling, deep in thought. "Oliver and Taylor will be among the passengers on the B-52 that will arrive in Irkutsk on October 9. With the help of some of our Soviet friends and dressed in their Stalin and Vlasik disguises, they will stir anxiety in the remote rural villages around Irkutsk where Stalin announced his policy of collectivization in 1927. The KGB will have its hands full tracking down the ghosts of Stalin and General Vlasik and trying to reassure the peasants that the harsh days of Stalin are not returning."

Ana laughed, relieving the tension. "Volkhov will be shocked, wondering if Khrushchev somehow summoned Stalin's ghost to be an ally."

Ana and Ed said the plan was a good one.

Kelly relaxed. He turned his attention to the ALSIB ceremony. By that afternoon, he informed Ana, Ed, and other key Posse members that the Soviet government had approved the B-52 involvement in the

ALSIB celebration. The plan to extract Meg and Jesse from Siberia had commenced.

Chapter 8
The Escape

Mongolia, Irkutsk, Lake Baikal, October 10, 1962

JESSE RUBBED HIS neck until it turned red after the Trans-Siberian crossed the Russian-Mongolian border early on October 10. Meg, seated next to him, gazed out the window at the clear blue sky, boundless horizon, and mountainous terrain. He knew that she was anxious too. They had discussed the transparent KGB plan to keep them in Mongolia after the trip ended. They had also talked about their detailed memories of the Leningrad shipyard and Kronstadt naval base. It was clear that what they had observed was the reason for the KGB attention.

Jesse wondered if the Sheriff and the Posse had picked up on their alerts and had a rescue plan in the works. He regretted not telling his mom and dad about their spying.

There were perhaps two hundred passengers on the train, including the thirty students. The happy, rambunctious group seemed to love train travel, time zone changes, the diversity of peasant faces that appeared outside the train's windows every time it halted, and the breathtaking scenery of rivers, steppe, and snow-topped mountains. Every time the train stopped at a station, passengers got off to exercise and buy local food to supplement the train's menu of dark bread, cucumbers, pirozhkis, pickles, borscht, gray colored chicken, sodas, and stale oatmeal cookies.

The train curved and opened a view of the tracks ahead. Meg turned to Jesse and tilted her head forward, indicating that there was something on the tracks. She was being discreet because Bobkin and Putin were watching her. Jesse nodded. The train was slowing down. It might be a Posse rescue plan. It seemed to him that Meg thought so too.

As the train braked to a crawl, it entered a thousand-yard-long tunnel of yurts, strung together, made of wool, yak hair, and willow and birch saplings. The wall of the tunnel featured Disneyland-like highlights of Mongolian history and had a platform that extended to the train.

The train's engineer stopped at the midpoint in the tunnel and announced that the Mongolian government wanted the passengers to disembark for a proper welcome and to view the highlights of Mongolian history. The passengers got off the train and found bowls of koumiss or airag made of fermented mare's milk, fresh milk, soft drinks, tea, and water.

Jesse watched Putin down three bowls of koumiss. He looked tipsy. Jesse lost track of Bobkin. At the same time, he saw his Mongolian friends, Altan and Dureen, beckoning to him and Meg. He led Meg toward them. When Jesse and Meg reached the spot where they had been, they were gone. A hand extended through a hidden slit in the wall.

Jesse and Meg slipped through the opening and found their friends standing with four shaggy ponies tied to a hitching post. They hugged each other. Altan pointed to the yurt tunnel.

"Our father arranged this Potemkin village to abet your escape. Someone he knows called him on a secure line and asked him to get you off the train without the KGB's knowledge before it reached Ulaanbaatar, about twenty miles away."

Then pointing to the horses, he continued, "We do not have much time. We must ride to an airfield where the Beaver is waiting to fly you to Lake Baikal."

"What's the Beaver?" Jesse asked.

Khulan's son smiled. He told Jesse and Meg that the Beaver was an amazing plane equipped with wheels, floats, and skis. It could land and take off on short runways made of dirt, sand, water, snow, or ice.

Altan said the Beaver was in Mongolia because a Canadian trade delegation was promoting its sale to the Mongolian government. In a large, sparsely populated country like Mongolia with isolated settlements in the Gobi Desert, the grassy steppe, and the snowy western and northern mountains during winter, the Beaver would be a godsend. It could fly and land anywhere in any season, including the ancient Lake Khövsgöl, home of the Festival of Ice.

"We'd better go," Dureen said. "The train will be departing soon."

The four teens mounted. Altan led at a gallop. Jesse and Meg, having grown up on a Texas ranch, were at home on horses. Hearing Meg's name over the pounding hooves, Jesse turned around. Bobkin was calling them to stop. Jesse told Altan that the KGB had spotted them.

§

BOBKIN HAD FOLLOWED Meg and Jesse. He lost them temporarily at the slit in the yurt wall but heard someone talking about a "Beaver," which he didn't understand. He felt around until he found the opening and slipped through. Meg and Jesse and two other young people were riding away on horses. He called to them, but they didn't stop. The girl of his dreams and her brother had fled. He had strict orders to keep an eye on them for another two weeks. He'd been looking forward to spending time with Meg.

He didn't understand why she had left. He had been kind to her and had feelings for her, and he thought that she had liked him. He had a good job and a bright future. She must know, he thought, that his loyalty to the Communist Party was a priority and that her fleeing was a betrayal of him that placed his career in jeopardy. She had to be taught a lesson on loyalty.

Bobkin slipped back onto the train platform and ran to the caboose, where the KGB had an office and an A-7 VHF transceiver and telex. He informed the agent in charge that Meg and Jesse Byrnes had escaped from the train and were riding horses with two unknown others in a southerly direction, maybe to a village called "Beaver." The agent immediately sent out alerts to KGB stations as far south as Ulaanbaatar. He told Bobkin the KGB would have horses and BRDM-2 scout cars flooding the area along the tracks south to Ulaanbaatar and would soon capture the runaways and their accomplices. Bobkin asked the agent to send the news to KGB headquarters in Leningrad and Moscow and mention "the Beaver." He thought it was important that Smirnov and Volkhov knew what he had done.

He returned to the train car and saw Meg's gold cross and *The Sound of Music*, which Meg had given to him and which he had just started to read. He suddenly regretted informing on Meg. He didn't know why. He picked up the cross and *The Sound of Music*. Maybe they had an answer.

§

AS SOON AS Jesse said the KGB had seen them, Altan turned west, away from the tracks. He and Dureen knew the land.

When the teens rode around a tree-covered mound, Jesse saw five uniformed soldiers on horseback on a course to intercept. Altan saw them at the same time and turned north into the hills, pushing the horses to a full gallop. The Russians followed, although their mounts could not keep up with the mountain-bred horses carrying the teens.

Altan led them into a valley with a rock wall to the east and high pines and rugged terrain to the west. They kept riding north.

An all-terrain BRDM-2 appeared on the crest of a hill in front of them. It fired warning shots. They quickly turned east toward the rock wall. It looked sheer and impenetrable. The riders were now caught between the armed vehicle to the north, the KGB riders to the south, the rugged terrain to the west, and the rock wall. Altan rode as if there were no rock wall. He rode across an outcrop of rock, which left no trace, and then vanished into a grove of trees. Dureen, Meg, and Jesse followed. They slowed the horses to pass through a crease in the rock wall, invisible except inside the grove, which also looked solid and an unlikely doorway to a passageway.

Altan said that in a little more than one mile they would reach the Beaver. The KGB would spend hours in the hills looking for them.

When they reached the plane, Jesse and Meg said goodbye to their friends and boarded the Beaver. "Good luck, and please come back," Altan said. Dureen hugged them.

The Beaver took off immediately. The pilot had permission from Soviet authorities in Irkutsk to land on different parts of Lake Baikal to demonstrate the plane's adaptability. His first stop, two hours after departing from the airfield outside of Ulaanbaatar, was a hidden cove near the lakeside village of Listvyanka. He planned to drop Meg and Jesse out of sight of a Soviet trade delegation patiently waiting to welcome the Beaver. When he taxied toward the shore, a Soviet naval patrol boat appeared. It closed on the Beaver, preventing Meg and Jesse from disembarking.

The officer on board the naval craft wanted to search the Beaver. The pilot said he was late for his rendezvous with Soviet officials, and he could search the plane later. The officer insisted, saying that he had a report that the Beaver might be carrying passengers from Mongolia.

The pilot told the officer that there were Canadians on board, and he could talk to them later. He told Jesse he was going to take off and come back. He turned his Beaver around and gunned the engine. The naval boat tried to get in front of the Beaver, but the plane was faster and was soon aloft. The naval boat shot a flare at the Beaver, but the plane replied with a wing-wave and climbed toward a bank of gray clouds.

"We will soon lose them," the pilot said to Jesse.

Jesse marveled at the versatility and speed of the Beaver. It flew east toward the other side of the lake, some fifty miles away. He heard the boat accelerate to full throttle in pursuit of the plane and saw the naval commander waving wildly and talking on a radio phone, probably to alert Soviet officials that the plane had not been searched and that it was headed to the eastern shoreline. Jesse watched the boat fade in the distance.

The pilot led the naval patrol on a wild goose chase. He increased his altitude, disappearing above a layer of gray clouds, and then altered course. He told Jesse and Meg that he was going back and would cut the engine when he went over the pursuing naval boat so that it would not know his destination. He told them he'd inform Soviet officials that he misunderstood the naval officer and thought the naval boat held a welcoming committee that wanted to witness the dexterity of the Beaver.

Twenty minutes later the Beaver landed near the Listvyanka village, put Jesse and Meg ashore, and took off.

Two Posse members met Meg and Jesse on the shore. They had watched the showdown unfold and were impressed by the pilot's courage and cleverness. They gave the teens passports with new names and had them put on army fatigues. They joined a nearby sightseeing bus full of American veterans who had come on the B-52 and were now returning to Irkutsk airport for the flight home.

At the Irkutsk airport, Soviet passport officials stopped the bus. One official, who could speak English, got on the bus and spot-checked passports. Everyone was dressed in US military fatigues. He stopped in front of Meg and checked her passport. "You're not a veteran of the Great Patriotic War, are you?"

Jesse swallowed hard. He thought the jig was up, but then he watched Meg, who he knew could think on her feet, smile, and say, "Of course not, officer. I'm the proud daughter of a veteran who is not with us."

"I'm sorry, young lady," the official said softly. "The war took many lives, and I respect you for coming to honor his memory." He looked around, nodded his approval, got off the bus, and waved it through security. He saluted the bus as it passed.

The bus passengers, including Meg and Jesse, joined the other veterans on the B-52. It had offloaded its cargo of jeeps, fighter planes, and other Lend-Lease aid for the ALSIB commemorative museum. Meg and Jesse were delighted to be greeted by Oliver and Taylor.

Thirty minutes later, the B-52 was on its way to Washington. Even though it was early in the afternoon, Jesse and Meg were tired and wanted to sleep on the long flight home. Oliver and Taylor were also tired. They decided to wait until they reached Washington and saw Kelly and other Posse members before discussing what the teens had seen.

Jesse was about to drift off when he heard Oliver and Meg talking. Oliver said he had seen the ghosts of Stalin and Vlasik moving among the peasantry in the villages around Irkutsk and thought that they had lit a fuse for popular rebellion against authoritarianism in the tradition of the False Dmitrys and Pugachev, who had led rebellions against the tsars in the seventeenth and eighteenth centuries.

Meg replied that the ghosts of Stalin and Vlasik were lucky that gun ownership was outlawed in Russia. The peasants would surely have shot Stalin and Vlasik and made them real ghosts. But then Jesse was dreaming.

§

"IOSIF, I THINK the ALSIB celebration was a spectacular success," Volkhov said. "The Americans left Irkutsk smiling, and Washington seems unaware of our ongoing missile deployment in Cuba." He sat in a comfortable chair behind his desk in Lubyanka holding a cup of hot black tea flavored with fresh mint and honey.

"I agree," Grigulevich said. "You have pulled the wool over their eyes."

Volkhov abruptly changed the subject. "There are only two developments that mar my contentment. Your collective farms around Irkutsk are restive, and your police have not found the Byrnes kids." He knew his use of "your collective farms and your police" would annoy Grigulevich. He liked tormenting his deputy.

"I don't know what happened in the villages around Irkutsk," Grigulevich said flatly. He must have been irritated by Volkhov's gratuitous taunting. "There are reports that some peasants saw a vision of Stalin and Vlasik asking for forgiveness for their sins, praising Khrushchev for his reforms, and linking food shortages, violence, and repression to the KGB. It sounds absurd, but the rumors are persistent."

Volkhov laughed, which relaxed Grigulevich. "It's not only absurd but fantastic. The day that Stalin praises Khrushchev is the day that I repent and believe in miracles. It's clearly some hooligans, drunks, or drugheads who are high on Afghan opium."

"What do you wish me to do?" Grigulevich asked.

"I want no unrest in the countryside with the missile ploy underway," Volkhov said. "Increase the vodka rations on the collective farms. Keep the peasants inebriated. Send some agents out to see if a False Stalin is lurking around Irkutsk. I have a cell for him in Lubyanka Prison where I will teach him with a knout what it means to be Stalin."

Grigulevich shifted his weight. "I will call the KGB office in Irkutsk to get an update."

"What about the Byrnes kids?" Volkhov asked.

"I will check with Ulaanbaatar and get you an update on the search for them."

Volkhov's hand pounded the desktop. "If they don't show up, their parents and the American government will be all over us."

"I will pull out all stops to find them," Grigulevich said, his voice tense.

§

GRIGULEVICH LEANED AGAINST the wall in his small office in Lubyanka looking out at the cameras attached to the apartment building across the street. KGB eyes were everywhere. There was no privacy, he thought, except when the cameras malfunctioned. That happened frequently, but it was nerve-racking trying to guess when they failed.

He favored dark clothes. They seemed to intimidate lower-ranking KGB agents who wanted his job. His reputation as a killer also kept the wannabes in line, but he had to be wary because the KGB was a magnet for psychopaths.

Bookshelves filled with old and new books in many languages lined the walls, filling the office with a woody smell. He got away with keeping his literary treasures because, he told Volkhov and others, he must read the classics to understand the mind of the enemy.

He held a phone receiver in his right hand. He had been on the phone for thirty minutes, trying to get through to the KGB office in Irkutsk. He knew the phone system in the USSR was unreliable, but he had hoped to quickly take care of the rumors about Stalin's appearance.

"Hello," a deep voice finally said.

"This is Grigulevich. What's with the rumors of a Stalin specter appearing at the collective farm villages outside Irkutsk?"

"This is Officer Vovitch, sir. A dozen KGB agents from Irkutsk found no trace of the Stalin imposter. He doesn't exist. I chalk it up to a hooligan who ran away as soon as the secret police showed up."

"Good work, Vovitch, and goodbye," Grigulevich said. He then called the KGB office in Mongolia and got through immediately. That was the result of Batu Khulan's insistence on a modern phone system for Mongolia to support his yurt and horseracing businesses.

"Stefanovich here," a rough voice answered, on the second ring.

"Grigulevich. What's the latest on those two American teens?"

"We're searching. So far, no luck. We'll call you as soon as we have something."

Grigulevich hung up, puzzled. He wondered how two foreigners could disappear in Mongolia, one of the most isolated corners of the world. There was no sign of them anywhere. It reminded him of Ana Cortez, who could evaporate into thin air.

Grigulevich called Volkhov and said the Stalin imposter, if there ever was one, had disappeared and was no longer an issue except for some traumatized peasants who would expel the nightmare with vodka. On the Byrnes kids, he reported that the KGB was scouring the countryside for them. Volkhov was furious, but he relaxed when Grigulevich said there was no evidence that they had left Mongolia. No need to worry about them informing American officials on their observations at Leningrad Harbor. "We're not free of concern, because the kids' safety rests on us," Grigulevich said, "but I think we're free of the fear that they will talk."

Volkhov thanked him and told him to call the American embassy and inform the ambassador that the Byrnes kids had gone off with friends in Mongolia. As soon as they were found, the police would inform Spaso House.

Grigulevich harbored his own fears. He thought the teens could have escaped, using the Beaver to reach the B-52 that was about to land in Washington. He sent an encrypted telegram to Victor Petrov to watch the entrance of the State Department on October 10 and 11 on the chance that the kids showed up. He hoped they had escaped for their own sake and the cause of peace. He also worried about the Cuban missile gambit. The more he thought about it, the more he decided it was inane to provoke a nuclear confrontation over communism, which he knew wallowed in absurdities. His disillusionment with communism was taking hold.

Chapter 9
Some Evidence

Washington, October 10,-11 1962

THE SHERIFF STOOD in the air traffic control tower of Andrews Air Force Base and watched Angel, a beautiful black and white female border collie with big brown eyes, chase a flock of Canadian geese off the runway. Angel was the Air Force's secret weapon to keep birds from colliding with aircraft landing and taking off at Andrews, the home of Air Force One.

Kelly walked over to Ana and Ed Byrnes, who sat behind an air traffic control operator and watched a flight radar screen.

"The B-52's approaching," Kelly said gently. Ana's pursed lips told him she was still angry over his use of Meg and Jesse. He desperately wanted to regain her confidence.

"Yes," Ana said tersely. "It's on time, and we know Meg and Jesse are safe. For that, we're grateful."

Kelly turned to the large, slanted window of the control tower. Ana and Ed stood next to him and watched the B-52 touch down. "They're here," Ed said with relief. "Let's go get them."

Fifteen minutes later, Kelly watched the teens and their parents embrace at the gate. He smiled. Then he heard Ana and Ed scold Meg and Jesse for not telling them about their work for the Posse and for keeping them in the dark when they were in danger. His smile evaporated.

"Never go off script again," Ana said. "We're a family and we communicate. The Soviet Union is a dangerous, authoritarian state where life is cheap. There's no rule of law. My mom and dad, your grandparents, were brutally murdered there. Do you understand?"

The Sheriff felt Ana and Ed's pain again and now the shock of the kids, who had expected to be received not only as a beloved son and daughter but also successful spies. He wished he could ease their disappointment and take the punishment for what he had done. But family relationships were none of his business. He tried to show his shame for causing the strain and anger by hanging his head down. He waited until Ana and Ed signaled that the issue was settled.

Meg and Jesse apologized and asked for forgiveness. Kelly was glad they were taking this first step in healing. Ana and Ed hugged Meg and Jesse. Ana took a deep breath and let out a sigh of relief.

"We love you," Ana said. "We'd be lost without you. The Sheriff shouldn't have involved you without our consent. He knows he made a mistake, but you are old enough to know that you should have told us."

Meg and Jesse had tears in their eyes. They again asked for forgiveness. They didn't push the blame on Kelly, which he thought showed maturity. Ana and Ed hugged them again and then reached out to Kelly who joined in the embrace.

"I'm so sorry," he said.

Ana said it was time to move on and find out what Meg and Jesse had discovered. She turned to the Sheriff. "It's your show now."

He smiled. He said he admired what Meg and Jesse had done and was as happy as Ana and Ed that they were safe. Ray Charles's "I Can't Stop Loving You" played softly in the background over the gate's speaker system.

Kelly knew the teens were hungry for American food. He wanted them well fed and at ease for interviews. He asked them if they would like to rest and have dinner before they discussed their trip. They said they were rested after sleeping on the plane but were starved.

Kelly led Ana, Ed, and the teens to a private dining room off the main mess hall at Andrews. Dinner was ribeye steaks, twice-baked potatoes, cranberry goat cheese salad with walnuts, grilled asparagus, corn on the cob, and garlic bread. Lemony iced tea and water helped wash down the feast. Chocolate tres leches cake and hot coffee followed. The conversation was light and warm. Jesse told a funny story about Leningrad's notoriously bad water, and Meg mentioned the Inquisition exhibition at the Museum of Religion and Atheism with a stake that opened a trap door when pressed down.

After dinner, the Sheriff escorted the family to a secure conference room in the base commander's suite. He had forensic artists from the FBI and intelligence agents from the Pentagon, CIA, and State Department come into the room. He asked Meg and Jesse about their observations and to work with the FBI artists to draw pictures of the Soviet ships and their cargo and the freight on the docks.

By ten o'clock, the Sheriff said he had a solid picture of what they had observed, and it reinforced his worst suspicions. He asked Jesse and Meg to come to an early morning meeting the next day at the State Department to review what they had observed for some Posse members. He then thanked them and encouraged them to get a good night's rest. The Byrnes family stayed at the Cloister, a twenty-bedroom safe house in the Kalorama neighborhood that the Posse used for overnight meetings and events.

§

THE SHERIFF PEERED out a window on the first floor of the State Department early on the morning of October 11. The air was cool but warming up as a tangerine sun climbed above the horizon. He saw Viktor Petrov of the TASS news agency sitting on a bench, pretending to read a newspaper while keeping a sharp eye on the building's entrance. Petrov had also been there the evening before. He wore a dark business suit and coughed uncontrollably. Kelly wondered if his cold had turned into pneumonia.

The benches around the State Department were under constant surveillance. No one sat there, especially two days in a row, without drawing the CIA's attention. Kelly laughed when told and said Petrov likely hoped to see if Jesse and Meg would show up. It indicated to him that Volkhov was worried about their disappearance.

Kelly took the opportunity to increase pressure on Volkhov. He called Ana and Ed and told them his idea. They endorsed it.

At eight o'clock sharp, a black limo pulled up in front door of the State Department building. Ed climbed out of the vehicle. Ana, Jesse, and Meg had already entered the building through a back door. A State Department employee rushed out to meet Ed, who looked irritable and angry.

"The Russians have kidnapped my children!" Ed shouted. "I want the FBI to investigate their itinerary, starting in Leningrad. Now!"

"Yes, sir," the official said. "The secretary of state is calling Moscow."

Petrov dropped his newspaper and nearly fell off the bench when he heard them. He caught a cab to the Soviet embassy and sent a telegram to Volkhov and Grigulevich that the American government wanted the FBI in Leningrad to start a search for the Byrnes kids. The Posse gave Kelly a copy of the transmission minutes later.

§

THE SHERIFF STOOD in front of a conference table on theseventh floor of the State Department. Posse members and analysts from the CIA and the Department of State sat around the table. The honored guests were Meg and Jesse Byrnes who sat with their parents near the head.

Kelly welcomed everyone. Then he turned to Jesse and Meg and thanked them for their work. He shared that the KGB was searching for them and now feared that the FBI wanted to come to the USSR to join the search. The group grinned. Kelly then asked Meg and Jesse to highlight their observations at Leningrad Harbor.

Meg said there were many workers near the warehouses and on the loading docks and that the cargo being loaded on freighters had the shape of missiles or missile parts.

Bone, a former KGB agent who had studied Soviet missile technology, asked how long the suspected missiles were. The USSR'S undefeated boxing champion until he met Kelly, he could break bones with the swat of hand. He was now a key Posse member and a B-list Hollywood actor known as "El Toro" who starred in Spanish-language versions of spaghetti westerns. Kelly valued him for his uncommon strength, fluency in Spanish, knowledge of Soviet missile systems, and popularity south of the border.

"About twenty-one to twenty-three feet," Meg said. Jesse nodded his agreement.

"The size of Soviet mid-range and intermediate-range ballistic missiles," Bone said.

Kelly asked Meg and Jesse to describe what else they had witnessed. After the teens completed their reports, Kelly stood up, rubbed his forehead, and looked down the length of the table. He seemed forlorn but resolute.

"Thank you, Meg and Jesse."

Kelly then said the Posse, along with the CIA and Department of Defense, had studied the global pattern of Soviet ships and determined that the main destination of Soviet shipping since July was Cuba. He added that CIA observers on the ground in Cuba had noticed intense activity across the island. "I'm sending Ana, Ed, and Bone to Cuba to get firsthand information. Then we'll make a recommendation to the president."

Chapter 10
Bienvenido a Cuba

Cuba, October 11, 1962

ANA, ED, AND Bone looked out the windows of the Mexicana jet on its approach to José Martí International Airport.

"So far," Bone said, "I haven't seen anything that looks like a missile site."

The trio craned their heads. They agreed that what they could see of the island looked placid, peaceful, and laid back.

"Look at that old Piper parked on the beach." Ed pointed. "A PA-20 Pacer. So reliable in its day."

Ana chuckled. "We're looking for missile sites, not old planes, but it'd be surprising if missile sites were visible. Air traffic control wouldn't let our final approach anywhere near hidden missiles sites."

Their mission was simple but dangerous: obtain photographic evidence and eyewitness accounts of what the Russians were up to. They would report their findings over the radio phone to US F-4 Phantom jet pilots from Guantanamo who would monitor the S-phone transmissions from international airspace around the island. Then get out. They had a return flight the next day to Washington via Mexico City.

The plane altered course and flew west around San Cristóbal, then approached the airport from the north. "Looks like the Cubans don't want any flights over the San Cristóbal region," Bone said.

The trio disembarked from the plane at three p.m. on October 11. It was hot and humid. The azure sky was cloudless. The sunlight was hot upon their faces. A light trade wind gave some relief from the heat.

Ana wore a yellow blouse tucked into a tan pantsuit. Ed, a big man, wore a blue polo shirt and cuffed jeans. Bone was a giant. His sage-green guayabera hung loose over tan slacks.

"Welcome to Cuba, Teresa Esperanza Garza Perez and Guillermo Puente Perez." The official looked over the tops of their passports at Ana and Ed. "You are married?"

"Yes, of course." Ana said.

"And welcome to you too, Roberto Torres Martínez." He eyed the Bone. "What part of Mexico are you from?"

"Mexico City," Ana said. They had decided to speak only Spanish.

"Where's your luggage?" the official asked.

"It's a brief trip for us. We have only a small valise and a briefcase. We're planning to buy some luggage and clothes in the market."

"Wonderful!" He beamed. "We love tourists from Mexico." After Cuba ran afoul of the United States and allied with the Soviet Union, Mexico had not broken diplomatic relations with the island country. The trio knew that Cuba was desperately trying to cultivate its tourist industry.

They thanked him.

"Do you have anything to declare?"

They each told him no. The valise held a black cape, a change of clothes for one night for each of them, and a British S-phone disguised as a bound sketch book. It had a two-way communication range of thirty miles, ground to air. The briefcase held a state-of-the-art Canon 50mm f/0.95 camera, a Polaroid Land Model 95, film, high-powered binoculars, and notepads.

"Fine. How about listing a hotel on your declaration form?"

Ana told the official they would take their chances and find a hotel after sightseeing. She had a small casa in mind, not far from the Plaza de la Catedral where they were to meet the Posse asset at five-thirty that afternoon. She did not want to be easily tracked or found.

"Okay. You are free to go!"

The trio took a taxi from the airport to the Plaza de la Catedral. The driver described some of the city's highlights along the way. Cicadas trilled love songs to the hot Cuban sun.

The taxi driver dropped them off at the Plaza de la Catedral. Ana led her two companions down a narrow, cobblestoned street to the Casa de las Tres Guitarras in Old Havana, about a five-minute walk from the plaza. It was also near the Floridita Bar, one of Ernest Hemingway's haunts, famous for its ropa vieja—a stew of shredded beef, onions, tomato sauce, and peppers. Legend had it that Hemingway often had his ropa vieja with a cold beer or a cup of café Cubano.

Ana, Ed, and the Bone registered at the casa, and Ana told Ed to pay in cash for two nights even though they planned to stay only one. She wanted to mislead any trackers. They freshened up and met ten minutes later in front of the Floridita Bar. Bone carried the valise and briefcase. They wanted to eat before meeting their contact and setting out for the night's work.

When they entered the Floridita, they were surprised by the presence of Russians. They ordered ropa vieja and coffee. It was going to be a late night. They sat on swivel cushioned stools at the bar. Hemingway's statue, holding up one end of the bar, smiled at them.

Three Russians sitting at a nearby table looked at them. Ana, sitting between Ed and the Bone, sensed the Russians staring at her. "Cuba, My Love," a saucy, romantic tune written by the USSR's top songwriters to express Russia's newfound love of Cuba, played softly in the background.

"Heh, beautiful," one of the Russians said in accented Spanish, looking at Ana, "would you dance with me?"

"No, Señor," Ana said, without turning her head toward the Russian. "My husband would not like it."

"Who is your husband?" the Russian said.

"I'm the lucky man, amigo," Ed said.

"You don't mind if I dance with your wife. We're from Russia and lonely."

"Maybe another day, amigo, we're in a hurry," Ed said. The bartender placed the stew and coffee on the bar.

"No," the Russian said. "I dance now." He got up and moved behind Ed. Ana glanced at Ed. She knew the Russian's teeth would be on the floor shortly if she didn't intervene, but then Ed handled it.

"I'll tell you what, amigo. I'll arm wrestle you. If you win, I will give my blessing to your request, but the decision to dance will reside with my wife. If I win, you will go back to your chair and leave us in peace. Our food is here."

"Korosho," the Russian said. He took the empty chair next to Ed and put his arm and his elbow on the bar.

Ed looked at him. "We have s deal?"

"Si," the Russian said.

Ed put his arm on the bar opposite the Russian and then locked a viselike grip around the Russian's outstretched hand and fingers. The Russian was strong and immediately tried to pin Ed's arm. It didn't budge. Ed deflated him by asking him if he were ready to start. The Russian glared at Ed and tried again to drive Ed's arm down. Instead, Ed smiled and then flattened the Russian's arm so hard the bar quivered.

"Ah, you bruised my knuckles," the Russian cried out.

"I'm sorry, amigo," Ed said, "but we have a deal." The Russian went back to his table, and Ed, Ana, and the Bone finished their meal. As they got up to go, another Russian spoke up.

"Wait a minute. You hurt my friend, so I'm going to hurt you." He was a big man with bulging, tattooed muscles. He walked over to

Ed. Ana feared another contretemps would get out of hand and draw unwanted attention.

The Russian stood behind Ed. "Get up, amigo."

"Compañero, go back to your seat," Bone said.

"Shut your mouth," the Russian replied.

Bone looked at Ana. She nodded. She thought they could risk teaching a drunk Russian a quick lesson in manners. She didn't want a donnybrook, only a quick knockout and a quiet exit.

Bone got up, towering over the Russian. The Russian rubbed his eyes and squinted as if he could not believe what he saw. For a moment he lost his nerve, but then he came at Bone with arms flailing. Ana felt sorry for him.

Bone, left arm raised to block a punch, threw a powerful right uppercut that caught the Russian on the chin and sent him crashing to the floor unconscious.

The other Russians had seen enough. They lost their appetite for dancing. They dragged their comrade to their table and revived him.

Ana didn't want to leave the situation so raw. Word could spread quickly about pugnacious strangers. She decided to restore the Russians' dignity and perhaps elicit some information. She walked to the table where the Russians were seated.

"My friends," she said in Russian. "I'm so sorry about this altercation. I'd be happy to dance with you, but I have an appointment. I'm an admirer of the Russian people."

The three Russians appeared to Ana to be awestruck. "You speak Russian," the Russian who was not hurting said. "We love Cuba with its freedom, love of life, and sunny beaches. My friends did not mean to be rude."

"We're glad you are here," Ana continued. "We have seen thousands and thousands of our Russian brothers and sisters around." She wanted to find out how many Russians were in Cuba.

"We have over forty-two thousand personnel here," the Russian said, smiling.

"Wonderful." Ana nodded. "Maybe I'll see you tomorrow. We must leave now. Goodbye, my friends."

"We will be waiting for you," the unhurt Russian said. "Perhaps we could do more than dance."

Ana smiled but wagged a finger to quell any thoughts of intimacy. She then led Ed and Bone out of the bar. After making sure they were not followed, she headed for Plaza de la Catedral to look for a man wearing a Boston Red Sox cap. The setting sun colored the old stone buildings orange and pink, and the rich smell of cigar smoke and guava filled the air. Salsa music played softly from somewhere on the plaza.

As Ana, Ed, and Bone approached the plaza, Ana saw the Red Sox cap, worn by a well-built man in his thirties. He waved and walked from the plaza down a side street. Ana and her companions followed. He stopped in front of an old, olive drab four-wheel-drive Jeep. He opened the door, and four FAR soldiers (*Fuerzas Armadas Revolucionarias*—Revolutionary Armed Forces), lurking in the shadow of a nearby building, emerged, and surrounded him. Ana, Ed, and the Bone stood back and watched.

"I'm Lieutenant Rodriguez. Your ID, señor."

The man pulled his identification from his shirt pocket and handed it to the officer, who studied it. "Why are you driving this old Jeep?" the officer said suspiciously, standing in front of the Jeep and resting his right hand on its frame.

The man smiled. "Because I can't afford a new one."

The soldiers laughed.

The man followed up. "Ever since the damn Americans imposed that embargo on us, I've been stuck driving this jalopy. Needs a new roof and a tune-up."

"Why a Jeep?" the officer said, regaining his composure. "They are usually used by military personnel."

"I work in the sugarcane fields and need a four-wheel vehicle to get around," the man said. The lieutenant nodded and gestured to Ana, Ed, and Bone.

"Who are they?"

"Mexican tourists I met on the plaza," the man said. "They want to see the highlights of Havana."

"Do you have a taxi license?" the officer said.

"No." The man looked dejected. Ana decided to step in.

"Lieutenant," Ana said, smiling. "We asked this gentleman to drive us around. We're from Mexico. He's so knowledgeable about Havana and Cuban history and has a delightful sense of humor."

The soldiers looked at Ana. She sensed they were impressed by her appearance, perfect Mexican Spanish, and respectful tone. They smiled.

"We're happy you're here," the lieutenant said with a bow. "Are these gentlemen your brothers?"

"No," Ana said with a twinkle in her eye. "One is my husband and the other one is a friend who loves Latin America."

"Bien. Bienvenido a Cuba!" the officer said. "Camaradas, let us move on. It is a pleasure meeting you, señora. Here is my card. If you need any assistance, please call on me."

"Thank you, lieutenant." Ana nodded. "We appreciate your kindness and hospitality."

The soldiers stood back. "Have a safe and pleasant stay while you are here," the lieutenant said. Turning to the driver of the Jeep, he added, "And señor, show them a good time!"

"You can be sure of that, lieutenant," the driver said. He opened the door for the trio and took a seat behind the wheel. Ana sat in the front next to the driver and Ed and the Bone, valise, and briefcase filled the back.

Soon they were on the main road heading north out of Havana toward San Cristóbal. The Jeep turned off the highway, cut through a forest of palm, and drove onto a cattle trail that appeared out of nowhere. The declining sun painted the western sky flaming red. Shadows advanced toward the east.

"Amigos," the driver said, "No names." Then he told them what to expect of the coming night. The Jeep's rebuilt engine could power through swamps, jungle, and rough terrain. It was tough, durable, fast, and versatile. They would use unmarked trails, paths, and roads to reach the San Cristóbal complex, about sixty miles away. He would get them as close as possible to the sites where the Russians were building. There were other complexes with building sites at Guanajay, Sagua La Grande, and Remedios, but it was impossible and unnecessary to visit them all. There were no missile sites near the deep-water US naval base at Guantanamo.

He told them the San Cristóbal complex was representative and the largest missile base. Eyewitnesses reported that the other complexes looked like it but were not as big. It was heavily militarized, and at night floodlights illuminated the area. There were at least eight building sites at the San Cristóbal complex that he knew of, and inspecting them should give them what they needed. They should inspect the sites quickly, moving from south to north and ending up close to the coastline. They should not establish any pattern that could be detected or timed. They would return to Havana by a different route to avoid running into security patrols.

"Good," Ana said. "Once we have the evidence, we want to stop on the coast and radio a description to F-4 Phantom jets from Guantanamo that will be flying in international waters."

"Okay," the driver said nervously, "but it will expose us. The Russians have radar, listening devices, motion detectors, cameras, guards, and dogs, and the FAR has naval and air patrols. FAR troops in trucks, sometimes with a Russian officer on board, patrol the backroads."

"We will be quick," Ana said. "And we will go to an unguarded beach. We saw Playa de Guanímar on the flight in. There was an old

Piper Pacer there, but no visible patrols. The Russians will stay where the military sites are, and the FAR naval and air patrols will likely stay in Cuban waters and airspace. The F-4s will be in international airspace. The Russians or FAR forces might get a bead on us when we transmit, but we'll have disappeared into Havana by the time they arrive at Playa de Guanímar."

The driver said Playa de Guanímar wasn't far. He was familiar with the old Pacer. It had been modified to hold four passengers, could take off and land on the beach, and was used to fly tourists on sightseeing junkets. He added that the two-lane road from there to Havana was paved.

He slowed down and stopped the Jeep. Darkness crept over the jungle. Twinkling stars and a nearly full moon appeared.

"We're here," the driver said, "and our timing is right. The guard dogs will be in kennels eating dinner. Luckily, we're downwind."

The driver got out and walked to the back of the Jeep, where he opened a small compartment. As instructed, he said, he'd brought three Makarov pistols, a wire cutter, three flashlights, and three FAR military uniforms—a large colonel's uniform, an extra-large major's uniform, and a medium, female captain's uniform—and ID. He pointed out the first site, behind the barbed wire fence visible just beyond the tree line. He would stay and guard the Jeep with an AK-47.

Ana, Ed, and the Bone slipped the uniforms over their clothes, took the guns and flashlights, and moved quickly to the tree line. Ed carried the briefcase with their equipment. They stopped at the metal mesh fence with barbed wire on top.

Bone bent a fence pole to the ground, taking twelve feet of fence with it. He then cut a two-foot pathway through the barbed wire. They gingerly walked through the opening and stopped about one hundred feet from a building site, keeping behind bushes and out of sight of the sentries. They moved quietly into viewing positions. They each took turns with the binoculars, focusing on the first site.

Ana whispered that she saw four SA-2 SAM batteries already in place. Ed nodded and murmured that some were manned by Russians and others by FAR troops. Ana was not disturbed by SAMS because they were viewed as defensive missiles with a slant range of about twenty-five miles.

Ana noted that there were runways in the distance where MIG-21s and Il-28 light bombers were parked. She was surprised because there was no record of such advanced planes in Cuba. Ana signaled to Ed to photograph everything, including the SAM sites, planes, and the large number of Russian and FAR troops.

After seven minutes, Ana looked at the Bone, who had kept the binoculars focused on a missile site beyond the SAM batteries. He had not spoken. His notepad with descriptions of the site's terrain, layout, and security was on the ground in front of him. He had a look of shock on his face. She wondered if something was wrong.

"It's a launcher for an R-12 MRBM!" he breathed. "They are installing launchers for medium-range nuclear ballistic missiles!"

"My God," Ana whispered. "Let me look." The Bone handed her the binoculars. He was visibly shaken.

"You're right." She handed Ed the binoculars. "I see the R-12 or what the CIA calls the SS-4. They can reach most major populations in the US! The Russians are threatening nuclear war! It is reckless and insane!"

Ana picked up the Canon and took photos from different angles. "I see other MRBM launchers and missiles being assembled to the left and right," she whispered. "It appears they're trying to disguise the launchers and missiles as palm trees." She took more pictures, while Ed scribbled notes and Bone focused the binoculars on the newly discovered missiles and launchers. They also saw bunkers and storage buildings that could hold missiles and nuclear warheads.

"I've got enough pictures and evidence of what the Russians are doing.," Ana said in a muted tone. "Let's get out of here and head to

Playa de Guanímar. We don't have to go to any other sites. The sooner we get the information to Washington, the better. Ed, can you fly that Pacer to Guantanamo?"

"I can hotwire the starter," Ed said. "It should have plenty of fuel because it's in daily use for tourist trips."

The trio walked back through the fence. The Bone lifted it back into place and propped up the bent pole with a large branch. Minutes later, they were driving on a back road toward the beach. But Ana thought she saw something.

Chapter 11
El Toro

Cuba, October 11-12, 1962

A RUSSIAN MAJOR in civilian clothes watching passport control thought he recognized Bone. But the Soviet government said Grigori the Bone Crusher had died on assignment in the United States in 1953. Out of curiosity, he decided to double check.

He found out from Cuban passport control that the big man he thought might be the Bone had a Mexican passport in the name of Roberto Torres Martínez. He wired a KGB acquaintance in Moscow and asked about the famous Bone, an undefeated boxer in the early 1950s whom the KGB had paraded around the Soviet Union to prove the superiority of the communist system. The agent referred the query to the research department at Lubyanka.

The department chief looked through the file and discovered that the Bone Crusher had died in Texas in 1953 on assignment. There were no other details, which made him suspicious.

Before replying to the major, he showed the wire to Volkhov. When Volkhov read it, he too was wary. Cuba was center stage because of the missiles. He wondered if it was a case of mistaken identity. Or could the Bone be alive and working for the Americans?

Volkhov told the research chief that he would handle the issue. He immediately notified the head KGB agent in Havana, asking him to fast-track a background check on Roberto Torres Martínez.

The Havana agent went to Cuban customs and asked where Martínez was staying. Apparently Martínez had arrived with a Mexican couple. The three of them had not listed a hotel destination on their customs form. He also learned that they had taken a taxi to Plaza de la Catedral.

The agent called two other agents and asked for help locating three Mexican tourists—one female and two males—who'd been dropped off at Plaza de la Catedral and were likely staying at a hotel or casa in that vicinity. He told the agents that the trio would stand out. One of the men was huge and resembled the legendary Grigorii the Bone Crusher.

The three agents met at the Floridita Bar, not far from the plaza, and then spread out. One decided to go into the bar on the chance that the trio was there or had been there.

Three Russians sat at a table drinking beer. He introduced himself and asked if they'd seen a huge man with a couple. Yes, they had. The huge man had knocked out one of them out. The other man had bruised a second's knuckles. And the beautiful lady spoke flawless Russian.

The agent sat down and got descriptions. He asked where they went. The Russians said they didn't know, but the lady had said she was coming back tomorrow to dance with them. The agent thanked them and found his companions. He relayed what he had heard. The lead agent thought it was odd, even if the big man were not the Bone. He left the two agents to stake out the neighborhood and told them he would send relief agents to set up a twenty-four-hour watch.

At the office, one of the agents called with the news that the trio had booked two nights at the Casa de las Tres Guitarras. He also said the owner of the casa had taken a picture of the woman with a hidden camera because he found her attractive. He had forwarded a wirephoto copy. The lead agent returned to the office and sent a telegram and the wirephoto copy to Volkhov.

Volkhov's antennae went up. He thought it highly suspicious that a big man resembling the Bone was in bar in Cuba with a woman who spoke fluent Russian. He showed the woman's picture to Grigulevich, who identified her as Ana Cortez. Grigulevich had tried to capture her for Stalin. He added that she was somehow involved in Stalin's demise. Her presence in Cuba meant trouble. He recommended that the trio be arrested and interrogated.

Volkhov ordered them murdered. His order must have grated on Grigulevich. He challenged Volkhov. "Killing Ana Cortez and her associates is counterproductive. It'd be better to keep them as hostages for negotiation."

Volkhov scratched his head and looked intently at his subordinate. He wondered about his commitment to the cause. "I want no complications when I have Khrushchev where I want him. Kill them." He told Grigulevich to handle the hit. His deputy sent out an urgent order to the KGB office in Cuba to find, interrogate, and kill the trio, but make the murders look like an accident. He sent a separate telegram to double security around the missile bases. Volkhov was satisfied that Grigulevich seemed to be back on the team, but he still planned to keep an eye on him.

The lead agent published a description of the trio and a warrant for their arrest. Before long, KGB agents and FAR troops were combing the streets around the Plaza de la Catedral and the Floridita Bar. The four FAR soldiers who'd interacted with the trio saw the alert and reported that the suspects got into an old Jeep with a Cuban man they'd hired to show them the highlights of Havana. They had the name and address of the driver, but they turned out to be fake.

§

THE DRIVER OF the Jeep was going as fast as he safely could on a heavily forested backroad about five miles from Playa de Guanímar when Ana saw distant, flickering headlights in the Jeep's sideview mirror. It was the first vehicle she'd seen all night and it was gaining on them. It must be in pursuit, driving that fast through such difficult terrain.

"We have company," she said. "Back into the dense part of woods and turn off the engine and headlights. I'm going to try to convince them to turn around."

"How are you going to do that?" the Cuban said.

"We'll see. I have an idea that I think will work. Keep your guns handy in case we must fight our way out." Ed and the Bone had learned long ago to follow her instinct.

She told the Cuban to take a position in the woods and cover her and the road with his AK-47. She told Ed to hide on the Jeep's back floor with a flashlight. She told Bone to put on his black cape, stand on the hood of the Jeep, and raise his hands high as if he were about to fly. She said when she yelled "El Toro, action," she wanted the flashlight to shine on Bone's upper torso, bathing his massive silhouette in a spotlight. She said she thought she could convince whoever was in pursuit that they were shooting a film and that the pursuers should go back the way they came. She wanted just enough time to reach the Piper Pacer.

Five minutes later a small pickup truck approached and stopped about fifty feet from where Ana was standing in the middle of the dirt road. Its headlights silhouetted her in the FAR captain's uniform. A Russian major got out of the passenger side, followed by a FAR major on the driver's side. Five FAR soldiers jumped to the ground from the truck's bed. The seven soldiers walked warily toward Ana. They held AK-47s and had sidearms strapped to their waists. An iguana dropped from a tree and raced across the road into the brush. The men jumped and raised their weapons, startled by the reptile.

"Stop," Ana yelled in Spanish. "We're filming an El Toro picture here. You must go back."

"El Toro!" the Cubans shouted. "Is he here?"

"He is, but he's in the middle of a scene. The Ministry of Culture has cordoned off this area for one hour until the scene is complete. No one is allowed here while filming is in progress."

The Russian major was perplexed. Everyone seemed to know El Toro except him.

"Who is El Toro?" he asked in accented Spanish.

"El Toro," the FAR major said, "is one of the most famous movie stars in Latin America. He is a badman but with a heart for the poor. We love him."

The Russian was impressed. Looking at Ana, he said, "Captain, has a Jeep come through here in the past ten minutes or so?" A fly buzzed around his face, and he swatted at it with a closed fist.

"No," Ana said. "We're making a film. No vehicles have passed here. I did see headlights flickering through the trees about ten minutes before you arrived. Maybe it turned off into the jungle, and its passengers moved the traffic cones and the road closure sign."

"Major," the Russian said, "let's go back about two miles or so and check for tracks. The Mexicans might be hiding there."

"Yes, a good idea," the FAR major said and then pleaded with Ana, "Captain, can we glimpse El Toro?"

"We're filming and behind schedule," Ana said. "One quick glimpse when we test the effect of a flashlight on his cape, but then you must move back." Ana turned toward the hidden Jeep.

"El Toro, action!" Ana shouted.

A light flashed on Bone, who appeared bigger than life, hovering in the air, in a black cape. The light went out. Two or three cocuyo beetles jumped in the air and glowed green.

A gasp went up from the six Cubans and the Russian. A few looked around. Then they yelled, "El Toro!"

"Can we come back in an hour to get an autograph?" the FAR major asked.

"Yes," Ana said, "but you must leave now so that we can finish the scene."

"Get back into the truck," the FAR major said. "We will return later." The FAR truck turned around and peeled out, its taillights disappearing around a curve.

Ana, Ed, Bone, and the Cuban hopped in the Jeep and sped in the opposite direction, toward the Pacer. The stars sparkled and the moon hung like a lantern in the night sky, illuminating the passing dark forms of trees, bushes, and rocks along the dirt road. The evening's natural beauty was only checked by the nightmare of what they had seen.

Fifteen minutes later, as they approached Playa de Guanímar, Ana told the driver to stop. She held her hand up near her ear, as if asking everyone to listen. They sat there, not moving a muscle, listening to the night sounds.

"It's too quiet," she whispered. The crickets, katydids, and tree frogs aren't singing."

Headlights flashed behind them. "It's a trap. There's an ambush ahead and a patrol behind us. Is there another way to the beach?"

The Cuban nodded. "It's about a half mile down the road. There's an old trail through the jungle that the sugarcane workers used to pull wagons before trucks took on the hauling work. It's probably covered with fallen branches, overgrown grasses, and a dead tree trunk or two, but the Jeep is a tank. It can get through."

"Take it," Ana said, as she, Ed, and Bone armed themselves with the Makarov pistols and the AK-47. The Jeep's powerful motor sprang to life.

A shot rang out and the bullet cut through tree branches above the road. "Keep going." Ana gripped the dash. "They want to capture us, not kill us."

Four pairs of flashing headlights came on like lightning bugs caught in a spiderweb.

"Is the Jeep strong enough to plow through them?" Ana asked.

"We don't have to," the Cuban said. "We're at the cutoff and turning into the jungle."

Tree branches whipped the windshield and frame of the Jeep but did not slow it. It was a bulldozer. Ed and Bone in the backseat kept their heads down. The windshield protected the driver and Ana from the lashing bushes and tree branches. Suddenly, the Jeep stopped.

"There's a huge tree on the path," the driver said.

Ed and Bone jumped out of the Jeep. They used the stump to pivot the tree just enough to allow the Jeep to pass, then jumped back into the Jeep.

"No," Ana said. "Move it back. It'll slow down the pursuit."

Fifteen minutes later, the Cuban drove up to the Piper Pacer. Ana, Ed, and Bone climbed out of the Jeep with their valise and briefcase. They slipped out of the uniforms and gave them to the Cuban along with the AK-47, Makarov pistols, wire cutter, and flashlights. The Cuban reached under his seat, grabbed a binder full of eyewitness reports on the Russian installations, and handed it to Ana.

Ana thanked him and asked him to wait until she made sure the plane was operational. She asked Ed to start it up. He climbed into the cockpit, hotwired the starter, and brought the engine to life. When she got closer to the Pacer, she saw that the wheeled landing gear was chained to an anchor sunk in concrete.

"Bone, please break the chain," she said. "I'll radio the F-4s that we will be in the air in a few minutes and need an escort to Guantanamo." Ana turned to the driver.

"Thank you for helping us. Have a safe trip to Havana. We're praying for peace."

"Thank you for coming," the Cuban said. "We are all praying for peace." The driver sped off.

Ana and Bone climbed into the plane with the valise and briefcase and took seats behind Ed, who was revving the Pacer's engine. Ana focused on Ed.

"Is there enough runway?" Ana asked.

Ed nodded. "Looks like over 1,500 feet of beach. The engine sounds tuned, with a smooth hum and good horsepower. Despite our embargo, the Cubans keep their small planes and cars in great working condition."

Ana sat back and relaxed. Ed released the brakes, increased the engine to full power, and guided the sturdy Pacer down the runway. As the plane ascended, two supersonic F-4 jet fighters, carrying air-to-air and air-to-ground missiles, flanked the Pacer. Three Cuban-piloted MIG-20s appeared to the north but turned away when the F-4s circled and closed on them. Twenty minutes later, Ed set the Pacer down at Guantanamo.

Ana, Ed, and Bone transferred with their light luggage to a North American X-15, modified to hold four passengers, and landed two hours later at Andrews Air Force Base. It was just after midnight. Ana was pleased that the Sheriff and officials from the CIA and the National Photographic Intelligence Center were there to meet them and take their film and reports.

Ana briefed the officials on what the trio had found. She said the dire situation grew more perilous with each passing hour. Ed and Bone reinforced her judgment. While the trio climbed into a van for transport to the Cloister, the Sheriff said the CIA and NPIC's analysis of the pictures and reports would be available in the morning. He thanked them for their work and told them to get a good night's rest. All hell was about to break loose.

§

GRIGULEVICH LAUGHED IN silence. Ana Cortez and her two associates had melted away again. When he'd issued the order for her murder at Volkhov's insistence, he sensed it would never happen. He was half convinced she was a spirit.

Upon further investigation, he discovered that a woman who was dressed in a FAR uniform and looked like Ana had convinced a FAR patrol and a Russian major around Cristóbal that she was directing a film starring the famous El Toro, the Robin Hood of Latin American cowboy movies. When he found out that a Piper Pacer had been stolen and flown to Guantanamo, he put it together—Ana Cortez had once again proven to be the bane of his espionage career. She had help, he thought, and maybe some of that help came from a higher power.

He had had her cornered in Mexico in 1940, and she had escaped. Then he had dealt with her when he was in Rome in 1953 trying to influence the pope to reach out to her and influence her to accept Stalin's hand in marriage. She turned up in Moscow, and Stalin turned up dead. There was no trace of her.

Now she had appeared in Havana with someone who looked like the Bone, just when the Cuban missile operation seemed to be trending in Soviet Russia's favor. He had made a half-hearted effort, using Cuban allies, KGB agents, and Russian military personnel in Cuba, to catch her. But once again she had vanished into thin air. He was not unhappy that she had escaped. Somehow, he'd known that she would get away. He began to think of her as a symbol and invitation to a better order for Russia. He wondered again if the two American teenagers who'd faded away in Mongolia were related to her.

Grigulevich told a very irritated Volkhov that the trio had help getting away, blaming inexperienced Cuban allies. Volkhov constantly nagged Grigulevich for his failure to capture the trio in Cuba. He also complained about the disappearance of the Byrnes teens and pressure from the FBI to search Leningrad Harbor.

Grigulevich tried to conceal his growing disillusion with communism from Volkhov. But his boss seemed uncomfortable around him. Had Volkhov perhaps realized Grigulevich's doubts? Nothing came of the strain because Volkhov's attention was soon drawn to the skies over Cuba, where he expected U-2s to blot out the sun.

Chapter 12
Answers

Langley and Washington, October 12–21, 1962

KELLY HUDDLED WITH Margo, Ana, Ed, Oliver, and Taylor in a cramped secure reading room around a mountain of reports, photos, and documents on a conference table at CIA headquarters in Langley, Virginia. The room had zero windows, green-painted walls, and uncomfortable metal furniture. Their faces showed strain and wariness. Danger lurked, and each of them was aware of it.

They had pored over the photos and reports that the trio had brought back from Cuba, the reports that Jesse and Meg had made, and extensive documents from the Posse's global network. They also had looked at NPIC and CIA analyses, photographs, and reports. They had studied three black books—thick, loose-leaf binders—containing pictures and user manuals for Soviet missiles. These had been collected by spies, most notably a source called IRONBARK, and journalists at events such as the Soviets' May Day parades where the Russians showcased weapons.

"I think they're planning a first strike," Ed said, sipping his coffee.

Kelly turned and looked at him. "No demands, just a preemptive strike?"

"Not yet. I believe they'll make demands but are working furiously to get to first-strike readiness."

The air conditioning clicked on, wafting tepid air through the stuffy, windowless room.

"It's so reckless," Ana said. "The Soviets are counting on law-abiding countries to appease them rather than call their bluff and risk a nuclear disaster."

The tension in the room, Kelly knew, reflected the tension felt across the US government, especially in the White House. The Posse had unequivocal proof that the USSR was placing SS-4 medium-range nuclear missiles at one site in Cuba's San Cristóbal region and had tens of thousands of troops and advanced jets and bombers in Cuba. The eyewitness reports that the Cuban asset had given to the trio had indicated that the Russians were doing the same thing at other sites in Cuba and possibly installing long-range missiles. They also knew the Soviet Union was lying through its teeth by insisting that the weapons in Cuba were defensive.

Kelly shook his head and looked intently at his fellow Posse members. "We must answer three questions for the president before he can decide on the US response to the Soviet aggression: Is the USSR ready for war? Are the missile installations extensive and operational? Are nuclear warheads in Cuba?"

Ana leaned back in her chair. She took a deep breath and pursed her lips. "To answer the first query, do we have to expose IRONBARK?"

"Yes," Kelly said with a sullen face. "Colonel Oleg Penkovsky is in position to find out whether the USSR's national strategic arsenal is in offensive position with missiles ready to launch. The answer will tell JFK whether he has flexibility in confronting the Soviets."

Ana nodded. "He'll have to drop his cover to make a clear and swift report. The KGB will be watching. He'll likely die."

Kelly caressed his chin. "I know, and I think he knows, but the information will potentially prevent a nuclear war and save millions of lives."

Ana took a deep breath. She had never met Penkovsky but knew he was an invaluable asset. Ed said he knew him—a courageous and patriotic Russian who worked to grow democracy in his homeland and who would sacrifice his freedom and life to help the Posse. Taylor and Oliver reinforced Ed's view, saying they knew and valued him as an intrepid advocate of democracy.

Margo then turned to the second question. "How do we obtain current information on the status of Soviet missile installations in Cuba?"

Kelly had been thinking about this question since the return of the trio from Cuba. "We must have aerial photographs of not just the entire San Cristóbal region, but also of all other areas where we suspect missile launchers are being built. Then the president would have a full picture of the threat."

"How quickly can we get a U-2 photo shoot? Margo said.

"The past few days the cloud cover and bad weather in parts of Cuba have prevented recon," Kelly said, "but tomorrow the forecast is for cloudless skies. Major Richard Heyser will take off before sunrise from Edwards Air Force Base in California in a U-2F, modified for in-flight refueling. He'll be over Cuba on a sleepy Sunday morning. US Navy jets from Guantanamo will help protect him, if necessary."

The group nodded. He smiled. "We are fortunate the Posse has friends and resources."

"And the third answer that calls for logic?" Ana asked.

Kelly sat back in his chair. "The CIA thinks they're no nuclear warheads in Cuba now and will not be for three or four days. I think the warheads are there."

"Why?" Ed, Taylor, and Oliver asked simultaneously.

"If I were sneaking missiles into Cuba," Kelly said, "I'd ship the warheads first because they can be carried unobtrusively in the holds of freighters. Once in Cuba, they can be stored easily in warehouses where they'd be available for use. Then I'd rush in the missiles at the last minute. They're bulky and must be carried above deck, where they can be seen, much as Meg and Jesse documented. They would likely stir a response that might lead to a blockade. I'd want to limit the time and opportunity for the US to respond, and even if it were to respond eventually, some of the first missile ships would have probably gotten through. It's better to have the payload in place before sending a shot across the bow."

"It's possible they're not there," Ed said.

Ana shook her head. "I agree with Kelly. Besides, if we apply a variation of the Pascal wager to the problem, it's better to act as if the nuclear warheads are there than to gamble that they're not. If they're there, we're already at the most dangerous time in world history and must act decisively. Our freedom hangs in the balance."

§

THREE DAYS FOLLOWING the flight of the U-2, Ana's last five words still rang in Kelly's ears. She had summed up the stakes in a single phrase.

The Sheriff entered the Cabinet Room of the White House. President Kennedy sat with the heads of the CIA and the National Security Agency, the Secretaries of Defense and State, and the so-called ExCom committee that JFK had set up to spearhead the US response to the Cuban crisis. The president's chief of staff directed Kelly to an empty chair near JFK at the head of the table.

Kelly knew JFK was determined to see the crisis through. He had set up ExCom to keep the military in check until diplomacy had a chance to work. He had ordered no public opinion polls to prevent politization of the crisis before the upcoming elections. He also demanded no demonization of Khrushchev, so that he had freedom to negotiate with the Kremlin leader.

"Thank you for coming, Kelly." JFK looked around the table. "We're facing an existential threat to the United States, the Western Hemisphere, and the world. The peril is unprecedented. Everyone here has seen the evidence that the Posse, working in close collaboration with our defense and intelligence experts, has gathered. Many of you have made recommendations to me, particularly from the defense and intelligence agencies. I asked Kelly to study the recommendations and then to provide us with answers to three questions." The president gestured for Kelly to begin.

Kelly turned to the first query regarding the Soviet readiness for war. He said, according to the Soviet asset code-named IRONBARK, the USSR was neither positioned for a first strike nor ready for nuclear war.

JFK zeroed in on the point. "Since the USSR hasn't put its forces on a war footing, it's likely placing missiles in Cuba for political purposes."

The Sheriff confirmed IRONBARK's report and JFK's conclusion. He saw relief in JFK's face. The information gave the president a tactical advantage.

Kelly then answered the second question. He reported that the photos from U-2 flights showed the Soviets had both medium-range and intermediate-range ballistic missiles. They could hit most major cities in the US and South America. They also revealed launchers, missile bunkers, transport trucks, and support personnel. He stressed that IRONBARK had provided plans and descriptions of the nuclear rocket launch sites in Cuba, which allowed the US to identify some missile sites in pictures from the U-2s that were blurry or low-resolution images. He said the photos provided overwhelming evidence of a systematic and wide-ranging deployment of Soviet ballistic missiles in Cuba and the transformation of Cuba into a heavily militarized Soviet base. He added that the USSR would, if not stopped, eventually gain a significant military advantage and a first-strike capability.

Kennedy wanted to know if the missiles could be taken out with air strike with 100 percent certainty. Kelly said he doubted it, but he would defer to the Secretary of Defense.

JFK turned to the Secretary of Defense and pressed him. The military chief said the US Air Force could guarantee that most of the missiles would be wiped out with a massive air strike. But it could not guarantee that all of them would be.

JFK shook his head. "An air strike is off the table for now."

Finally, Kelly explained why he and other Posse leaders thought nuclear warheads were already in Cuba. Besides logic, he said the photos showed that certain storage facilities were guarded around the clock. He believed the Russians would only do that to safeguard nuclear warheads.

Kennedy thanked Kelly. He then opened the discussion for questions and options. After tense and heated discussion, the choices presented to JFK included diplomacy, naval blockade, naval quarantine, and an invasion of Cuba accompanied by an airstrike on the missile sites and their supplies. Kelly noted that the military leaders persisted in wanting a preemptive air strike followed by an invasion.

When asked for his opinion, Kelly advised a less aggressive approach that prepared for action but allowed first for diplomacy. He recommended that JFK set up a quarantine, which the Secretary of Defense had proposed, and simultaneously send a letter to Khrushchev demanding that he remove the missiles.

Kelly said a quarantine was preferable to a blockade because it was not an act of war, like a blockade, but would achieve the same result—the US Navy could prohibit Soviet ships carrying offensive missiles from entering Cuban waters but might allow nonthreatening cargo to pass. He did not believe that Khrushchev intended to attack the US.

"Khrushchev is under a great deal of pressure from Yuri Volkhov and the Kobaists, a neo-Stalinist faction of the Russian Communist Party." Kelly presented a photo of Volkhov speaking to Khrushchev in an office. He also pointed again to the information from IRONBARK that showed the USSR was not ready for war.

President Kennedy and the ExCom members asked Kelly a few more questions. Then the president thanked the group for its advice and ended the meeting. He said he had enough information to respond to the Soviet threat. He'd send them his decision in a few days and inform the American people of his decision on October 22.

On October 19 the secretary of state told Kelly that Soviet Foreign Minister Andrei Gromyko had met with the president in the Oval Office. Gromyko had boldly asserted that Soviet aid to Cuba was purely defensive and no threat to the US. The secretary told him that Kennedy, who knew Gromyko was lying, informed the Russian that the greatest consequences would ensue if Soviet offensive weapons were introduced into Cuba. Kelly appreciated that JFK had played his cards close to his vest.

On October 22, television and radio networks advertised throughout the day that the president of the United States would address the nation on radio and live television that evening on a sudden and imminent threat to world peace. Kelly knew that citizens everywhere held their collective breath.

The Sheriff hoped JFK would deliver a speech that gave the Soviets pause in their wild escalation of tension and warmongering. The president needed to rally global opinion behind the US. He wasn't expecting a tour de force.

Chapter 13
The Lion

Washington, October 22, 1962

THE SHERIFF ENTERED the White House, Margo on his arm, shaken by the growing realization that the United States could be wiped off the face of the earth. But the Posse had assembled what the president needed to formulate a response to the Soviet menace.

Kelly and Margo sat, together with other Posse members and government officials, in front of the television in the newsroom of the White House. They were there to hear Kennedy's address to the nation and the world on the Soviet Union's impulsive, perilous behavior.

"It's a day for the history books," Kelly said, "if we survive this crisis."

"Unbelievably reckless," Margo said. "The Soviets have thrown down the gauntlet."

"The US has an advantage," Kelly said. "They don't know that we know they're running a bluff. If JFK is the commander I think he is, he will convince the Soviets to back down."

Kennedy appeared on the screen, speaking in a clear, no-nonsense, confident voice. He said the Soviet Union had secretly installed nuclear missiles in Cuba, lied about it, and now threatened the United States, the Western Hemisphere, and the world with nuclear war. That there was absolutely no bargaining with a gun to the head of the US. The missiles, he stressed, had to be removed immediately or the US would remove them. Period.

He further said the US had moved forward with steps to force the USSR to capitulate: imposing a naval quarantine on Cuba, moving the US nuclear arsenal to DEFCON2, and warning that any attack from Cuba would be considered as having come from the USSR. It would be answered with a full retaliatory attack on the Soviet Union. Kennedy ended by appealing for peace and stressing that the crisis could be ended if the Soviet government removed its nuclear weapons from Cuba.

Kelly thought Kennedy's speech was an astute, measured mix of diplomacy and force—just what the situation called for. The tone was stark, balanced, and pointed, but not unreasonable given that Moscow had initiated the threat. The equation was simple and clear—remove the missiles or the missiles would be removed.

News reports poured into the newsroom at the White House, showing that American and democratic public opinion across the globe had rallied behind Kennedy. The OAS and NATO leaders, whom Kennedy personally engaged and kept in the loop, announced their unqualified support of Kennedy's stand. It cast Soviet Russia as an irresponsible pariah state that could not be trusted. But uneasiness surfaced. Suddenly, the nation and the world, shocked and focused, faced the possibility of global nuclear war.

Fifteen minutes later, Kelly told the Posse members that he and Margo were heading to the Cloister. They would ponder what the Posse could do to end the Cuban missile crisis and help Khrushchev get out of the hole that he had dug. He said he'd like to meet with all available Posse members at the Cloister at eight-thirty the next morning.

When Kelly reached the front door of the White House, the president's chief of staff told him that the president wanted to see him in the Oval Office.

"Come in," President Kennedy called out when Kelly knocked. Margo waited outside.

The president sat at his desk, on the phone with General Eisenhower. He motioned for Kelly to sit down. Kelly did, the historian in him admiring the oak of the nineteenth-century desk. He knew that it was made from the timbers of the British Arctic exploration ship the HMS *Resolute*, a gift from Queen Victoria to President Rutherford B. Hayes.

Kelly didn't know if this was a short or long meeting, and he wanted to be prepared for any eventuality. The president's Welsh terrier Charlie relaxed on a rug near the desk. A Swedish ivy plant, its leaves shaped like shamrocks, rested on the mantle above the fireplace.

Kennedy wiped his forehead with a handkerchief. "Thanks for calling, Ike." He hung up and put his glasses on the desk.

"Good to see you, Kelly, or should I call you the Sheriff?" the president said, smiling.

Kelly laughed. "Call me by any name you want, Mr. President, but don't call me late for dinner."

"OK, Kelly," Kennedy chuckled. "I wouldn't want to miss a meal by Margo either. How is she?"

"Fine, thank you for asking."

Kennedy smiled, picked up his glasses, and pointed them at Kelly. "These are dangerous times. I should feel fear, but I don't. We're in the right. I will bend here and there to give peace a chance but will not snap."

Kelly shifted. He was looking at a man who held the future of the world in his hands. Dictators thought they could bludgeon the representative governments into surrender. "It's an old story, but democracy, freedom, and the rule of law will prevail."

JFK nodded. "I have bad news on IRONBARK. He was arrested and will probably be executed."

"I'm sorry to hear that, but what he did might help prevent nuclear war."

The president agreed and changed the subject, "Khrushchev is a puzzle."

Kelly stared at the president, who raised an eyebrow. He realized it was a question.

Kelly ran a hand through his hair. He said that Khrushchev had grievously miscalculated. The USSR faced annihilation or an image-damaging defeat.

"Why?" Kennedy asked.

Kelly shook his head. "The underpinnings of authoritarian government are lies foisted upon people by force, fear, and violence. Weakness or defeat reveals not only the foolishness of backing such a government, but also the truth of what makes a country strong."

JFK stared at Kelly for a minute. "You think Khrushchev will be cashiered if he removes the missiles?"

Kelly nodded. He said Khrushchev had made a fundamental mistake in the lexicon of dictatorship. He had miscalculated the strength of democracy.

JFK scratched his head. "Khrushchev has a dilemma."

Kelly nodded and said it was important for the US to help him stay in power for the short term. His reformist agenda could end communism and change Russia into a responsible power that would support the rule of law and democracy.

"That is quite a balancing act," Kennedy said shaking his heads, "but if anyone can square the circle, it'd be Dr. Miller."

"What do you mean?" Kelly was surprised to hear his alias from the president.

"Thirty minutes ago," Kennedy said with a wry smile, "a telegram from Khrushchev addressed to Dr. Robert Miller arrived at the State Department. Hand-delivered by a Washington-based Russian with the TASS news agency, a confidante of Alexei Adzhubei, Khrushchev's son-in-law. He added a verbal warning: 'watch your back.'" Kennedy passed the telegram to Kelly.

Kelly held the telegram tightly and stared at it. The message was cryptic: Miller, come quickly to the place that served a good purpose in the past!

"What does Khrushchev mean? What can he want?" The president's tone was earnest.

Kelly explained he had met Khrushchev in 1953 in the courtyard of the only Catholic church in Moscow. The Vatican had asked him, as Dr. Robert Miller, to serve as its representative in the delicate matter of Stalin's wooing of Ana Cortez. He had done research in Rome and was well known among select, discrete Vatican leaders who specialized in foreign affairs. He said Khrushchev and he had hit it off and had kept in touch. He said the Soviet leader knew him as an academic from the DC area who occasionally served as a State Department consultant.

JFK grinned. "I guess he didn't know you were the Sheriff."

"True." Kelly laughed. "As for what he wants, it sounds like a plea for help. It might even involve the pope as a mediator in the Cuba affair."

JFK stood up. He said his back hurt. Then he met Kelly's eyes. "I agree. Khrushchev might be reaching out to the pope. I want you to go to Moscow, and to Rome if Khrushchev so desires. I think the pope might be helpful. I already asked him to pray and to make a plea for peace."

"Excellent idea," Kelly said. "He has great moral authority."

"I think so," Kennedy said. "I was particularly impressed with his speech at the opening session of Vatican II. He is an optimist who thinks differences are not a reason for war, alienation, or separation but are part of God's plan to bring people of the world together."

Kelly nodded. "Khrushchev clearly admires him too."

"Apparently." JFK paused. "I sent him a stern note via our ambassador in Moscow, telling him that the Soviet Union had started this fight and had to remove the missiles immediately to end it."

Kelly leaned forward. "It's good to keep reminding him of that. Hopefully, we can settle this through diplomacy."

JFK handed Kelly a small box and a phone number. "You can contact me any time on this secure mobile phone from the American embassies in Moscow or Rome, and I can call you. Give Khrushchev its number if you want him to reach you."

Then JFK held out his hand. "Be careful!"

They shook. Kelly thanked the president and left the Oval Office.

§

"**WHAT DID JFK** say?" Margo said, once they were secure in their room at the Cloister.

"He understands what we're up against," Kelly said softly. He kissed Margo and they embraced tenderly.

Kelly looked into her eyes. He told her Kennedy grasped that the crisis was a pivotal battle in the ongoing struggle between democracy and authoritarianism and that history showed appeasement always made matters worse when dealing with greedy dictators. "He's a Lion and the perfect leader for the times."

Margo smiled. "What's he going to do?"

Kelly took a deep breath. "He wants me to go to Moscow to work with Khrushchev on a solution."

"Why you?" Margo was surprised.

Kelly explained the invitation from Khrushchev and the importance of swift action.

"It's too quick," Margo advised. "We need a backup plan to protect you."

"I'll be okay," Kelly said. "It's a straight shot to Moscow. Khrushchev will protect me. Maybe we can find a way out of this crisis before it blows up into a nuclear war."

"Take someone with you. I can go," Margo pleaded.

"No. I need you to manage the Posse. I'll be fine."

"Let's compromise," Margo said "I'll take a group of Posse leaders to Rome. From there, we can move to give you backup anywhere in Europe. If you don't need it, we will wait for you in Rome."

Kelly stroked her hair. "All right, that's a good idea, but I must leave immediately. The White House booked me on the next KLM flight to Moscow."

He sensed that Margo was unhappy but trusted him to make the right decision. He admired her creative flexibility and he felt better knowing she'd be in Europe. She packed him a carryon bag with clothes for cold and warm weather. Then she laid out an outfit for him that fit the academic profile of Dr. Miller—a white turtleneck pullover, a black winter raincoat with a zippered wool lining, a tweed Irish brown herringbone jacket, and a brown Ushanka hat made of rabbit fur. "It'll keep you warm. Plus it's an unlikely ensemble for a super spy."

"I'm also taking my white British style Fedora and my black Tony Lama boots because they're so comfortable."

Margo laughed. "You will certainly look like an eccentric professor, quite different from the cowboy attire you wore when you knocked out those two Russians agents at Casey's bar in San Marcos in 1953."

"Those two agents are now running the KGB office in Leningrad," Kelly said, shaking his head in disbelief.

"I know," Margo said, "and I'm glad Leningrad is not on your itinerary. They are brutes."

He smiled. "Maybe you should cut my longish hair."

She looked thoughtful, then shook her head. "Keep it. No spy would sport such a waggish hairdo. Be careful. I'll cancel the morning meeting with the Posse and will be waiting your call in Rome." They kissed goodbye.

Kelly's thoughts leapt ahead on his way to the airport. The meeting with Khrushchev might lead to an end of the Cuban missile crisis. He wished he had time to develop a proper backup plan for Russia, but the trip to Moscow under Khrushchev's protection was safe. In his haste, he forgot about Volkhov and the neo-Stalinists—who did not want the crisis to end.

Chapter 14
Who Is Miller?

Leningrad, October 23, 1962

VOLKHOV'S EYES BULGED. He had just read a copy of the telegram, provided by agent Viktor Petrov of the TASS news agency in Washington, that Khrushchev had sent to Dr. Robert Miller. He sat at his desk in his first-floor office at Lubyanka. The window, with black steel bars, looked out to the predawn darkness of Malaya Lubyanka Street. A solitary fluorescent light on the ceiling was buzzing, a sign that it was about to fail. He had a cup of hot black coffee. He had awakened early to hear Kennedy's speech. The warm days of early October had given way to freezing Arctic blasts and snowstorms that spread like an icy wave across the flat Eurasian plain. Crusty snow gave Moscow's gray buildings a new white coat. The office was stuffy and overheated, which he detested, but the thermostat was stuck on high.

Grigulevich sat across from him. The man's long hair looked uncombed, probably because he'd rushed to meet with Volkhov.

He too had a cup of coffee but had difficulty sipping it because his metal folding chair wobbled. Two of its legs were slightly shorter than the others. Volkhov called it "the torture chair" and used it when he wanted to make his subordinates suffer. It was four a.m. on October 23.

Volkhov was not concerned about Kennedy's broadcast, which he dismissed, but he wondered why Khrushchev had asked Miller to rush to Moscow.

"What's your read on Miller?"

Grigulevich said he'd met Miller in Rome in 1953 and introduced him to Khrushchev in Moscow. Miller was a naïve, low-level American professor around DC who was enlisted by the Vatican to work on Stalin's courting of Ana Cortez because he could speak Russian.

Volkhov nodded. "I don't know much about Miller, but I had Khrushchev boxed in when he sent that telegram to Miller. I don't like it."

Grigulevich, teetering forward, asked if Miller was a problem for the Cuban play.

Volkhov suppressed a snigger at his deputy, who looked ready to fall over. He didn't know why he liked to torment Grigulevich. He leaned back in his chair and told Grigulevich that the trap was about to be sprung, and Khrushchev seemed to be blinking. He thought Khrushchev had contacted Miller to get reassurance from the Americans that negotiations were still possible. Or maybe to look for a face-saving way out of the crisis.

Grigulevich smiled and leaned toward Volkhov, agreeing that the KGB leader's analysis was on target.

Volkhov liked fawning. "Where in Moscow did Khrushchev meet Miller in 1953?"

"In the courtyard of St. Louis Church," Grigulevich said with a forced smile.

"Interesting." Volkhov sipped his coffee.

"Is it important?"

Volkhov explained that it was a clue to what Khrushchev was thinking. "He may be planning to reach out to the pope about the Cuban quandary. Miller could be a conduit to Pope John XXIII."

Grigulevich shrugged. "So what? If the pope moves JFK to back off his threat, we win. If Khrushchev retreats, we dump Khrushchev, and still win."

Volkhov dismissed Grigulevich's points with a shake of his head. He said the pope was nothing, but Miller had ties to the American government. He didn't want to take any chances when he had Khrushchev on the ropes. He wanted Miller dead and Khrushchev isolated.

Grigulevich's eyes narrowed. He clearly was not enthusiastic, but Volkhov could not tell if that was because his chair was uncomfortable or he didn't like the thought of killing Miller.

"What's wrong?" Volkhov said.

Grigulevich shifted his weight again. "Nothing. How do you want to handle the hit?"

Volkhov decided it was the chair. "He's on a flight to Moscow. Khrushchev has the Army and the Foreign Ministry with him and will be able to protect him if he gets to Moscow. Force the plane to land in Leningrad on grounds of an anonymous bomb scare. Take him to the Astoria Hotel to keep up the appearance that we want him comfortable because he is an American with a diplomatic passport. Use torture to squeeze him for information and then dump his body in the Neva."

"No problem," Grigulevich said, clenching his teeth and slowly standing to give his legs a chance to stretch and free himself from the chair.

Volkhov stared at him. Grigulevich was a cold-blooded killer without scruples but a brilliant planner. He needed Grigulevich but didn't trust him and enjoyed making him suffer.

"What's your plan?" Volkhov said. He watched Grigulevich breathe out unhurriedly, seeming glad to be free from the chair and to share his thoughts on the hit.

"I'll give the job to the local KGB team in Leningrad. Smirnov and Brodsky are tough guys. One was a boxing champion, and the other was an Olympic wrestler. I almost feel sorry for Miller."

"That's wicked," Volkhov said. "You are going to turn two hard-bitten musclemen on a pipsqueak. I'd love to be a fly on the wall for that interview."

"He will suffer and divulge what he knows," Grigulevich said. He turned toward the door to leave.

"I hope for your sake that you're right," Volkhov said. "You failed to catch and kill Ana Cortez and her friends in Cuba, and you still haven't found the Byrnes kids."

Grigulevich didn't turn back.

Volkhov was disturbed by the KGB's inability to capture the trio in Cuba and the Byrnes teens in Mongolia, but he had a more pressing issue to deal with. He wanted Miller killed and looked forward to a report of Miller's body parts floating down the Neva River. He didn't expect to see Miller in Moscow.

§

WHEN THE KLM flight entered Soviet-controlled airspace, the Sheriff, who was holding a diplomatic passport in the name of Dr. Robert Miller, awoke from a deep sleep and leaned back in his window seat. A flight attendant named Anke, whom he had come to know on the trip over the Atlantic, stood in the aisle. The older blonde woman was a distant relative of a Dutch foreign minister who had helped build NATO. Good looking, she spoke English fluently and had an outgoing personality. They chatted on and off during the flight about postwar Europe and the hope that Europe could find both economic and political unity. He had asked her to wake him up when the plane crossed the Soviet border. She handed him a cup of hot coffee. He thanked her with a smile. She smiled back, said the plane was an hour or so ahead of schedule because of a strong tailwind, and returned to the galley.

He read again the telegram from Khrushchev. He wondered if the Soviet leader was still in control and looking for a way out of the crisis or had lost power to Volkhov and the Kobaists.

When the plane suddenly made a roll left, straightened out, and began to descend, Kelly looked out the window and recognized the Baltic Sea and frozen Lake Ladoga in the distance. The late morning sun was aglow but fighting a losing battle to break through a thick ceiling of dark blue-gray clouds.

The plane was landing at Pulkovo Airport in Leningrad, not Sheremetyevo Airport in Moscow. Before he had left Washington, he had sent an encrypted message to Khrushchev that he would meet him at three p.m. on October 23. He didn't want to be late. He was glad the plane was ahead of schedule.

The pilot announced on the intercom that there would be a stop in Leningrad because a bomb threat had been reported. The plane had to be searched and cleared. Kelly's eyebrows went up. He suspected that Yuri Volkhov and the KGB wanted to block him from meeting Khrushchev.

He should have prepared a backup plan, but he'd been impatient. He now tried to correct the mistake. He had Posse assets in Leningrad, Helsinki, Tallin, Riga, Vilnius, and Moscow, and Margo and other US Posse leaders were in or on their way to Rome, but he had no way of contacting any of them without arousing KGB suspicion. He also assumed Khrushchev had the Soviet Foreign Ministry or Defense Ministry monitoring his trip. Would they take measures to rescue him? He knew the Soviet leader wanted their meeting to be low key and private.

Kelly leaned forward in his chair and called Anke. He showed her his diplomatic passport and said he was the reason for the diversion, not a bomb.

He told her that he was on a mission to meet with Khrushchev in Moscow to help defuse the Cuban missile crisis, which involved NATO, and that the KGB wanted to stop him. He asked her to have the pilot radio air traffic controllers in Helsinki to inform the State Department in Washington that "Miller needs help." He also asked her to call the US consulate in Leningrad once the plane had landed with the same message. He hoped one of these maneuvers would bring the Posse.

She said she'd be happy to. She and everyone else in the Netherlands wanted the Cuban missile crisis resolved peacefully. He thanked her and said maybe he could get back on the plane before it departed for Moscow. She smiled. He asked her to watch his bag and deliver it to the US embassy in Moscow if he failed to reboard. The phone that JFK had given him to use in an embassy was in the bag, and he didn't want to risk losing it in a KGB search.

Kelly sat back in his seat and hoped for a lifeline from the State Department or Khrushchev. In the meantime, he was on his own and would have to use his wits to escape the KGB in Leningrad.

Entering the terminal, Kelly was met by four KGB agents. Kelly recognized Smirnov and Brodsky, wearing overcoats and scarfs. He sensed that they were unnerved by his physical presence. Kelly was a big man with well-toned muscles, fit without a hint of fat. The long hair, though, softened his tough guy image.

"Were you in Texas in 1953?" Smirnov said in Russian, uneasily, thinking he looked familiar.

"I'm from Washington, my friends," Kelly said in perfect Russian. "Why are you here and why did you divert the plane?"

"We need to talk to you," Smirnov said. "We will put you on a later plane."

"May I call the American embassy in Moscow and inform them of this situation?"

"No," Smirnov said. "It's a minor issue and can be resolved quickly. If you would accompany us to the Astoria, we have a room there where you can freshen up."

Chapter 15
Another Lesson

Leningrad and Moscow, October 23, 1962

KELLY FROWNED. WORRIED, he looked through the window of his first-floor room in the Astoria Hotel and studied the cars in a fenced parking lot, waiting for a car to move to show him an exit. No car moved, and no tracks marred the blanket of snow covering the parking lot. The snowed-in cars, in the faint light under purple-black clouds, were more like potted plants than working vehicles. It was a ploy that the Soviets often used to impress foreigners, creating a Potemkin village to fool the naïve into thinking that the Soviet Union was a modern society.

The Posse leader was now a hostage of the KGB, Volkhov, and the Kobaists. He kicked himself. He knew better and should have planned for this possibility. The hotel phone had no dial tone. If he wanted to reach Moscow in one piece, he had to make his own opening. He had no weapons, and the KGB knew that because an agent had searched him at the airport. He hoped that his SOS had reached someone.

Suddenly, the door opened. Kelly turned away from the window and waited. A beautiful blonde closed the door behind her. She was scantily clothed, and her low-cut blouse gave an ample view of her cleavage. She twirled around. Her short shorts looked like they were painted on and left little to the imagination.

"Is it Dr. Miller?" the blonde said in a sweet, low voice, turning to face Kelly.

Kelly knew she was a siren, a Russian specialist in what the Russians called *kompromat*. "Yes, I'm Dr. Miller."

The lady moved closer to Kelly. "You're wearing big cowboy boots. Is your gun as big as your boots?"

Kelly laughed. "I left my gun at home, with my wife."

"Maybe you didn't," she said. "Maybe you have it with you and just can't find it. I'd be happy to look for it and fire it if I find it." She turned around, bent over, and slapped her behind. "Maybe it's here."

"Miss, you hold no interest for me," Kelly said. "I have a plane to catch. You're wasting your time."

The wind blew snow against the window. An icicle slid from the roof and stabbed the snow-covered ground outside the window.

"Sweetie," she said, "you can either have some fun while you talk, or my comrades who are outside in the hallway will beat you until you spill your guts. What's it going to be?"

"I'd suggest you leave. Otherwise I'll throw you through that window and you might freeze to death."

"The window is locked," she sneered.

"I didn't say I was going to open it," Kelly said.

Her eyes were hard, searching, yet admiring. She didn't seem to know what to do.

"You wouldn't hurt me, Dr. Miller, would you?" She looked up at him through her eyelashes.

"I would." He cracked his knuckles and flexed his hands. "You'd best leave, right now!"

"Have it your way," she sneered as she walked out and slammed the door.

Kelly sat on a swivel chair in front of the vanity. The vanity's mirror gave him a view of the door. He expected visitors, and he wanted to see what he was up against before he acted. There was a knock.

"Come in." He tipped his Ushanka hat forward to cover part of his forehead, which he thought could distract his interrogators.

The door opened. Smirnov and Brodsky walked into the room. He looked them over in the mirror. They had taken off their coats and had rolled up their shirtsleeves. They evidently planned to beat him to a pulp. They looked confident, strong, and menacing. He was surprised that they were alone and apparently unarmed, but perhaps they wanted full credit for any information that they were able to extract from Dr. Miller.

Kelly smiled. He planned to give the agents a dance lesson, a reprise of their meeting in 1953 at Casey's bar in San Marcos, Texas.

"Stand up, Miller," Smirnov said. "You insulted our friend and made her cry."

"I can't hear you," Kelly said. He wanted the two agents close. They moved directly behind him.

"Get up, Miller," Smirnov shouted. "Can you hear me now?"

"Da, comrades," Kelly said. "Do you remember the Texas two-step?"

Kelly watched their faces contort into anguish and fear. They seemed to realize that a Siberian labor camp loomed in their future.

Kelly pivoted on the chair, moving upward as he turned. His right elbow found Smirnov's nose and shattered it with such force that the man hit the floor out cold. Kelly stepped forward and delivered a crushing left hook to Brodsky, who fell to the floor unconscious. These boys clearly needed more practice dancing the Texas two-step.

Kelly straightened his Ushanka hat, buttoned up on his raincoat, and walked toward the lobby. It was filled with men in dark suits whom he took to be KGB agents. The blonde was sitting in a chair covered with a blanket. Unseen, he turned around and found an exit at the end of the corridor. He cut through the parking lot and headed down Nevsky Prospekt.

He made his way to the Art Nouveau Singer House with its mansard roof. Built in 1904 by Singer, the sewing machine maker, it now was the House of Books, one of the largest bookstores in Russia.

The Posse sometimes used it as a drop-off point for messages. There was no public phone there, so he couldn't call the consulate. But if his plea for help had reached someone, there would be a message for him at the book counter.

Kelly approached a young lady at the counter near the abacus machine and asked if there was a book reserved for Dr. Miller. She said there was. She pulled a copy of Tolstoy's *War and Peace* from a shelf and handed it him. He thanked her and said he would like to examine the book. She told him that that would be fine. He walked toward a small reading table, opened the book before he reached the table, and found a note inside with the words "Kutuzov Kazan, push the stake" typed out in Russian.

Kelly was perplexed by "push the stake," but he knew what "Kutuzov Kazan" meant. It was a reference to Field Marshall Mikhail Kutuzov. In the war against Napoleon in 1812, he used retreat to drain the French and their allies when they invaded Russia. Kazan was the Kazan Cathedral, now called the Museum of the History of Religion and Atheism. He was being told to retreat to Kazan Cathedral.

He put the note in his pocket and returned the book to the saleslady, then headed down the street to the atheist museum.

Four cars pulled up and some twenty men in dark suits jumped out just as Kelly reached the entrance. The two men he'd knocked out at the Astoria, their heads wrapped in bandages, appeared to be leading them. One of the KGB agents must have seen him on the street. He was in trouble.

Kelly joined a French tourist group in front of an exhibit, Yuri Gagarin looking out the window of the Vostok spaceship saying, "There's no God up here."

The tour leader was a young Russian man who Kelly surmised was not a member of Komsomol because of his casual dismissal of communist ideology. Speaking in French, which gave him cover from Russian ideologues, he told the group that the museum exhibits did not actually reflect the realty of religious belief in Russia. He demonstrated his point with a story.

"A student," the guide said, "was about to graduate from the School of Militant Atheism and came before his professor for his final exam.

"The professor asked him the key question, 'Who is God?'

"The student said God is a creation of the exploiting class. God is s tool that the capitalists used to keep the masses impervious to social injustice.

"'Very good. You have passed,' the professor said.

"'Thank God!' the student said.

"'Amen,' the professor answered."

Kelly and the tourists laughed, but the police agents were approaching. He strode toward the rear of the museum. It was an unfortunate choice. No exit. Two sides of a circular walkway led to where he stood, but a column of agents was advancing down each of the approaches. Their Kalashnikovs had sharp bayonets attached.

As they moved forward, they yelled out and poked their bayonets into exhibits as they passed. It was a tactic geared to scare spectators or someone hiding to move, and it worked. People scattered. There was neither a place to hide nor a group to get lost in.

Kelly crouched in front of an exhibit. One agent, bayonet extended, was coming toward him. Kelly fell to the floor. The man approached, confused. Kelly turned, wrapped his legs around the man's, and then twisted his body, slamming the man down to the floor and knocking him out.

The two lines of converging KGB agents looked around, puzzled that their comrade had been taken down by an unseen enemy. In that instant, Kelly glimpsed the exhibit in front of him. He had initially paid no attention to it, watching the deadly columns moving toward him. Now he turned to focus on it. It was the Inquisition exhibit with a heretic being burnt at the stake. He recalled Meg's story. Thank God he'd listened. Meg was his backup.

He jumped on the exhibit and pushed the stake to the floor. A trapdoor opened, revealing a ladder to the basement. He slipped through the opening and closed the trapdoor behind him, sliding the lock into place and climbing down the ladder. He spotted an exit door and pushed it open.

A car in the alley flashed its lights. He ran to it, recognizing Steve Wright, an American consular official and Posse member. Kelly jumped into the passenger seat.

"Glad you made it, sir," Wright said. "We got your message from Anke at KLM. The flight is waiting for you and everybody is back on board. Our ambassador in Moscow informed Khrushchev, who had the Red Army commander for the Leningrad oblast take control of airport security. They'll hold the plane until you get there. Khrushchev told the ambassador that he was sending the two KGB agents who annoyed you to Labor Camp Ninety-Eight on the Kamchatka peninsula."

Kelly chuckled. "They're alumni."

"I take it you gave them another lesson on the Texas two-step?" Wright said.

"Yes," Kelly said, "but they need practice."

Wright smirked. "They worked hard to redeem themselves since their release in 1958 and move up in the KGB. They made our life difficult with their blanket surveillance. They should've been practicing their moves."

Kelly beamed. "How did you manage?"

"Today, it was easy," Wright said. "The entire KGB office was either babysitting or chasing you."

Both Kelly and the consular official grinned.

"We're here," Wright said. "The Red Army officer at the main entrance will escort you to the KLM flight. Good luck and God speed."

On the plane, Anke greeted him with enthusiasm. "Welcome aboard!"

He thanked her for her help and took his seat. She smiled and announced over the loudspeaker that the plane was cleared for departure and should be only an hour or so behind schedule. She served Kelly a huge breakfast and urged him to eat and stay hydrated because he'd need his strength for the critical work ahead.

A little over an hour later, Kelly landed at Sheremetyevo airport in a snowstorm. He was greeted by a diplomatic delegation from the US embassy, including a retired US Army intelligence colonel named Bill Fillmore, who went by Fill, who was a Posse member and a bodyguard for Kelly. He also saw a dozen security troops from the military wing of the KGB. Unlike KGB intelligence and counterintelligence agents who wanted to remain inconspicuous, the security troops wore uniforms like the Red Army, distinguished by royal blue piping and shoulder boards marked with GB for state security.

If Volkhov didn't already know, he'd soon learn of Kelly's arrival in Moscow and would be quite unhappy. But the KGB would not move against him in Moscow. Khrushchev was protecting him and could use the Red Army against the KGB.

He was pleased that Red Army troops provided an escort for him and his entourage to Spaso House, the residence of the US ambassador in Moscow and not far from the Kremlin. He freshened up, discussed the mounting Cuban crisis with the ambassador, and prepared to meet Khrushchev. The clock was ticking. He knew Volkhov would be watching his every move and was likely pulling out his hair over the failure of the KGB agents to murder him in Leningrad. He was still not safe, and the world was closer to annihilation. He pushed himself forward. Failure was not an option, no matter what the cost.

Chapter 16
Volkhov's Response

Moscow, October 23, 1962

VOLKHOV SLAMMED HIS fist into the wall when he discovered that Miller was on his way to Moscow. Grigulevich had failed again. But he would deal with them all later: Grigulevich, Miller, and, if necessary, the pope. He did not want to lose momentum on Cuba.

He had initially dismissed Kennedy's menacing broadcast and private letter to Khrushchev as perfunctory and unalarming. Now he believed the American demarche had to be countered. Khrushchev must knock the wind out of Kennedy's sails and churn the waters around Cuba. Volkhov felt responsibility for the revolution. He believed in his heart that this was his moment.

At his desk in Lubyanka, Volkhov had started to draft a response to Kennedy but found himself with writer's block. He seethed over Miller's escape, Grigulevich's negligence, and Khrushchev's scheme. He wanted to vent, breathe in fresh air, and find inspiration.

He exited Lubyanka through a rear door, got behind the wheel of his car, which was usually driven by a chauffeur, and drove toward the Kremlin. He entered Red Square, passed through the main entrance into the Kremlin in Spassky Tower, and parked his car not far from the Armoury Museum with its riches from the tsarist era. There was fresh snow on the ground, and he could see his breath's vapor in the cold wind. He, like Stalin, found the cold to be invigorating.

He loved Russia's seat of power. He always was refreshed being among its skeletons: the dead tsars buried in Archangel Cathedral, now a museum; Lenin's mausoleum, holding the embalmed body of the founder of the communist state; and the Kremlin Wall Necropolis, the burial place of the icons of the Communist Party.

He walked by the Ivan the Great's bell tower, the tallest structure in the Kremlin. He headed in the direction of Stalin's grave. More snow started to fall. Not fluffy snowflakes, but ice balls the size of BBs. A thrush nightingale warbled in the distance, an unanswered mating call.

The guards everywhere were his troops, the military wing of the KGB. The secret police had sole authority to protect the Kremlin and Soviet leaders and their dachas.

Stalin had set that system in place to balance the power of the professional military officers in the Red Army. The Army was charged with protecting the external borders of the state, but the security police controlled domestic security. Stalin didn't trust the military officers. Neither did Volkhov.

The KGB guards knew Volkhov. When he passed them, they saluted and stood straight as arrows. He saluted back and trekked on. Many times, he thought about using his troops to overthrow Khrushchev, but he knew the Army was with Khrushchev. It was how he had catapulted himself into the Kremlin following Stalin's unexpected death. The Army was not far away, and Khrushchev was in constant communication with its officers. He had to be careful.

Volkhov ambled outside Spassky Tower to Red Square, named not for the communist movement but for its beauty. He strolled over to Lenin's mausoleum. Stalin used to be buried there with Lenin. Khrushchev had his body moved for reburial in the Kremlin Wall Necropolis in 1961. For Volkhov and the neo-Stalinists, Khrushchev's action, a symbol of his massive effort to remove Stalin and his violent, authoritarian policies from Soviet Russia, was galling. Stalin's reign was the apogee of Russian history.

Volkhov trudged through the accumulating snow to Stalin's grave along the Kremlin Wall. He stood in front of the tomb. Tears rolled down his cheeks. He felt inspired and determined.

"Vozhd," he whispered, "you were the greatest ruler in history. I vow to punish Khrushchev. I vow to bury him here and to rebury you with full honors in the Lenin-Stalin mausoleum. I also want you to know that we have 162 nuclear warheads on Cuban soil. More than Khrushchev authorized. I'm prepared to turn the US into a wasteland."

Volkhov was now excited. A flock of crows, Moscow's most ubiquitous bird, flew overhead and cawed. Volkhov picked up a stone and threw it in the direction of the birds. He made a mental note to call the crow chasers, a special regiment of KGB soldiers that shooed crows and other pesky birds away from the Kremlin's medieval walls, and tell them to keep the birds clear of Stalin's resting place. He raced back to his office and quickly penned a draft letter that he wanted Khrushchev to send to Kennedy to rebut his threats.

§

KHRUSHCHEV'S FRONTAL VEIN bulged on his bald head. Two members of the Presidium sat in front of his desk, staring at him. The room was cold. No one smiled. No one drank the hot black tea on the desk. Their red faces looked like volcanoes ready to explode.

The Soviet leader had decided not to make a direct reply to Kennedy's October 22 television speech and private note. They insisted that he had to respond and that others on the Presidium agreed with them. They argued that anything less than a hardline response to Kennedy's threats was a sign of defeat. They had Volkhov's letter that they wanted him to sign and send to Kennedy. He countered that he preferred to deescalate the confrontation rather than engage in a round of angry exchanges with Kennedy.

Khrushchev knew Miller was coming to meet him. It'd be awkward to convince the American that he was looking to ease the crisis while simultaneously intensifying it. He eventually decided to sign the letter to appease the Kobaists. He would take other steps to show his willingness to ratchet back the pressure, including stopping freighters on their way to Cuba and meeting with Miller.

On October 23 Khrushchev sent Kennedy the letter, charging that Kennedy's broadcast and letter embodied grave threats to the security of nations and violations of international law. The US had entered upon a policy of grievously violating the United Nations Charter, of impinging on the freedom and navigation of the seas, and of aggressive threats to the nations of Cuba and the Soviet Union. It was clearly interfering in the internal affairs of Cuba, the USSR, and other states. The letter said the United Nations Charter and international norms gave no state the right to set up in international waters the inspection of ships bound for the shores of the Republic of Cuba.

In addition, the letter said the Soviet Union did not recognize any right of the United States to establish control over armaments that were necessary for the Republic of Cuba to strengthen its defensive capability. It went on to say that the Soviet Union affirmed that the weapons, regardless of the classification to which they belonged, were only for Cuba's defense against an attack of an aggressor. It concluded by stressing that Khrushchev hoped the US would wisely abandon its threatening policies that could lead to catastrophic consequences for world peace.

Volkhov jumped for joy. He was convinced that the forceful letter would keep Khrushchev in a box and infuriate the Americans. He was ready to meet with Grigulevich and deal with Miller and the pope. He failed to appreciate who Miller was. He was about to find out.

§

GRIGULEVICH STOOD AKWARDLY in front of Volkhov's desk, grimacing and shifting his weight from one leg to the other. Standing was painful on his arthritic knees. It was just past two p.m., and this was his second meeting with Volkhov that day. The ashen daylight coming through the snow-encrusted bars of the window projected a grid of shadows into the room.

The acting director of the KGB sat in his overstuffed armchair behind the desk, sipping a cup of hot black tea. An ashtray filled with cigarette butts filled the room with its stale fumes. He seethed. "What are you looking at?"

Grigulevich looked startled. "Nothing. I was just struck by the crisscrossed pattern of the light and shadow in the room. It's like a metaphor of Soviet life."

Volkhov stared at Grigulevich as if he were nuts. He shook his head. He had no time for iconography. He moved to the Miller problem. He told him that he had done a good job of diverting Miller to Leningrad but had failed to kill him. "Why?"

Grigulevich hesitated. He decided to blame the local agents in Leningrad. He told Volkhov that Miller was resourceful and lucky. The agents in Leningrad had not anticipated his ability to reach out to Khrushchev, who employed the Red Army to snatch him away from the KGB and land him safely in Moscow. "You know he's here, don't you?"

The question infuriated Volkhov. His face screwed up and turned red. "Yes, I know. My question to you is why is he meeting with Khrushchev at St. Louis Church, next door to where you are standing?"

Grigulevich pulled on his left ear, thinking about the question. He wondered why Volkhov didn't know the answer to his own question. He asked the KGB leader if he had installed recording devices at the church or had tried to use Lubyanka's parabolic microphones and antennas to listen in.

Volkhov rubbed his chin and said flatly that a platoon of Red Army troops had blocked his agents from planting recorders. They had employed some type of ambient noise system to interfere with Lubyanka's receivers.

Grigulevich rolled his eyes. He said he didn't know why they were meeting, but given Miller's background, it probably had something to do with the pope, Kennedy, and Cuba.

Volkhov resented what he perceived as a condescending attitude. "Of course. I don't need ears to hear what's going down. I told you earlier Khrushchev wants Miller in Rome, and Miller will soon be on his way. He is going to ask the pope to mediate the Cuban crisis." Volkhov pointed to the torture chair in front of his desk for Grigulevich to sit down.

Grigulevich defied him. "I'll stand."

"Sit down," Volkhov repeated, in an imperious voice. Grigulevich sat down and shifted his weight to find some comfortable position but looked distressed. Neither tea nor water was offered.

Volkhov didn't want to know why Miller and Khrushchev were meeting, but why it mattered. He wanted Grigulevich's insight. He was the closest thing to an expert on the Vatican that the Kremlin had. He told Grigulevich he was mystified as to why Khrushchev would reach out to the pope for help on Cuba. He said the pope had no clout and, although Kennedy might be a Catholic, he was like all so-called religious politicians, a hypocrite. He reminded his deputy that Stalin dismissed the pope as a political force because he had no army. Besides, Khrushchev persecuted the Catholic Church.

Grigulevich furrowed his brow. He told Volkhov that he was underestimating the pope. Pope John XXIII was enormously popular and influential not just in Catholic countries, but also among Orthodox, Jewish, Protestant, Buddhist, Hindu, and Muslim believers. He was even admired in the communist world. His influence came from moral authority, openness to ecumenism, humility, dedication to peace, and the belief that all people are salvageable because they are loved by God.

Volkhov looked at Grigulevich with astonishment. "You sound like an admirer. Or perhaps a convert."

"Nyet," Grigulevich retorted. He was trying to tell Volkhov that the pope had standing. Under him, the Catholic Church was a danger to communism. He pointed out that it was a worldwide organization that had diplomatic relations with some 185 countries. Its values underpinned Western democracy, the market system, and international law. The Catholic Church had influence in Soviet Poland, Czechoslovakia, Hungary, Latvia, and Lithuania and had played a role in the Hungarian Revolution and in the continuing unrest in Soviet Eastern Europe. Grigulevich finished by stating that several leaders of NATO countries and the European Economic Community were Catholic.

Volkhov eyed Grigulevich, his lips pressed together. He swept the air with his right hand, dismissing Grigulevich's points. "The future belongs to communism. The Catholic Church and this pope are regressive forces and will disappear as communism advances."

"What do you want to do?" Grigulevich asked.

Volkhov said the best way to deal with lingering malignancies is to cut them out. "I want Miller and the pope dead. That will close the door on the problem."

The deputy KGB director glanced at Volkhov with a slight frown and pursed lips. "You want me to go to Rome and take care of it?"

Volkhov sat back in his chair. He ran his hand through his hair. Grigulevich seemed to disapprove of the double hit but appeared ready to carry it out. "Yes," Volkhov said sharply. "I want you to take charge in Rome."

Grigulevich nodded. He looked away and shifted his weight on the uncomfortable chair. He was ready to go.

Volkhov didn't want him to leave. He needed to hear more, not only to be sure of his deputy's conviction, but also to delight in watching Grigulevich's logistical mind work. "How do you think it should go down?"

§

GRIGULEVICH DID NOT reply. He simply dipped his head and then looked steadily at Volkhov like a master chess player, moving his pieces mentally into position.

In fact, he was wary. Volkhov could have him shot, but he had doubts about murdering the pope and Miller. He didn't point out the acting director's contradiction—if communism were the future and the pope so anemic, why kill him? If Miller's trip to Rome were so inconsequential, why murder him to prevent a meeting with the pope? He kept these questions to himself. He decided to offer Volkhov what he wanted: a plan to murder the pope and Miller.

Grigulevich said he wanted to use the four sleeper agents among the Russian Orthodox delegation attending the Second Vatican Council and the sniper in the Lithuanian Catholic delegation, whom they both knew by reputation.

Volkhov agreed and said he'd put them at his disposal. He smiled. Grigulevich could see he anticipated more detail.

Grigulevich told Volkhov the pope would be easy because tomorrow was Wednesday, and he'd be walking among thousands of pilgrims in St. Peter's Square giving the papal blessing at ten-thirty a.m. He'd place two assassins from the Russian Orthodox delegation among the pilgrims. One would shoot the pope. The other would kill the shooter and call himself the pope's avenger. Volkhov would denounce the killer and blame Khrushchev for the assassination because he was the one who'd approved the Russian Orthodox delegation. The KGB would also float rumors that the shooter was a mafia hitman hired by conservative elements of the Catholic hierarchy. They opposed the pope's reforms and effort to modernize the Church. These seeds of doubt would split the Church. Miller would be more of a problem because he was resourceful, and they didn't know his itinerary.

Volkhov chuckled loudly. He enjoyed Grigulevich's intricate plan. As for Miller, he told Grigulevich that he'd just learned that Miller would be flying to Rome today. The US ambassador had placed his

Lockheed JetStar at Miller's disposal. The pilot, a retired US Army colonel called Fill, had filed a flight plan with Rome's Leonardo da Vinci-Fiumicino airport as a destination.

Grigulevich formed the fingers of his right hand into the shape of a gun and pulled the imaginary trigger. "Boom, he's dead." He'd arrange a sniper hit between the airport and the city center.

Volkhov hit the desk with his fist. "Ingenious! Get Miller before he can meet with the pope."

Grigulevich nodded. "Perhaps, then, there's no need to need to kill the pope. He'd not be informed of Khrushchev's hopes."

"Nyet," Volkhov said. "We must kill him because he's a potential lifeline for Khrushchev. I want no lifelines."

"Khorosho," Grigulevich said without enthusiasm.

Volkho sat quietly for a moment, then said he hoped that the sniper in charge of Miller wouldn't be caught. If he were, he could also be disavowed and denounced as a conservative Catholic who hated Miller because he was advising the pope on modernizing the Church.

Grigulevich laughed. "That'd be sweet, but the sniper will not be caught. He was trained by Ivan Ivanov, the expert sniper who wiped out battalions of Nazis at the Battle of Stalingrad. There's no one better. If he is tracked, he'll kill his pursuers. He never misses. He's that good."

"I've heard that," Volkhov said, "but Miller, as you said, is resourceful."

Grigulevich leaned back in his chair, trying to find a comfortable balance. He just wanted to leave. He told Volkhov not to worry. The sniper was also resourceful. He said he'd track Miller at the airport, the hotel, and the Vatican. He said no matter where Miller was, the sniper would find him. "He will erase the Miller problem."

"Excellent." Volkhov smiled again. "The plan is infallible. I have a good picture of Miller. Take it with you and give copies to the agents. If you leave now, you will reach Rome before Miller. Use the new Caravelle jet that the KGB purchased last year from the French."

Grigulevich nodded. He stood and tried to look buoyant as he walked out of the acting director's office. Once outside, he relaxed. He stood for a few minutes, taking deep breaths. For the first time in his life, he had doubts about the doctrine of communist inevitability. He felt a piercing, humbling ambivalence. He heard the crescendo drumbeat of two middle spotted woodpeckers high in the branches of the large oak trees in the courtyard of St. Louis Church.

When he turned to look at the birds, he caught a glimpse of the barred window in Volkhov's office. The KGB director stood in front of a map of Cuba, perhaps trying to figure out new ways to stoke the crisis. Grigulevich was glad he was flying to Rome. He knew many people there. But he would need to use an alias because he sensed that the most important people might know he was a Soviet spy and assassin.

The plan was not infallible. But it was good enough, he thought, to get the mission accomplished. He regretted having the pope killed. He liked the man personally and as a moral leader, but he had his orders.

As for Miller, the professor was way out of his league and had been fortunate to escape Leningrad. Grigulevich believed he would be easy to dispose of, but once again he and Volkhov had failed to perceive with whom they were dealing. On a whim, he decided to send a copy of Miller's picture to Victor Petrov in Washington to see if he knew him.

Chapter 17
Hard Facts

Moscow, October 23, 1962

BEFORE THE SHERIFF left Spaso House for his meeting with Khrushchev, he was briefed by the Department of State on new or impending developments in the rapidly intensifying Cuban crisis. He learned that US Navy ships, joined by naval ships from OAS nations, had moved into position to enforce the interdiction of boats approaching Cuba starting at two p.m. on October 24. Soviet submarines gathered in the Caribbean were poised to break the blockade.

He found out that the OAS was meeting to officially endorse and support the quarantine of Cuba. UN envoy Adlai Stevenson was presenting photographic evidence showing that the Soviet Union was installing offensive nuclear missiles in Cuba and threatening the Western Hemisphere with aggression.

He was also briefed on Khrushchev's letter to JFK in which the Soviet leader had rejected the American demand that the missiles be removed and had claimed that the weapons were "intended solely for defensive purposes." He saw JFK's brief, blunt response of October 23 to Khrushchev's missive. It stated the Soviet leader had started the crisis by secretly sending missiles to Cuba and warned that he must stop Soviet ships before they reached the quarantine or risk an intensification of the situation that would lead to dire consequences.

Finally, Kelly learned just as he was going out the door that Soviet freighters carrying armaments to Cuba appeared to be halting just west of Africa, but that the Soviet oil tanker *Bucharest* was proceeding toward Cuba.

The Sheriff felt whiplashed by the quick-moving events. He hoped that the impulsive, often contradictory actions and decisions would not jeopardize what seemed to him to be Khrushchev's sincere effort to defuse the crisis. He hoped his meeting would open a door to a peaceful resolution.

§

AT 2:45 P.M., AFTER a quick late lunch with the ambassador, Kelly climbed into the backseat of an embassy car and told Fill, who was driving, to proceed to St. Louis des Français Church. Heavy snow had recently fallen, and the streets were slippery and rutted. Kelly wore the same clothes that he had had on the plane but now added a green vest, a red wool scarf, and fur-lined gloves. He left his bag at Spaso House. He was anxious but hopeful.

Fill passed the Bolshoi Theatre toward Dzerzhinsky Square. He then turned left into Malaya Lubyanka Street and parked in front of St. Louis Church with its six white Doric columns and mustard-colored stucco walls. A splendid example of Gallic-Greek architecture from the early nineteenth century, it was nestled in a towering forest of police buildings collectively called Lubyanka, the central headquarters of the KGB.

The church still existed and was open only because the Soviet government, which was determined to wipe out all religions, had an arrangement with the French government to tolerate it. The French reciprocated by permitting Moscow to maintain St. Alexander Nevsky, a Russian Orthodox Church in Paris, which the Kremlin used as a base for espionage.

Kelly climbed out of the car and asked Fill to wait for him.

From the sidewalk in front of the church, he saw Khrushchev, bald as a mushroom, sitting on the bench in the front courtyard of the church in a dark blue overcoat. A contingent of Red Army soldiers in olive green uniforms and fur hats with flaps formed a standing cordon around the courtyard. The soldiers were not within hearing range of the bench but served notice that the Soviet leader was protected.

It was clear to Kelly that Khrushchev wanted a private conversation in the open air. He assumed that audio jammers had been installed around the courtyard to block eavesdropping and that any bugs had been swept up.

To the right of the courtyard was the main office of Lubyanka, the mother nest of the KGB. Kelly imagined Volkhov looking out a window and grimacing, having failed to prevent the meeting and unable to eavesdrop.

Soviet plows had cleared Malaya Lubyanka Street of snow but, unlike their usual practice, had not piled it in front of the church. It was a meaningful gesture because the Soviet government tried to make life as wearisome as possible for believers. Kelly took it as a sign that Khrushchev wanted to impress the pope.

The chain of soldiers split, opening a path into the courtyard for Kelly. He walked through, and the guards closed ranks.

"Good afternoon, General Secretary Khrushchev," Kelly said as he approached the Soviet leader. He hoped to win the Soviet head over to a face-saving retreat. He knew him to be bullheaded but also practical. Light snow flurries fell silently to the ground.

"Good of you to come on short notice, Miller," Khrushchev said. There was perspiration on his forehead. "I'm sorry about the delay in Leningrad. I am sending the two KGB agents who accosted you to a Siberian work camp. They kept mumbling about the Texas two-step."

"It was not a major problem," Kelly said, smiling. "Thank you for rescuing me."

"Please sit down," Khrushchev said. Kelly sat next to the Soviet leader. The bench quivered slightly.

"Are you still teaching?" Khrushchev asked, closely looking at Kelly.

"I'm still an academic," Kelly replied. It was important to reestablish rapport with Khrushchev because he planned to ask him to surrender.

Khrushchev nodded, thanked him for the telegram, and moved on. He explained his problem with the Kobaists, Volkhov, and Cuba. He said he'd made a mistake by putting offensive missiles in Cuba. He'd thought he could manage to gain leverage with Kennedy but couldn't. "There are too many moving parts, and Volkhov and the Kobaists have powerful allies in Russia and agents in Cuba whom I cannot control. The military is with me for now, but I cannot appear weak. Can you help?"

"That's a tall order," Kelly said, somewhat stiffly. "I'm happy to help in any way that I can, but why me? Why are we meeting here? Kelly wanted to see if his cover had been compromised—and if Khrushchev had a role in mind for the pope.

Khrushchev told Kelly he had connections in Rome and Washington and could possibly ask the pope to influence Kennedy, who was a Catholic, in this Cuban matter. "I wanted to meet here because this place has served good purposes in the past and it sends a positive message to the pope. In a sense, I'm on his terrain. I also think I can trust you."

"You can trust me," Kelly said, encouragingly. "And maybe the pope can help, but I must ask about your paradoxical policies. I read your menacing letter to Kennedy, but then I heard Soviet cargo ships headed for Cuba were stopping in the water."

Khrushchev shifted his weight on the bench. He turned and met Kelly's eyes. "I must follow an ambivalent path to hold power. I mingle the tough stance with concessions, sometimes doing anomalous things, to signal a willingness to resolve the crisis and return to the status quo."

The air was frigid. Kelly could see their breath vapor. He smiled. "That's what I was hoping for. I'm going to explain some hard facts and then suggest a way out."

Khrushchev coughed and shifted his weight again. "I should tell you before you pontificate about hard facts that I cannot accept the quarantine and have moved submarines into the Caribbean area to challenge it. I do not appreciate the way Kennedy has made this into a worldwide crisis by painting the Soviet Union as an aggressor and calling upon the OAS, NATO, and the UN for support against us. And I think it is quite menacing, illogical, and unjustified to say a missile launched from Cuba would be answered by a nuclear attack on the Soviet Union. Cuba is a sovereign nation, and Castro is an independent actor."

Kelly sat back against the bench. It shook again.

"Thank you for telling me your parameters, but I'm going to give you the hard facts anyway. There is no way out without the immediate removal of the missiles. Let's deal with your last point first. Everyone knows Castro doesn't control the missiles, bombers, jets, or submarines. The Soviet Union does. So Kennedy's statement that the US will retaliate against the USSR if a missile is fired from Cuba makes perfect sense.

"Let's turn to the contradiction at the heart of your foreign policy in Cuba, of your wish to gain leverage to negotiate with Kennedy. You claim you pursue a policy of peaceful coexistence or competition with the US, yet you're installing offensive nuclear missiles in Cuba. That's not peaceful.

"You want leverage with Kennedy to facilitate your expansion. You wouldn't need leverage if communist values were popular. Most people in the world, including Russians, do not want food shortages, violence, authoritarianism, and Stalinists. They desire freedom, rule of law, tolerance, justice, and democracy. Do you think the Russian people rebelled against the tsars because they wanted to be enslaved by the communists?"

For a minute Khrushchev sat still. He clearly didn't like what he had heard but he wanted to find a solution. "My intention was not to threaten the US but to get it to help me solve my problems."

Kelly didn't relent. He turned and looked at Khrushchev. "Your problems are largely the result of pushing a totalitarian ideology at home and abroad."

Khrushchev held up his right hand, as if asking for a break. "I'm trying to change that."

"I know." Kelly made his tone reassuring. "That's why I'm here. You reforms are a tacit admission that communism is deficient."

Khrushchev bucked. His right fist smashed into the palm of his left hand. "Deficient but not dead. We will bury the West."

Kelly shook his head and laughed. "Communism is a deadly disease. It produced Stalin and Stalinism. You see the disease and address some of its symptoms, but you are blind to the cure. The Kobaists see neither the disease nor the cure and think your treatment of symptoms is a threat to them, so they target you.

"Your treatment is a plea for help. The dilemma has a short-term exit that keeps you in power for two years or so and a long-term exit that leads to the removal of communism. The fix embraces values that resonate with human nature and experience, the values that Russia started to embrace at the beginning of the twentieth century before the Bolshevik Revolution."

Khrushchev's head shot back as if hit by an unseen blow. "What do you mean 'two years or so' in power? I can turn the tables on the Kobaists now and stay in power well beyond two years if the US would give me something in return for removing the missiles."

Kelly extended his two hands forward to emphasize his point. "The Kobaists pushed you, and you took the bait. They have you in a corner.

If you keep the missiles in Cuba, you will ignite nuclear war, which is idiocy, so you will remove the missiles. When you withdraw the missiles, the Kobaists will say you are weak and demand your removal."

"Precisely," Khrushchev said, irritably, "and the reason I called you."

Kelly took a deep breath. He had to win Khrushchev over to accepting his fate, to stop and think about the crisis, a solution, and his future. "The way out for the short term is to play the China card. When you remove the missiles, the Chinese, like the Kobaists, will blister you relentlessly. They want the USSR to get into a fight with the US because then Russia will have to arm them with nuclear weapons to make them a credible and powerful ally against the West, but once you do that, they no longer need Soviet leadership and will become your rival.

"You can use Chinese outrage to silence the Kobaists, who would not want to be allied with China against Russian leadership of the world communist movement. The Army will stand with you against the Chinese, and the Kobaists will fall in line and wait until later to try to take you down. I would say if you played the Chinese card shrewdly, you would retain power for about two more years or so, finally being removed when the Chinese obtain nuclear weapons on their own."

Khrushchev sat stunned, or so it appeared to Kelly. "An interesting analysis for someone who claims to be a naïve academic. You seem to be very well informed about politics and Soviet affairs." His voice indicated uncertainty about who the American really was.

"I just read a lot," Kelly said with a wave of his hand.

"What about the long-term option?" Khrushchev asked suspiciously but earnestly, seemingly accepting that he had access to a smart, well-read professor.

Kelly appreciated that Khrushchev understood that he'd been outmaneuvered by the Kobaists and would be lucky to stay in power for two more years. He needed a plan to continue his reform policy for the long term.

"You must move now," Kelly said, "to cultivate a successor who will eventually outfox the hardline communists and continue the reform policy."

"It will not work," Khrushchev whispered. "The hardliners will not allow any of my acolytes to succeed me."

"Not anyone in your inner circle," Kelly said. "Find someone bright who foresees the USSR evolving into a responsible power, free of Stalin's repressive policies and free of his aggressive foreign policy. Is there anyone who comes to mind?"

Khrushchev narrowed his eyes. "Mikhail Gorbachev," he said slowly. "He's doing a fantastic job in Stavropol. He's far down the food chain, but I can boost him over the next few years without tinging him with my endorsement."

"Good," Kelly said. He knew of Gorbachev. A perfect candidate, and someone who would begin the Posse's long-range plan to transition Soviet Russia from communism to democracy. He sensed that the KGB hardliners would replace Khrushchev with someone like Brezhnev or Kosygin. Those two stolid, unimaginative bureaucrats would maintain the status quo and keep the Russians in dire straits and the Communist Party elite on the lookout for a leader with a new perspective like Gorbachev.

Khrushchev sat back. He shrugged and then rubbed his bald head. Kelly could tell that he was tense and dissatisfied. "Your assessment is too one-sided. Kennedy must give me something."

Chapter 18
Peacemaker's Role

Moscow, October 23, 1962

KELLY STIFFENED. HE said a trade-off wasn't on the table. Khrushchev must remove the missiles first. The US doesn't want war, he said, but it will not bend. The US is on fire. "You have lit the match, and the US is responding with unity, resolve, and staggering power."

The Soviet leader said he had underestimated Kennedy but needed something to save face. He said the Soviet ambassador in Washington had hinted that the US might be willing to remove its Jupiter missiles from Turkey.

Kelly shook his head. "Not simultaneously. Down the road, perhaps."

Khrushchev complained that the missiles in Turkey were obsolete and had already been surpassed by the Polaris submarines. Kelly dismissed that and stressed that the missiles in Cuba must be removed without any quid pro quo.

Khrushchev fumed. "I can't just concede. I'll be thrown to the dogs. I will not last one day, let alone two years. The Red Army will not support surrender."

Kelly nodded vigorously. "Of course not. You prevent immediate removal by embracing the role of the peacemaker. Choosing peace over war will bring respect and honor. It will buttress the Army's support of you. You can even deliver a blow to the Kobaists by pointing out that Lenin made peace with the Germans in 1918 and then with the peasants in 1921."

Khrushchev shook his head. "I don't know how I can embrace the role of the peacemaker in the face of Kennedy's threat."

Kelly smiled. "The peacemaker puts the interest of the community before self-interest. You'd be seen as a winner, and the Soviet Union as a mature, responsible state—unlike madman Mao, pushing for nuclear war."

Khrushchev was not convinced. He said he'd look weak if he announced he was removing the missiles because he was a peacemaker.

Kelly agreed. "But it wouldn't be seen that way if you and Kennedy both endorse the prayer for world peace of a third party, a man of immense moral authority like the pope. Once you show your willingness to pull back, the US will help to bolster your image and will not gloat or try to depict you as a loser."

Khrushchev shook his head. He said he had been persecuting the Catholic Church and other religions and couldn't credibly reach out to the pope.

Kelly faced Khrushchev. He reminded him that he had sent Pope John XXIII birthday greetings when he turned 80 years old in 1961. The pope had sent him a thank-you note. He invited Russian Orthodox clergy to observe the meetings of the Second Vatican Council. Khrushchev had sent not only a Russian Orthodox delegation, but also Catholic clergy from Soviet Lithuania and some of the satellites in Soviet Eastern Europe.

"That's different. There was mutual advantage," Khrushchev said. "With a plea now, I would appear to be on my knees."

Kelly leaned forward. He told Khrushchev that he wouldn't be making a plea. "Let the pope make the offer. You and Kennedy will simply respond."

"How can that happen?" Khrushchev said, perking up.

Kelly realized that Khrushchev wanted him to act as an intermediary. His estimation of Khrushchev increased dramatically. He saw that the Kremlin dictator clearly understood his predicament and wanted Kelly to find a face-saving solution, even if it were only for the short term.

"I'll go to Rome," Kelly said.

Kelly's offer must have relieved Khrushchev. He sweetened the request that Kelly would carry to the pope. "If you privately persuade him to make an international appeal for peace, I'll embrace the appeal. Down the road, I'll show my gratitude by permitting Catholic Ukrainian Archbishop Josyf Slypyj, who presently is in prison, to go into exile and live in Vatican City."

"I'll ask him to draft an entreaty for peace," Kelly said. "If he does, you and Kennedy can review a draft and then endorse it. That would get the diplomatic backchannel moving."

Kelly knew Kennedy had already sent a private note to the pope asking for prayers for peace. He had faith that the pope could find a way for Khrushchev and Kennedy to step back from the mounting crisis and end the threat.

Khrushchev shrugged. "When can you leave?"

Kelly said he'd depart immediately on the American ambassador's new Lockheed JetStar, piloted by a retired US Army colonel assigned to the embassy. "If I'm airborne soon, I should be in Rome, given the two-hour time difference, by dinner time."

Khrushchev nodded and offered to send someone from the foreign ministry or military intelligence with him.

Kelly shook his head. That would generate too much publicity. But he promised to keep the Soviet leader informed.

Khrushchev grinned. He told Kelly that there was one more thing. He wanted him to play the role of referee and explain his alarming, seemingly contradictory moves to the American government.

The Sheriff was silent for a moment. He leaned back against the bench. "I'll do it because I trust that you sincerely desire to settle the crisis. Give me a secure, emergency phone number to talk to you at any time."

"Khorosho!" Khrushchev said, clearly relieved. He pushed a paper toward Kelly. On it he had written his private number. "Be careful. Volkhov does not want this crisis to end. You will be in danger if he thinks you're a problem solver."

Kelly nodded. "I'll be very careful." The Sheriff was not about to tell Khrushchev about the Posse. He then handed the Kremlin leader the number of the phone that JFK had given him, which was connected to his Miller persona. "You can reach me at any time when I'm in an American embassy."

"Thank you, Miller," Khrushchev said. "Give my best wishes to Pope John. He's a humble, good man in touch with the needs and hopes of people around the world. No wonder they call him 'Il Papa Buono.'"

"By the way, I handpicked most of the members of the Russian Orthodox delegation and the Catholic delegations from the satellites in Eastern Europe to attend the Second Vatican Council. But I had nothing to do with the Catholic delegation from Soviet Lithuania. I signed off on it, but Volkhov selected its members. He also added four people to the Russian Orthodox delegation."

"Good to know," Kelly said. "I'll be in touch."

As Khrushchev and Kelly stood up, a Red Army officer approached the bench. "What is it?" Khrushchev said.

The officer whispered in Khrushchev's ear. Kelly stepped away to give the Soviet leader privacy.

"Miller," Khrushchev said. "I was just told that Grigulevich, who you knew as Teodoro Castro, is on his way to Rome to visit with the Soviet religious delegations at the Second Vatican Council. He's flying in the KGB's new Caravelle jet. He'll be there before you. I should have handled him the way I dealt with Beria. I urge you again to be careful."

Khrushchev's revelation about Teodoro Castro being Grigulevich was known to Kelly, but he told Khrushchev that that was news, that he had thought that Castro had dead years ago. Khrushchev said that he had recalled him from Rome in 1953 and that he was now Volkhov's right-hand man.

"That's interesting," Kelly said, with a look of surprise, which was partly feigned because of the Soviet leader's disclosure that Castro was Grigulevich, but also genuine because it meant trouble. "And he's visiting the Soviet religious delegations?" Kelly continued. "That's curious, too. Out of the blue he's going to Rome. He must be up to something."

"Maybe," Khrushchev said. "He and Volkhov might have slipped KGB agents into the mix."

Kelly sat down and leaned into the back of the bench, considering Grigulevich. The man was a charming diplomat, well known in Roman and Vatican circles, but he was also a butcher. Kelly wondered if Grigulevich planned a contract hit on him followed by a propaganda campaign to disrupt the pope's intercession in the Cuban upheaval.

The more he thought about Grigulevich, the more disturbed he became. His impatience and lack of preparation had nearly cost him his life. He needed more information, and Grigulevich was his best source. To squeeze the urbane KGB agent, he required help from the Posse.

Kelly stood up and turned to Khrushchev, who seemed puzzled over his sudden silence at the mention of Grigulevich's name."

"Does Grigulevich bother you?" Khrushchev asked.

"It's a complication," Kelly said, "but I can manage it. The bishops and envoys to the Vatican would recognize him. He must be using an alias and perhaps a disguise."

"He has a diplomatic passport in the name of Archpriest Stanislav Illich, assistant to the Russian Orthodox patriarch," the Russian leader said.

"That's helpful. I'd better depart for Rome immediately."

Khrushchev nodded. "Khorosho. When you are ready, I'll send a squad of soldiers to escort you."

"Fine," Kelly said. "I must make a brief stop at Spaso House."

Riding in the backseat of the embassy car with an army escort and Fill at the wheel, Kelly considered the delegation from Soviet Lithuania that Volkhov had put together. He was also concerned about the Russian Orthodox delegation. Even though Khrushchev was involved, Volkhov had added some people.

The Soviet government, as part of its antireligious campaign, had sleeper agents in the Orthodox Church. The KGB had inserted agents in seminaries who were ordained to the priesthood, and some of those were elevated to the episcopate. Such collaborationist clergy worked to undermine religion and moral behavior and act as spies. The Soviet groups at the Second Vatican Council could be used by Volkhov and Grigulevich to discredit the pope and his effort to mediate the Cuban missile crisis.

Kelly had not kept up with Grigulevich after Khrushchev had recalled him from Rome following Stalin's death. He was surprised to learn he'd found refuge with the Kobaists and Volkhov. The man was a legend in Russian intelligence circles. He was also the architect of Trotsky's assassination in 1940 in Mexico and had had Tito in his crosshairs in 1953 when Khrushchev removed him. He had been close to Stalin, who nicknamed him Grig.

Once Kelly was in Spaso House, he sent a coded telegram to the State Department to inform the White House what was afoot. He said he was on his way to Rome for a meeting with the pope on behalf of Khrushchev, but that Volkhov, Grigulevich, and the KGB were determined to prevent his meeting and damage the pope's reputation as a mediator. He asked for help and patience. Time was slipping away. The Cuban missile crisis was intensifying. He had to get information on the KGB plans in Rome. He had decided to target Grigulevich.

He called Margo on a secure phone and told her he was safe. He found out that she and key Posse members from the US had arrived earlier that day at Palazzo Margherita, the chancery of the US Embassy on Via Veneto. The group included Ana, Ed, Bone, Oliver, Taylor, Denise "the Warbler" Moreno, a beautiful Posse member with a dulcet voice and the shooting skill of Annie Oakley, and Fedor Axelrod, another Soviet KGB agent who had defected to the US and joined the Posse in 1953. Axelrod was fluent in Lithuanian and Russian. Kelly thanked Margo for her foresight in going to Italy. He told her he was on his way to Rome and wanted to meet everyone, including top Italian Posse members, at the embassy before dinner to help him implement a plan to pressure Grigulevich. He told her there was a good chance to end Cuban crisis, but "those who are steering the world toward nuclear obliteration must be stopped." They exchanged expressions of love, made smooching noises, and hung up.

Kelly then phoned the office of the Papal Secretary of State Cardinal Amleto Cicognani. He knew the cardinal from an earlier time when he had studied Stalin's collectivization and religious persecution policies at the Vatican archives. The office secretary passed him through.

"Good afternoon, Kelly," the cardinal said. "We are looking forward to seeing you. Where are you?"

Kelly explained that he was in Moscow and looking forward to meeting with the pope and to Rome's warm weather. He told Cicognani that there were some complications that required his help. He explained that the KGB would try to stop the meeting and that Volkhov had sent Iosif Grigulevich, formerly known as Teodoro Castro, to Rome. He also said there were likely Soviet sleeper agents in the religious delegations from Soviet-controlled countries attending Vatican II.

"So Grigulevich is still working on behalf of the Stalinists," Cicognani said. "Many people in Rome will be surprised. He's not using the alias of Teodoro Castro?"

Kelly told him that he had a Russian passport in the name of Archpriest Stanislav Illich and he might wear a disguise.

The cardinal said he had vetted the religious missions from the Catholic countries in Soviet-controlled East Europe. He knew they had some collaborationist clergy, but he didn't think they were active KGB agents because they were out of shape, ignorant of theology, and alcoholic. He told the Sheriff that he might be right about the Russian Orthodox and Catholic Lithuanian delegations from the USSR because they included some suspicious characters. "How can I help you?"

"I must have information on the KGB scheme tonight," Kelly said. He went on to explain his plan. The cardinal told him everything would be arranged.

As he walked into Sheremetyevo airport, Kelly had a gut feeling that he had missed something. He hoped that his ploy to pressure Grigulevich would give him the information he needed to stop the KGB from preventing a solution to the Cuban missile operation. But he didn't know about the sniper.

Chapter 19
Saint Grig

Rome, October 23, 1962

G RIGULEVICH ARRIVED IN Rome around five p.m. and met the five Soviet agents at a ristorante near the Vatican and laid out the plan. He gave them each a picture of Miller and their assignments. He ordered the sniper and two agents to focus on Miller who would be landing soon at da Vinci airport. He wanted them to hit Miller that very day near the airport. Other KGB-affiliated officials from the Soviet embassy were at the airport and would keep them apprised of Miller's arrival.

If Miller somehow eluded them, the trio was to search for him at hotels on both sides of the Tiber near the Vatican, concentrating on the east or Roman side of the river where most of the hotels were. If they failed to find him that night, the sniper was to position himself early on Wednesday morning on the roof of Castel Sant'Angelo Museum, which overlooked St. Peter's Square, all streets near the main entrances of the Vatican, and, importantly, the only two bridges spanning the Tiber River from central Rome into Vatican City, which in Grigulevich and the trio's opinion, was the most likely way that Miller would approach the Vatican. The two agents, wearing black fedoras festooned with a red ribbon, were to serve as spotters for the sniper. They were to stand, one on each of the bridges, and the one who saw Miller was to wave both hands in the air. With the help of the spotter and his ambush location, the sniper should be able to shoot Miller wherever he appeared—on the streets around the Vatican, St. Peter's Square, or the bridges. They also agreed that Miller would come early because the clock was ticking on the Cuban crisis and the pope was available and wanting to help end the threat to peace.

Grigulevich told the other two agents that they were to shoot the pope in St. Peter's Square and then told each one separately and confidentially that he was the avenger and must kill the agent who shoots the pope. He told them to carry out the order without reservation or consultation. He said if anything happened to them, their families would be compensated. He also promised them that the Soviet government would get them released from prison if they were caught. He didn't explain how. Grigulevich knew the plan made it likely that the pope would survive and that the agents would either shoot one another or do nothing. He was showing signs of his disenchantment with totalitarian ideology and a willingness to use its demand for blind obedience against it.

§

AS THE JETSTAR flew over Tuscany, Kelly learned that the general in charge of the Carabinieri, Italy's military police, had ordered the plane to land at the US military base at Gaeta, halfway between Rome and Naples, instead of da Vinci airport. Kelly approved of the change. The general was a Posse member, and Kelly trusted him. The tangerine sun had set and a reddish glow appeared on the horizon.

When Kelly exited the jet, the American chargé d'affaires, the Carabinieri general, and the chief of the Polizia de Stato, who was also a Posse member, met him on the runway. The chargé told him that the airport was changed because the KGB was watching arrivals at da Vinci airport. He also said the Posse members from the US were at the US Embassy, and Posse assets from across Italy were in Rome, awaiting instructions.

The general informed him that "Stanislav Illich" had arrived at da Vinci airport earlier and was staying at a multi-story B & B with the Russian Orthodox delegation near the entrance to the Vatican Museum. The Posse owned and managed the B & B and had enticed the Orthodox delegation to lease it at the start of Vatican II by calling it the Russia House and offering a below-market monthly rate.

"Bene," Kelly said. "Let's get to the chancery."

The welcome party led Kelly to a helicopter. Twenty minutes later he walked into the embassy's conference room.

Ricotta and roasted tomato bruschetta with crumbled pancetta, garlic olives, biscotti cookies, Amarone red wine, water, and hot coffee were spread out on a side table against the wall. Kelly breathed it in. He and Margo embraced, and he smiled in the general direction of Ed, Ana, Oliver, Taylor, Denise the Warbler, Bone, and Axelrod.

"Greetings!" Kelly said to the large group gathered in the room, including the papal secretary of state, the US ambassador, the head of the Carabinieri and polizia, Posse members from the US, and Posse leaders from Italy. They warmly greeted him. The ambassador directed Kelly to a black leather armchair at the head of the table. Kelly, who was hungry, grabbed a plate of appetizers and a glass of cold water and sat down.

Kelly thanked everyone for coming. He then briefly outlined the danger that beset the world. He explained that both Kennedy and Khrushchev desired to retreat from the brink of war but were hampered by political perceptions and a hardline communist faction that wanted to bluff the US into debilitating concessions or, failing that, win a nuclear war. "One misstep and we'll all be toast."

He went on to say that the two leaders seemed to have embraced the idea of using Pope John XXIII as an off-ramp. "I'm here," he stressed, "to meet with the pope at eleven a.m. tomorrow to see what can be done, but there is a problem."

Kelly told them that Grigulevich and the KGB were in Rome to stop him and the pope. "There are," he said, "Soviet agents in the various delegations that came from Soviet-controlled states to attend

Vatican II. I think the KGB agents will attempt to run a massive propaganda blitz against the pope to discredit him as an intermediary in the Cuban situation. They might try more sinister things, perhaps try to kill me. The KGB does not want the Cuban fire to be extinguished."

The Sheriff then offered his solution. To neutralize the KGB, the Posse needed to get information on the makeup of the various Soviet-controlled delegations at Vatican II. The listening devices in Russia House had not generated any useful information, and the Posse had no ears in the apartment complexes where the Lithuanian and other East European delegations from Soviet-controlled East Europe were residing. "Our major effort to obtain details on KGB plans," Kelly said, "revolves around Grigulevich."

He made eye contact with the papal secretary of state. "Your Eminence, do you have the tape recording?"

The cardinal, next to Kelly, stood up. "I called Grigulevich earlier today to set up a meeting. I recorded the conversation."

The assembly was quiet. All ears were attuned to the tape recorder that the cardinal had placed in the middle of the table. They heard a phone number being dialed.

"Pronto," said a voice with a heavy Russian accent.

"This is Secretary of State Cardinal Cicognani calling for Archpriest Stanislav Illich."

"Solo un minuto per favore." There was a loud noise as if the phone had been dropped. A few minutes passed.

"Good day, dear Cardinal Cicognani," a voice said. "This is Archpriest Stanislav Illich. To what do I owe the pleasure of this call?"

"Ah, Teodoro, it's good to hear your voice again," the cardinal said.

There was silence. Then deep breathing. It was clear that Cicognani's casual divulgence must have jarred the dean of Soviet espionage and foul play.

"How did you recognize me?" Grigulevich asked.

"I saw your picture on our security cameras when you entered Russia House. I never forget a face. You didn't say goodbye. Most people think you were murdered by the mafia."

"Well, I had a nervous breakdown and had to depart immediately for health reasons. It's so good to hear your voice. What can I do for you, your Eminence?"

"I want you to meet someone who is impressed with you."

"Who?"

"He calls himself the Inspector General. He's come a long way." There were a few moments of silence again. "Why me?"

"As I said, he's impressed with you."

"Where would I meet him?"

"Here at the Vatican in the Tower of the Winds."

"What time?"

"He'd like to meet you at eight-thirty p.m. before he retires for the night. He's an old timer who likes to get to bed early. If you come to the archway next to the main entrance to St. Peter's Basilica, I will have a staff member escort you to the Tower of the Winds. It's within easy walking distance of where you're staying. It will not be a long meeting."

"All right, I'll be there, and you will guarantee my safety?"

"Yes, of course, Teodoro. You have nothing to fear. It'll be like old times."

"I'm looking forward to seeing you again," Grigulevich said. "Arrivederci."

The cardinal turned off the tape.

Kelly grinned. He then said the Posse would try to push Grigulevich for information on the KGB plans by giving him a road-to-Damascus moment, featuring Oliver and Taylor as the disembodied ghosts of Stalin and Vlasik, respectively.

"I hope you have something else to offer him," Cardinal Cicognani said. "He's a hardened, practical man."

Kelly nodded. "We'll deal for solid information."

The Sheriff said he also wanted Bone and Axelrod to impersonate senior clerics from the papal household and attend a reception organized by Cardinal Cicognani for the Russian, Eastern European, and Lithuanian delegations. Their goal, he said, was to find out who among the delegates we can count upon to support the pope in case of a propaganda attack and who was likely a covert KGB agent.

"Once we understand the KGB operation, we will meet here later tonight, say around ten, to plan. We don't have much time."

§

GRIGULEVICH SEETHED OVER the phone call from Cardinal Cicognani. He had not expected to be so easily identified as the former Costa Rican ambassador but, as far as he knew, the cardinal still didn't know he was Iosif Grigulevich, Soviet spy extraordinaire. He probably should have worn a disguise, but he thought the false passport and residing at Russia House was adequate cover. He wondered if he were slipping.

He also fumed because the call happened against the backdrop of Miller changing airports and foiling the attempt on his life. He didn't know where Miller was. He knew the whereabouts of the sniper who had called and told him after Miller failed to appear at da Vinci airport that he was moving to the backup plan that involved the Castel Sant'Angelo Museum and the spotter agents on the bridges. But he also knew the sniper was creative and independent and could strike out on his own. His plan for taking down Miller and the pope was not going well, but he didn't mind. For a reason he could not pinpoint, he felt restive about the plan and the asininity of stoking a nuclear nightmare.

He wondered if the "old timer" the cardinal had called about was Miller. If so, he would not be displeased. He wondered who he really was and why Khrushchev trusted him. He was happy to go to the Tower of the Winds, a sixteenth-century astronomical observatory. He knew it well and felt it was a safe place, above the Gallery of Maps and deep inside the Vatican. He wondered why Petrov had not commented on the picture of Miller that he had sent him.

At a quarter after eight, Grigulevich approached the main entrance to St. Peter's Basilica. A priest in a black cassock and black biretta with a red tuft greeted him, introduced himself as a staff member of the secretary of state, and bade him to follow. They walked through the archway where four Swiss Guards, wearing blue doublets and blue berets, stopped them, checked their identities, and searched them. Finding everything in order, the guards directed them to proceed.

Grigulevich watched the priest carefully as he climbed the steps and paused at the door of the Tower of the Winds.

"Please enter, Ambassador," the priest said.

"Aren't you coming in?" Grigulevich asked suspiciously.

"I'm not worthy," the priest said. He bowed and retreated down the stairs.

Grigulevich shrugged, opened the door, and walked into a blinding white light. He stood there, unwilling to proceed because he couldn't see who or what was in the room. The Warbler was singing "Let There Be Peace on Earth, and Let It Begin with Me." His spine tingled as the voice filled the room with its soulful intensity and harmonized with a choir of soft voices. He had always been a sucker for beautiful voices and music. Kelly carefully observed him from an adjoining room through a pinhole in the portrait of Pope Gregory XIII, which hung on the wall.

"Cardinal Cicognani, are you here?" Grigulevich called out.

He heard a familiar voice. "Sit down, Grig." It sounded like—it couldn't be. Stalin was dead. The bright light faded to a soft glow. The singing melted to a whisper.

"Is that you, Koba?" Grigulevich asked. Was someone pulling his leg?

"Yes, Grig. Sit down."

"Grig" was a term of affection that he thought only Stalin knew. As his eyes adjusted to the reduced light, he saw two men who looked like Stalin and his bodyguard Vlasik seated at the far end of a conference table. They were dressed in sheer white chasubles with parallel rows of gold banding on the front and back. They appeared translucent and likely to evanesce with a gust of wind.

"I thought you were dead, Koba," Grigulevich said, recovering his wits and sitting down in a comfortable, black velvet covered armchair.

"Yes, many have thought so." It sounded like Stalin's voice. "As you can see, I and Vlasik are very much alive. We have a new purpose. We've been assigned a new mission by the Inspector General."

"Who?" Grigulevich said brusquely.

"He who provides for the birds, fashions the laws of nature, and shepherds the flock, even to the point of trying to save the lost sheep," Oliver said in a clear voice.

Grigulevich smiled. He was being played. "Are you referring to Uncle Sam?"

The Stalin figure laughed. "You have not lost your sense of humor, comrade. In this case, I'm referring to God."

Grigulevich decided to play along. He was curious. He felt safe. "How did it happen, Koba? You were always a persecutor of religion."

"You remember, Grig, that I met Ana Cortez at Spaso House. I talked with her. She touched my soul, and I have never been the same. She led me to alter my life, to atone for my sins."

"I remember Ana Cortez," Grigulevich said. "Are you trying to change me?"

"It's your choice. You have led a life of deceit and violence."

Grigulevich laughed, "Talk about the pot calling the kettle black."

"Look to the future," Oliver said. "The Inspector General is giving you a choice. The gospel says, 'He who is not with me is against me and he who does not gather with me scatters.' What road do you choose?"

"I always look to the future," Grigulevich said. "Recently, I decided communism isn't the wave of the future. I have seen how autocracy easily slips into pettiness, narcissism, deceit, and rending of the community. I'm ready for a change."

The singing became louder, and the blinding white light returned.

"Who is singing?" Grigulevich asked. "It's moving."

"Close your eyes." Oliver said.

Grig closed his eyes. He heard the door at the other end of the room open. The singing and the light softened.

"Open your eyes, Grig," a soft, feminine voice said.

He opened his eyes and saw Ana Cortez in a dazzling garment of white. Oliver and Taylor were gone. He bowed to Ana. "You do get around, Ana. I'm so sorry for trying to capture and kill you."

"Stand up, Grigulevich," Ana said. "You must repent to God, not me. Confess and abandon whatever treacherous mission you are on. Turn your life around!"

Grigulevich got up. He smiled. "I enjoyed the show. Why are we here?"

Ana looked at him closely. He was not having a Damascus moment. She saw no point in beating around the bush. "We want to know what the KGB is planning in Rome."

"That's reasonable," Grigulevich said. "I'm open to a new perspective. I was not joking when I told your movie stars that I'm sick of communism. But I'll need a concrete inducement."

"What do you want?" Ana said.

"I have a love child in Rome. I want her and her mother to be given an annual pension of one hundred thousand Swiss francs, adjusted each year for inflation. And I'll need a quarter million dollars in my Swiss bank account."

"I don't think it'll be a problem," Ana said, "but it depends partially on the quality of your information. Not to mention your continued work and effectiveness once you return to the USSR."

"I'll tell you what the KGB has planned in Rome if you guarantee the pension for my child and her mother. I'll listen to what you want me to do in the USSR before I commit to anything else. Then we can talk more about my Swiss bank account."

Ana nodded, inviting Grigulevich to speak.

Grigulevich held up his hand. He said he respected her influence, but he must have confirmation from an American government official. Ana left.

Ed stepped in. "I guarantee the pension."

Grigulevich recognized Ed as the head of the State Department's Russian desk. He knew he was talking to someone who could make a commitment. "I'm here to arrange the assassination of Miller and the pope. A sniper came with the Lithuanian Catholic delegation to Vatican II. He is in the wind. He intended to kill Miller earlier today, but Miller arrived at a different airport. The sniper might be hunting him at hotels or wherever he's staying. If he does not find Miller, he will position himself on the roof of Castel Sant'Angelo Museum at the crack of dawn tomorrow. From that vantage point, he will have a clear shot at Miller when he crosses the Tiber on the only two bridges into Vatican City, either the Ponte Sant' Angelo, the pedestrian only bridge, or Ponte Vittorio Emanuele, the main artery for automobiles and trucks.

"There are also four KGB agents in the Russian Orthodox delegation. Two of them will be on the bridges early tomorrow morning, one on each bridge, to signal the sniper when Miller approaches. They'll be wearing black fedora hats with a red ribbon around the band. The one who sees Miller will wave both hands above his head.

"The other two will be in St. Peter's Square tomorrow when the pope visits with the pilgrims. They will be wearing the clerical dress of the Russian Orthodox Church. They plan to assassinate the pope."

"Description?" Ed said.

"One has a full black beard and is tall, and the other is short and sports a blonde goatee."

"Who is the trigger man?"

"They both have the assignment, but the one who actually kills the pope will be shot by his comrade, who will then claim he's the pope's avenger."

"Is there anything else?" Ed said.

"No" Grigulevich said, "but Volkhov aims to have the Cuban missile crisis balloon into a fiery test of communism and democracy. He has a marksman in the US who will target Kennedy if the president proves to be a problem."

Kelly was astonished at the revelations. The KGB plan was more pernicious than he had imagined, but Grigulevich's confession and apparent transformation into a potential ally was equally shocking. Could he be trusted, he wondered. It was worth giving him what he wanted to see how he reacted. He continued to watch the exchange.

"Anything more?" Ed asked.

When Grigulevich shook his head, Ed told him to sit down. He said he had to check on what the US government would offer him.

On a hunch, mainly because the FBI pressure to search Leningrad Harbor had not been persistent, the Soviet spymaster said, "I'm glad your children made it home safely."

Ed nodded and left the room. He returned ten minutes later and told Grigulevich that the pension for his love child and her mother would be set up tomorrow. Then he said when he returned to the USSR, four things must happen. He must help Khrushchev end the Cuban missile crisis, help him survive as the Kremlin leader for as long as possible before retiring, work inside the KGB to push the career of Mikhail Gorbachev, and reconnect Russia with its Judeo-Christian roots.

Grigulevich rested his hands on the table. "So, you not asking me to spy for you?"

"No," Ed said. "We know you wouldn't spy, but we do think that you'd be willing to improve the future of the people who live in the USSR. We will put the quarter million in your account upon the successful end of the Cuban missile crisis. We will add another quarter million in two years if you work effectively with Khrushchev and Gorbachev."

Grigulevich beamed. "I'll do it."

The door behind Ed opened. He walked out and the door closed.

Grigulevich looked around. No one was in the conference room. He sat down in the armchair and felt a weight lift off his shoulders. He had been frank because he didn't want to murder the pope or Miller and opposed the lunacy of threatening a nuclear confrontation. He also had concluded that Christian-based orders were far superior to ideologically-based dictatorships. He was comfortable, relieved, and confident. He smiled, got up, and opened the door behind him. The priest who had led him to the tower was standing before him.

"Father, thank you for escorting me," Grigulevich said. He felt relaxed. The crescent moon gave faint light, but he saw clearly. A tawny owl hooted from the woodlands near the Tiber. He smiled. "It's a beautiful evening," he continued. "I have a new mission."

He had done what he could to thwart the assassinations, and he hoped the Americans were successful. He now realized, too, that Cardinal Cicognani knew who he was. He breathed a sigh of relief that Stalin was indeed dead. But his feeling of new purpose was quickly disrupted. The sniper and assassins were loose and the Cuban missile crisis still mushrooming.

Chapter 20
The Sniper

Rome, October 23–24, 1962

AFTER GRIGULEVICH DEPARTED, Kelly expressed his surprise to the Posse members who were with him at what he had heard. He asked their opinion. Everyone was flabbergasted but felt that Grigulevich was telling the truth. Kelly, too, thought he had been candid. Kelly and the others returned to the American embassy to develop a counterplan.

When Kelly arrived, Axelrod and Bone informed him that four Russian Orthodox clerics and one Lithuanian Catholic priest had left their delegations and gone underground. That information matched what Grigulevich had said. They also told him that the rest of the delegates would support any effort by the pope to mediate the Cuban missile confrontation.

When the Sheriff entered the embassy's conference room at ten p.m., everyone was there, including the Italian defense minister, also a Posse ally. Kelly quickly described the KGB plan and laid out a counterplan to neutralize the threats.

Security was already tight around Vatican City because of Vatican II. He asked that it be boosted immediately with additional police, Carabinieri, Italian army troops, and metal detectors.

The police, Carabinieri, and Italian defense leader said that the metal detecting equipment was not yet operational at the Vatican but readily agreed to beef up security. They also said that the crowd in St.

Peter's Square would be divided, organized into manageable groups, and restrained by manned rope lines and checkpoints. The clergy would be directed to enter St. Peter's Basilica and then come down the stairs to the square to a roped-off, standing-only place at the foot of the stairs where the pope would pass.

Kelly said he thought the two Russian assassins, wearing the clerical dress of Orthodox clergy, would find their way to the reserved standing area. He and Posse members, wearing religious garb, would be waiting. He thought with luck that they could disarm and arrest the assassins based on the description that Grigulevich had provided. He also believed that Grigulevich, perhaps wittingly, had handicapped the assassins. Each of them would assume he was to be the avenger rather than the assassin, so neither would shoot the pope.

But Kelly wanted to take no chances. He asked Cardinal Cicognani to delay the pope's public visit with pilgrims in St. Peter's Square for fifteen minutes, until 10:45. Then he ordered the Posse to arrange a car backfire and commotion in the square at 10:30 sharp, before the pope arrived and not far from the roped off area where the Orthodox clergy were. The distraction might fool the assassins into believing that the pope had been shot, leading them to reveal themselves as they each tried to assume the role of the avenger.

The two Russians who intended to signal the sniper from the bridges would also be identified and stopped. Both bridges would be filled with undercover Posse and police officers. At 8:30 a.m. a Posse member wearing clothes like Miller and a bulletproof vest would walk onto Ponte Sant' Angelo and a mannequin, similarly dressed and seated in the backseat of a convertible with the top down, would be driven across the Ponte Vittorio Emanuele. When the Russians started waving, the Posse would surround them and the police would move in and arrest them.

As for the sniper, the Sheriff decided to send Bone, Axelrod, and two other Posse members to the Castel Sant'Angelo Museum before sunrise to take him down. He thought if they were in position, they would catch him when he climbed to the roof or, if he were already on the roof, they would surprise and disarm him.

The Sheriff also had assignments for Margo, Ana, Ed, Oliver, Taylor, and the Warbler. He asked them to work with the genuine members of the various clerical delegations from Soviet-controlled countries to boost the reputation of the pope as a mediator in the resolving the Cuban missile crisis.

The Sheriff went on to stress the importance of his meeting with the pope to end the crisis and the critical nature of what everyone had to do to ensure the pope's safety. He extended his thanks to the leaders of the police, army, and Carabinieri for their deployment. He wished everyone good luck.

After the meeting Cardinal Cicognani told Kelly that he was in danger because the sniper was still on the loose. He suggested that Kelly, instead of entering the Vatican through a public entry point, take the secret passage and tunnel into the Vatican from the interior of Castel Sant'Angelo, a building owned by the Italian government but managed by the papacy as a museum and mausoleum housing the body of Roman Emperor Hadrian from the second century. For centuries, the popes had used the secret tunnel to escape powerful politicians and kings who wanted to kill, imprison, or control the head of the Catholic Church.

The secret tunnel extended underground to an apartment deep within the Vatican. Kelly said he had heard of the secret passageway and would like to use it. Cicognani said the pope was also open to a meeting before his public blessing to discuss the Cuban issue and to give Kelly more time at St. Peter's Square.

Kelly applauded the idea and said he'd like to meet the pope at 9:00 a.m. The cardinal told him that two Swiss Guards would meet him at 8:30 a.m. at the front door of the Castel, lead him into the Castel to the door to the secret passage, and then escort him the length of the tunnel into the Vatican. He said the Castel was protected by St. Michael the Archangel, whose statue with sword in hand had adorned the top of the building since the sixth century. According to a vision experienced by then Pope Gregory the Great, God had St. Michael stop a plague pandemic that had afflicted Rome.

"St. Michael will give you a hand," the cardinal said, "if any trouble develops."

"I'll be there," Kelly said. He had his own idea for crossing the Tiber without using the bridges.

Before retiring that evening, Kelly received word that President Kennedy had sent another letter to Khrushchev on October 23. He stayed up to read it. JFK was frank and to the point. He wanted the missiles removed and blamed the Russians for the conflict.

Kelly was concerned that the tone would upset Khrushchev, but he knew Kennedy was being honest. There was no easy or face-saving way out of the dispute. He fell asleep in Margo's arms, hoping that Khrushchev could outplay the hardliners and come to terms with JFK. He thought he had outsmarted the sniper.

§

THE SNIPER HAD planned to kill Miller on the highway between the airport and the city center. When Miller did not show up at da Vinci airport, he was unworried. He had an alternative plan, which did not include searching hotels near the Vatican. He thought that was like looking for a needle in a haystack and he had wondered why Grigulevich had suggested such a weak option.

The sniper, at thirty-eight, was the best contract killer in the KGB. He could take the fuzz off a peach at thirty-five hundred yards. A Russian living in Soviet Lithuania, he spoke Russian, Lithuanian, Spanish, English, German, and French. With a small, soft physique that bordered on feminine, he was a master of disguise. He was one of many psychopaths that the communist system exploited—a man without scruples or compassion. His black pants, black soft-soled shoes custom made for silence, and dark shirt helped him blend into the background, day or night.

He approached his targets with care. He studied his prey closely and, if possible, followed them, observed their behavior, and then developed multiple plans of attack. Disappointment was not in his DNA. A missed opportunity only challenged his creativity. He would never stop.

His priority was to have a secure, last resort hideaway to snare Miller. He had been in Rome since October 11 when Vatican II opened, pretending to be a Lithuanian Catholic priest but really acting as an enforcer to keep the Soviet and satellite clerics from defecting, criticizing the Soviet empire, or praising the pope too enthusiastically. He was familiar with the sites around the Vatican.

When Grigulevich gave him the contract on Miller, he was relieved to be free, at least temporarily, of his babysitting job of monitoring clerics and focusing on what he did best—assassinating baneful foes of the USSR. He thought the best place to set an ambush of Miler was the roof of Castel Sant'Angelo. It provided an unrestricted view of the two main bridges over the Tiber that connected Rome's city center to Vatican City. He'd have a spotter on both bridges. The roof also had a view of virtually all the streets near the Vatican, including the only place where cars can enter and park in Vatican City, the parking lot next to the Church of St. Anne. Grigulevich, however, told him to hit Miller near the airport and hold the Castel Sant'Angelo in reserve. He wondered if Grigulevich was conflicted about spilling blood near the Vatican. He would have been happy to take out the pope, too, but that job was given to less experienced agents.

When his target failed to show up at the airport, he went to a bed and breakfast near the Castel Sant'Angelo Museum and rented an inexpensive room for one night. He didn't plan to sleep there. He just needed time and space to get ready to hit Miller. He decided to disguise himself as a nun. Such an outfit would help him blend into the background of the many holy men and women who walked around the Vatican. It would grant him unquestioned entry to the museum. He shaved three times to make sure his face was clear, and then shaved his forearms.

He donned a nun's black headgear with a veil and a long white surplice that fell to his shoes. He wore it over his black pants and camouflaged shirt. His costume was different from that of traditional sisters, but Rome had so many unconventional orders of nuns that no one could be sure if he were a nun from a new order that was waiting to be recognized by the Vatican or from some rural or desert monastic group that had no clue on how to dress in public. He called himself Sister Mary Garcia from Ecuador.

Once he was properly attired, he waited outside the entrance of the museum for a group of nuns to show up. His backpack held a hundred-foot-long tan rope ladder and a black and gray nylon sleeping bag. In his hand he carried a violin-style gun case with a rifle, pistol, a switchblade knife, and a bolt cutter hidden under a camera, lenses, binoculars, and a guidebook on the birds of Rome.

When a busload of nuns showed up, he joined them and was waved through security without a search. Once inside, he went to the basement and located a padlocked exit door that he had found earlier when he had studied the building from the outside. He cut the padlock with his bolt cutter and made sure he could open it from the outside. Then he returned to the main floor of the museum and climbed the stairs to an exit roof door that had a horizontal, spring-loaded push bar lock. He pushed the bar, stepped out onto the roof, scotch taped the bolt of the lock to prevent it from latching, and closed the door behind him. He could escape by entering the Castel and exiting through the basement, but he also had a rope ladder that he could use to climb down the side of the building into a grove of trees. He got out his binoculars and did a careful survey of St. Peter's Square, the streets leading to the Square and the Vatican, and the two bridges spanning the

Tiber. He knew security was tight around the area because of Vatican II, but his new vantage point made him realize that the police were everywhere. He looked around the roof and found a place to set up camp. He put away his nun garb, unfolded the sleeping bag, stretched out, and thought about Miller.

He had not had much time to study Miller's life after being ordered to kill him. He reflected now on what he remembered from the files to try to figure out where Miller would be.

He recalled that the KGB's information on him was sparse. That intrigued him. He recollected that Miller was multilingual, was athletic and brainy, and had access to influential people in the US government, the Vatican, and the Kremlin. He seemed to be a person who appeared and disappeared at will during crucial moments in international crises. He decided that Miller was more than an academic middleman between Khrushchev and the pope. He decided that he was an American spy whom Soviet intelligence had misclassified and misjudged as some neophyte diplomat.

When he examined Miller from that point of view, he calculated that he would probably stay at the US embassy in Rome. He decided on a change of plan because of the security cordon around the Vatican. He'd look for Miller just at or before dawn at the American embassy. He could always come back to the Castel if he were not there. He didn't inform the spotters of the change of plan because he wanted them on the bridges in case he couldn't find Miller With that thought, he turned over and slept soundly. The evening air was cool and pleasant.

Chapter 21
The Sword of St. Michael

Rome, October 24, 1962

THE NEXT MORNING before sunrise, the sniper left his ambush location on the roof, packed up his sleeping bag and nun's outfit, dropped the rope ladder to the branches of a large tree that shaded the museum, and climbed down to the tree. He had decided that it was too dangerous to reenter the Castel because of the possibility of night watchmen or security guards in the building. He hid the bottom part of the ladder in the tree branches. He had his gun case and backpack with him. He was ready to hunt down and kill Miller.

He was again surprised at the huge concentration of police and military troops around Vatican City and all visible approaches to the Vatican. He thought it was unusually extensive, even for the pope's impending public appearance, and wondered if he were the reason. He laughed to himself. No one would catch him, he thought.

He saw four men arrive at the museum's entrance. They looked in good physical shape and stood in the shadows conversing. One was huge, and another was speaking in Russian. They looked familiar. But he dismissed the thought. Bone and Axelrod had died in the US in 1953.

He hailed a taxi on a side street and headed for the US embassy. He found a perch on the roof of the Grand Hotel near the embassy with a clear view of the embassy's courtyard. Miller might appear there for coffee or a light breakfast.

When the sniper focused his binoculars on the courtyard, he was surprised to see Miller sitting with two beautiful women. They were drinking coffee and talking. It was an opportunity to take Miller out and avoid all the police commotion near the Vatican. A golden October sun was rising in the east, chasing away white, wispy clouds. The temperature was warm. He sighted his rifle.

§

ANA, THE WARBLER, and Kelly sat at a table in the outdoor courtyard of the embassy, enjoying a second cup of coffee. They and Margo had already eaten a savory dish of Italian-style eggs Benedict, fresh fruit, Italian hard bread, and strawberry jam.

Margo was in the kitchen talking to the chef about his recipe for spaghetti carbonara. Bone, Axelrod, and two other Posse members had already left to stake out Castel Sant'Angelo. Oliver, Taylor, and Ed had joined the Posse members who were converging on St. Peter's Square and the bridges across the Tiber leading into the Vatican.

The courtyard was partially shaded by olive trees, stone pines, and two trellises of purple grape vines. It had a Trevi-like fountain, frescoes on the walls surrounding the courtyard, and marble sculptures. Roses in bloom filled the courtyard with a sweet, pleasant aroma. It reminded Kelly of a small version of the Palazzo Farnese. A warm breeze gently stirred leaves around the embassy grounds.

As Kelly leaned back against the cane webbing of his chair and sipped his coffee, his eyes caught a flash of reflected sunlight on the roof of the nearby Grand Hotel. Instinctively, he fell sideways to the varnished pebble stone floor, pulling Ana, the Warbler, and the table with him. A bullet from the sniper's rifle ripped through the back of his chair. A second bullet ricocheted off the floor near him.

Ana, the Warbler, and Kelly kept the table in front of them and rolled it as they crawled behind the trellises covered with purple grape vines. Two more bullets ricocheted off the floor inches from Kelly as the sniper tried to guess where he was. They were pinned down but not exposed. The sniper had missed.

Armed US Marine guards with bulletproof vests and helmets appeared, formed a wall around Ana, the Warbler, and Kelly, and led them into the embassy. Polizia and Carabinieri officers swarmed the Via Veneto and buildings near the embassy.

They reported that they found spent cartridges from a Russian-made M1891/30 sniper rifle. The sniper had gotten away.

Kelly called Bone and Axelrod on a British S-radio phone and informed them that the sniper was probably headed for the Castel Sant'Angelo. They told him about evidence that the sniper had already been on the roof of the Castel.

§

THE SNIPER STOPPED to don his nun's garb and then headed to Castel Sant'Angelo for another try at Miller. When he arrived near the Castel, he could see that the police were everywhere. The two men he'd seen earlier and seemed familiar were holding his rope ladder.

He turned into an alley next to a souvenir shop that sold rosaries, plastic replicas of Michelangelo's Pieta, and cold water. He assembled his rifle and slipped it under his nun's dress, holding it against his body with his right arm. He then walked to the main driveway entrance into the Vatican.

He stopped some fifty feet from the entrance and leaned back against the Vatican's towering dark stone wall as if resting and people-watching. He set his open case on the sidewalk in front of him as if asking for alms from passersby and thought about Miller.

The sniper decided that he had few options now and would keep his eye on the main drive into the Vatican, which seemed to him to be the only entrance open. There were three Swiss Guards there checking identifications.

He thought he would be able to get a shot off if Miller showed up in a car and slowed to turn into the driveway. He could still get away in the nun costume in the pandemonium that would ensue. He looked at his watch. It was 8:20 a.m. He thought Miller would probably show up later, closer to the time of the pope's public blessing. He was ready.

Nonetheless, he was surprised to see Miller approach on foot. He was with five companions who surrounded him and blocked a clear shot. He watched the group closely. It passed him on the other side of the street and headed toward the Passetto di Borgo, the elevated walkway connecting Castel Sant'Angelo to the Vatican. He didn't know why Miller had not simply entered the Vatican through the Swiss Guard checkpoint that he had been monitoring. Perhaps he wanted to witness the pope's public blessing from the safety of the Castel. Or he was deliberately avoiding obvious entry points into the Vatican for fear of the sniper.

If so, the sniper thought, Miller had made a bad choice. He couldn't believe his luck. He made his way to the closed museum's basement exit door. He pushed it open and carefully closed it behind him. He peeled off his nun's garb and checked his weapons. He moved to the front of the museum.

He knew Miller now had to walk back across the Passetto to the Vatican. There was no other approach. He decided to monitor Miller's movements from a window near the entrance of the Castel and then break the window, shoot him, and escape through the basement exit.

To his surprise, the front entrance door of the Castel swung open. He hid behind a large statue of St. Michael the Archangel.

§

THE SHERIFF AND five Posse members, including Ana and the Warbler, had taken the A Line metro from Circo Massimo station to Octaviano metro station. The Sheriff thought the sniper wouldn't anticipate their using such a public transit system. He had a good idea that the sniper had probably retreated to the neighborhood around the Castel Sant'Angelo and was looking for him. He thought he'd fool him again by just walking into the museum and then disappearing via the secret passageway into the Vatican.

When he arrived at the entrance to the museum, he was informed by Bone and Axelrod that they had searched the roof of the Castel and found a rope ladder. Kelly said that that probably meant that the sniper was on the streets.

He told Bone, Axelrod, Ana, the Warbler, and the other Posse members to work with the police to secure the museum and its bridge and passageway. He thought the sniper, if he were not apprehended on the street, could be captured when he returned to the Lithuanian delegation to Vatican II. He asked Ana to call Margo and Ed, who were managing Posse communications at the embassy, and bring them up to date. He was focused on his meeting with the pope.

Kelly entered the Castel Sant'Angelo and was escorted by two unarmed Swiss Guards to the secret tunnel that led into the Vatican. One guard walked up to what appeared to be the middle of a solid stone wall and pushed it. A hidden door opened to a dimly lit tunnel. Both guards walked into the passageway ahead of Kelly to show him the way. One asked Kelly to close the door.

When Kelly pushed the door two-thirds of the way shut, he found the barrel of a rifle blocking the door and partially angled toward his face.

"Move back," the sniper said in Russian.

Kelly stood his ground, sensing that the sniper might not be able to get off a deadly shot with a rifle in such a cramped space. He wanted to crowd the sniper, knowing that the extended rifle barrel was to his advantage because he could push it away with the door or lay hold of it. But the sniper could still shoot, and a bullet could ricochet and hit him or one of the Swiss Guards. He decided his best option was to keep the sniper distracted.

"Don't shoot," Kelly said in Russian. "The Swiss Guards aren't involved."

"I'm not here for them and I know they're unarmed," the sniper said. "Now move back."

Kelly stiffened. He felt helpless. He should have had Bone and Axelrod search the interior of the museum. It was a critical mistake. Likely a fatal one.

Kelly backed up and saw the door open wide. He felt a stabbing from behind that made him collapse. A shot echoed thunderously in the tunnel. He wondered if he had been shot.

Turning gingerly, he saw that what hit him was the metal sword of a statue of St. Michael the Archangel, a duplicate of one on the roof. From a shiny spot in the tarnished metal, it looked like the sniper's bullet had ricocheted off it. Kelly's eyes followed the bullet's path to a chip off the stone wall. The bullet must have glanced off the wall and hit the barrel of the gun.

Kelly grabbed the dented barrel and jerked the gun away. He swung the butt handle of the gun at the sniper's head. The sniper had a Nugent pistol strapped to his body. He pulled it and fired, barely missing Kelly as he ducked the rifle handle. The sniper regained his balance quickly, but not quickly enough. Kelly swung the rifle again and knocked the pistol away.

Kelly moved forward, ready to pulverize the sniper. The sniper brandished a switchblade.

"You are a hard man to kill, my friend," the sniper said, "a modern-day Rasputin, but your time has come."

Kelly smiled, which seemed to confuse the sniper. Kelly had fought many men armed with knives. He allowed the man to come forward, swinging the knife back and forth. He watched his opponent close in. Suddenly, the sniper jabbed forward with the knife in his right hand and then quickly tossed the knife toward his left hand, apparently thinking that his prey would move left to avoid the right jab.

Kelly had seen that maneuver before. He went right with lightning speed and, as the knife was in the air, drove a slashing right uppercut into the man's solar plexus. The man staggered as if hit with a block of concrete. He missed the knife and slowly bent over, retching and trying to catch his breath. As he fell to the floor, his bare head hit the bronze base of the statue of St. Michael the Archangel with a dull thud. His skull cracked, he died instantly.

The tunnel entrance swarmed with polizia. The Sheriff picked up the knife and the rifle and gave them to the polizia. One of the Swiss Guards had summoned them on walkie-talkie during the melee.

"Take his body to the morgue," Kelly said in Italian, "and notify the Lithuanian Catholic delegation attending Vatican II of his death. They will know what to do with him."

A Posse member had news for the Sheriff. He informed him that the polizia had arrested two Russians, one on the Ponte Vittorio Emanuele II, who started waving madly when a mannequin dressed like Miller appeared on the bridge in a convertible, and the other on the Ponte Sant'Angelo who waved wildly when someone also dressed like Miller popped up and started walking across the bridge.

The Sheriff grinned. "The fishing is good on the Tiber."

Then Kelly turned to the Swiss Guards. "Let's go meet the pope. He's in danger, and the Cuban missile crisis is boiling."

Chapter 22
Il Buono Papa

Rome, October 24, 1962

WHEN THE SHERIFF exited the secret passageway connecting Castel Sant'Angelo to the Vatican, he entered one of ten sixteenth-century apartments that wrapped around the Courtyard of Sixtus V. He felt he had been transported back in time to the Renaissance, when the papacy supported and encouraged Europe's magnificent revival of learning and awareness of life's possibilities. His goal was twofold.

He hoped that Pope John XXIII, a humble and unassuming man nicknamed Il Buono Papa, would use his moral authority to help Khrushchev and Kennedy stop the Cuban missile crisis. The Soviets had put the end of the world on the table only to discover that free nations would never allow a communist victory. Khrushchev was reaching out for a lifebuoy, and Kelly and Kennedy were supporting him.

His other purpose was to protect the pope's life. He knew that Pope John XXIII would die soon, but he was determined to make sure his death was not at the hand of an assassin. The pope had been diagnosed in summer 1962 with advanced stomach cancer, given only a few months to live.

Cardinal Cicognani led Kelly into the Apostolic Palace, where the pope had a small apartment with a bedroom, kitchen, bathroom, and office. A window looked out at sunny St. Peter's Square. Often the pope opened the window and waved to pilgrims milling about the Square. When he did, the crowd erupted in applause and cheers. The window was not open now, but birds twittered, trilled, and whistled. A solitary cardinal sitting on the windowsill stood out against the muted colors of pigeons and sparrows.

The pope sat behind a simple wooden desk, writing. The room was bright with golden sun streaming through the window. The pope, wearing wire-rimmed bifocals, looked up and smiled at Kelly. He had met him when Kelly had spent time in the Vatican archives researching Soviet religious policy.

"Come in, come in." The pope beckoned enthusiastically, thrilled to see a dear friend. He came around to the front of the desk. He was short, dressed in a white cassock with attached Pellegrini, a pectoral cross suspended from a gold cord, and a white skull cap. His face was friendly.

"I was writing a letter to Cardinal Suenens of Belgium, one of the managers of Vatican II, to invite and include women in the proceedings of Vatican II. I was so focused on convincing the fuddy-duddies that we had to update the Church that I overlooked one of our most needed changes—including women in its leadership. Celibate men understand neither women nor the challenges of family. At any rate, that is not why we are here."

"Thank you for receiving me on short notice," Kelly said. He leaned forward to kiss the pope's ring, but the pope raised him up and thanked him for coming.

"No need for that." The pope gestured to a side table with refreshments. "Please help yourself to coffee, fruit, and pastry, and sit down. We have much to talk about and not much time."

Kelly smiled. He admired this pope's humility, apparent love of all peoples, and yearning for peace. He passed on the food and sat in front of the pope's desk.

Pope John also sat down. He had a coffee on the desk. Cardinal Cicognani sat in a chair just to the left of Kelly with a cup of black coffee.

The pope said he understood that Kelly had faced an ordeal to get there safely. "I'm so happy you are here. Evil has many forms, and the burgeoning Cuban missile crisis is one of them. How grave is the situation?"

Kelly told the pope that it was a delicate moment. He said both Khrushchev and Kennedy hoped for peace. Kennedy viewed the placement of nuclear missiles in Cuba as a provocative and intolerable escalation that threatened the security of the Western Hemisphere. He wanted the missiles removed immediately or he would use the US military to remove them. He asked that the pope pray for peace.

"Khrushchev, on the other hand," Kelly said, "knows he erred by placing nuclear missiles in Cuba but does not want to appear intimidated by removing them in the face of Kennedy's demand. He thinks he will look weak. The communist elite or the Red Army would move against him. He's looking for a face-saving way out of the clash."

Kelly outlined Khrushchev's hope that the pope, as a widely recognized moral leader, would make a plea for peace. Khrushchev and Kennedy would then accept the papal plea for the sake of civilization and world peace.

"To complicate matters," Kelly continued, "the hardline, neo-Stalinist element called the Kobaists led by Volkhov want conflict, even to the point of nuclear war."

"What is the rationale for Volkhov and the hardliners' bellicose policy?" the pope asked.

Kelly said part of it was the hardliners belief that Kennedy was feckless and would capitulate before going to war. Part of it was blind arrogance stemming from the belief that victory, even in nuclear war, was assured because of the inevitability of their ideology. And part of it was a calculation that even if the USSR were forced to remove the missiles, they could blame Khrushchev for capricious leadership and remove him.

The pope shook his head. He looked over the top of his glasses at Kelly. "My heart burns for the Russian people. They have had a history of exceedingly bad governments over the centuries. First the tsars, then the commissars.

"The great problem confronting the world after almost two thousand years remains unchanged. Men are either with Christ and enjoy light, goodness, order, and peace. Or they are without Him or against Him, and they suffer confusion, bitterness in human relations, and the constant danger of fratricidal wars. We can do nothing about the hardliners except pray for enlightenment. Let's focus on Khrushchev and Kennedy."

"Yes," Kelly said. "They're rational actors and the solution lays in making them appear as equals and agreeing as men of courage and prudence to prevent a worldwide disaster."

"Of course," Pope John said. "In anticipation of their hope, I have drafted a plea for peace. I want you to read it and give me feedback."

The pope picked up a manilla envelope and handed it across the desk to Kelly. The Sheriff pulled out a one-paragraph document written in beautiful Italian. He read it slowly to himself. Then he read it aloud to Cardinal Cicognani, who tilted his ear toward Kelly.

We beg all governments not to remain deaf to this cry of humanity. That they do all that is in their power to save peace. They will thus spare the world from the horrors of a war whose terrifying consequences no one can predict. That they continue discussions, as this loyal and open behavior has great value as a witness of everyone's conscience and before history. Promoting, favoring, accepting conversations, at all levels and in any time, is a rule of wisdom and prudence which attracts the blessings of heaven and earth.

"It's powerful and persuasive." Kelly said.

"No changes?" the pope said.

"No changes," Kelly said. "It's simple, brief, and to the point."

"All right," the pope said. "Cardinal Cicognani, give copies immediately to both the Russian and American ambassadors in Rome for transmittal to and approval by their governments. Tomorrow I will broadcast the appeal on Vatican Radio and release it for publication by newspapers around the world. I pray that the leaders will pull back from the brink of war and give peace a chance."

"It'll have a positive impact," Kelly said.

The pope went on to say that peace requires social and international justice and virtues that stress unity and respect. He said that fallible human nature combined with nuclear weapons would destroy nations. He strongly recommended as an interim step that a nuclear test ban treaty be negotiated.

Kelly nodded. That was a brilliant idea and he would bring it up to President Kennedy. Then he sat upright in his chair and changed the subject to the pope's safety.

"Your Holiness, you're scheduled to greet the pilgrims at 10:30 this morning. There are two assassins in the Russian Orthodox delegation who plan to murder you. I have a plan to stymie them. Please start your procession at 10:45."

"Yes, Cardinal Cicognani told me about the threat," the pope said. "Who wants to kill me? I'm old, humble, poor, and nonthreatening."

"Volkhov and his group," Kelly said. "The goal is to keep you from helping Khrushchev find a solution to the Cuban imbroglio."

"But it's too late. I am already reaching out to Khrushchev and Kennedy."

"Yes," Kelly said, "but that's not the same as a solution. You remain a safety valve for modulating this crisis. The assassins will try to kill you."

"I guess they don't know that I don't expect to live much longer." The pope crossed his hands over his midsection. "But all right. I'll enter St. Peter's Square fifteen minutes late. If you think I should postpone the event entirely, I will."

"Thank you, Holy Father," Kelly said. "Postponement will not be necessary. Your appearance will inspire the world to hope for an end of this crisis."

The pope nodded. Kelly moved to the edge of his chair.

"Holy Father," Kelly said. "I was so sorry to hear of your condition, but I so admire your determination to carry on and work for us."

"I'm a sinner," the pope said, "and my time is limited. I follow the exhortation of St. John of God: 'Labor without stopping. Do all the good works that you can while you still have the time.'"

Kelly smiled and nodded. He got up and bid goodbye to the pope and the cardinal. He headed directly to St. Peter's Square, where he would deal with the assassins.

§

THE TWO ASSASSINS walked up to the rope lines sectioning St. Peter's Square into spaces for about fifty people. They wore the costume of Orthodox Christian priests—black cassock, black clerical shirt, and a white clerical collar. One was tall and had a black beard with streaks of gray. The other was short and had a blonde goatee. They examined the security arrangements for the pope in St. Peter's Square. It was ten in the morning.

"Go to the standing area for religious," said the bearded man. "I will stay with the pilgrims. That way we will cover the reserved religious area and the other part of the square where the masses are gathering. I will float among the pilgrims looking for a good place to shoot the pope. I will keep an eye on you in case the pope comes your way first and you have an opportunity to take him out. I think the guards will permit me to jump the rope lines because I am in clerical dress and can tell them I'm trying to reach the roped-off section for religious."

The small man nodded. He entered St. Peter's Basilica and came down the front stairs to the area roped off for clergy. Many clergymen, including Orthodox religious from Greece, Syria, and Jerusalem, were already there. Women religious were in an adjoining space.

The short man stood near the rope separating the huge crowd of pilgrims from the clergy. When he saw his colleague among the pilgrims, he waved to him. He planned to watch him shoot the pope and then claim to avenge the pope by killing his fellow KGB agent.

§

THE SHERIFF REACHED the roped-off area for clergy in St. Peter's Square at 10:20. He'd been held by a call from JFK about the pope's plea for peace. Then he had to take time to don a clerical collar and a black cassock.

Hundreds of clergymen milled about, including many Orthodox priests, most with beards but all with some type of facial hair. Kelly had no facial hair and stood out like a sore thumb. He knew Posse members and policemen were there too in clerical disguise, but he couldn't easily identify them at first. There were too many clerics and little time to study faces closely. He had failed again to plan properly.

He saw an Orthodox clergyman with a beard outside the roped-off area, walking toward him. Was that one of the assassins? What was he doing outside the ropes? And where is the other assassin? I cannot protect the pope, his mind shrieked. He felt cornered, regretting that he had not planned to isolate and neutralize the assassins.

Kelly heard the bells of St. Peter's Basilica ring out a minute before 10:30, indicating that the pope was about to enter the square. As he began to scrutinize the faces of the clergymen near him, he recognized four Posse members spread out among the crowd. But there were too many men in Orthodox dress. And he was distracted by the bearded cleric, outside the ropes among the pilgrims but clearly moving closer to him.

Suddenly, he heard a loud noise that sounded like a gunshot and saw a commotion at the edge of the Square, perhaps only 150 feet from where the Orthodox clergy were congregated. It was the distraction that he had arranged to draw out the assassins. None of the Orthodox clergy near him moved. They looked concerned and confused.

"You're Miller," the bearded Orthodox cleric said, standing on the other side of the rope next to him. He had one of his hands inside his cassock holding something about waist high.

Kelly felt trapped. He had not expected the assassin to be outside the roped area or to recognize him. None of the Posse or police was alert to the man. As he turned to face him, he saw a small, goateed Orthodox clergyman walk toward him.

He remembered that each shooter likely believed he would be the pope's avenger. He gambled. "Did you shoot the pope?" Kelly shouted in Russian to the short Orthodox clergyman approaching him.

"No," the small man said. "He did," pointing to the bearded man. He then pulled out a revolver and shot the man dead. "I'm the pope's avenger," he said, and dropped his weapon on the pavement.

The man was immediately surrounded by police and Posse members, arrested, and charged with murder. His companion's body was removed by the polizia and taken to the morgue.

Kelly felt a cascade of relief. Grigulevich's lame plan for killing the pope had fizzled out. He believed Grigulevich had intended it to self-destruct, and that thought gave him confidence that the Soviet spy would follow through and help Khrushchev survive.

At 10:45 a.m. Pope John entered the square and greeted the pilgrims, who broke out in rapturous applause. The pope blessed them and thanked them for coming.

Kelly left the square and made his way to the US embassy, where he Ana, Oliver, Taylor, the Warbler, Bone, and Axelrod joined him.

Margo and Ed were already there. He had called and told them to set up a war room in the embassy to coordinate the complex tasks of removing the Soviet missiles in Cuba, keeping Khrushchev in power, and stopping Volkhov and the Kobaists from escalating the crisis. He had no idea that the KGB leader had secret plans to transform the Cuban missile crisis into a nuclear war.

Chapter 23
Volkhov's Move

Moscow, October 24, 1962

VOLKHOV POUNDED THE desk. He stood in his office in Lubyanka with his reading glasses on, holding a draft of the pope's plea for peace. Khrushchev had approved the draft and had Foreign Minister Gromyko communicate that fact to the Vatican through the Soviet embassy in Rome.

The office was hot and the outside cold, causing frost and an icy border on the window. Its pale green walls reeked of stale cigarette smoke. The dimming, late afternoon light coming through the bars of the window made the room feel restricted and small.

Grigulevich stood erect in front of Volkhov's desk, looking anxious but not cowed. His hair was long, his face unshaven. He had a complacent look on his face.

"What happened in Rome?" Volkhov said, controlling his anger and puzzled by Grigulevich's bearing.

"The agents were incompetent," Grigulevich said emphatically.

"The sniper who was supposedly so good that he never missed?" Volkhov said sarcastically.

"I saw his body at the morgue," Grigulevich said. "His skull was cracked. There were no other marks on him. He was in Castel Sant'Angelo when it was closed to the public. The police report said that he apparently tripped in the dark and hit his head on a museum statue. He was in the wrong place at the wrong time."

"And you believe it?" Volkhov said, putting his glasses on his desk and glaring at his subordinate.

"I do," Grigulevich said. "There is no other explanation. He had an arsenal of weapons with him, including his sniper rifle. The police think he was planning to assassinate the pope."

Volkhov pulled his chair out from under the desk and sat down. He pointed to the humiliation chair in front of his desk. He wanted Grigulevich to suffer. "Sit down."

Grigulevich slid a piece of cardboard under the chair to level it. He grimaced to make Volkhov happy.

Volkhov focused again on the draft of the pope's plea for peace. "Speaking of the pope..."

Grigulevich held up an open palm to indicate he had an answer to Volkhov's hanging but unspoken question. "It was a comedy of errors. The agents pulled guns on each other. One was shot and killed, the other arrested for murder. I interviewed the survivor. He said he thought the other agent had shot the pope and then he, playing the role of the pope's avenger, killed him."

"And these are your people?" Volkhov said bitterly.

"I didn't pick them," Grigulevich said unapologetically. "I only used them."

Volkhov's face tightened with anger. "What about Miller?"

"He was tracked to Rome," Grigulevich said, "but he apparently never left the American embassy. The two agents standing on the bridges crossing into Vatican City each thought he saw him and waved. The police arrested them. They were declared personas non grata and expelled from Italy."

"You take no responsibility for this band of fools?" Volkhov said.

"I take full responsibility," Grigulevich said, "but I can't perform miracles. I should have done it myself rather than rely upon others. Hold me accountable."

Grigulevich's surprising confession relaxed Volkhov. He was still seething but had a showdown to orchestrate. He needed Grigulevich to contain Khrushchev and stir the Cuban crisis. "We don't want this papal plea to defuse the confrontation. I wrote an indignant letter to Kennedy's blunt note of October 23. I want you to take it to Khrushchev and convince him to send it today."

"Do you think he'll listen to me?" Grigulevich asked.

"Yes," Volkhov said, "because you're a famous diplomat and hitman. You are my assistant, so you carry with you the full power of the Kobaists. He will be wise to do what you tell him."

"Khorosho," Grigulevich said.

"What's with the hair and stubbly face?" Volkhov said. "Did you decide to become a monk in Rome?"

"Nyet," Grigulevich said. "I have been busy. No time for appearances."

Volkhov laughed. "Well, don't fix up for Khrushchev. The unkempt look makes you seem more menacing."

§

KHRUSHCHEV NEARLY FELL off his chair when told Grigulevich wanted to see him. He knew him well. He had been Stalin's suave hitman, and now he worked with Volkhov. Khrushchev had closely followed the charade in Rome and wondered how Miller had managed to neutralize Grigulevich and have the pope issue his draft of a plea for peace. He looked forward to chatting with Grigulevich.

Grigulevich was ushered into his office at four p.m. on October 24. Khrushchev got up to greet him. The room was cold. A plate of ripened bananas on the desk, which were rare in the USSR, smelled musty. The light, melodic music of Glinka, Khrushchev's favorite composer, played in the background.

"Good to see you, Iosif," Khrushchev said. "You look like a wild monk."

Grigulevich smiled. "I would have groomed myself more appropriately for you, but Volkhov insisted that I come disheveled. He thought my mien would intimidate you. I thought you'd be amused and see that I'm a different person."

Khrushchev eyed him carefully. He didn't trust him, but he had to admit that Grigulevich seemed jovial and relaxed. "Have a seat, Iosif."

Khrushchev returned to his chair behind the desk. He watched the KGB hitman wait until he was seated, which he took as an unusual sign of respect. He thought he glimpsed a cross under Grigulevich's shirt. "Are you wearing a crucifix?"

"Da," Grigulevich said. "I lived with some genuine Orthodox clergy in Rome for a few days. I liked their approach to life."

Khrushchev shook his head. He looked at Grigulevich suspiciously. A charming, cold-blooded killer. He wondered if this was a trap. "What can I do for you?"

"I come as a friend who desires to help you resolve the Cuban impasse," Grigulevich said. "Volkhov sent me to you with this letter in response to Kennedy. It is confrontational, verbose." Grigulevich handed him the letter.

Khrushchev read it aloud. It rejected the authority of the US and OAS to impose a quarantine because such action violated international law, international norms, and Cuban and Soviet sovereignty. It claimed that a quarantine was an ultimatum that demanded that the Soviet Union and Cuba adjust their relations or face force.

It also claimed that US actions amounted to intimidation. It said that the Soviet Union abided by international law and universally recognized norms of conduct that regulate navigation of the high seas in international waters. It charged that the US was involved in dangerous political showboating because of ongoing election campaigning.

The letter concluded that the Soviet Union rejected American demands, would not respect the quarantine, and would take what actions were necessary to guarantee its international rights on the high seas.

Khrushchev looked intently at Grigulevich. "Are you advising me to send this?"

"Da."

"It will not defuse the crisis."

"No, but you can do other things to indicate that you are open to negotiations."

"For example?" Khrushchev said.

"You could recall more ships back to Europe," Grigulevich said. "You could endorse the pope's plea when he broadcasts it tomorrow on Vatican Radio. You could write a second letter."

"Reasonable," Khrushchev said. "What's the catch?"

"What do you mean?" Grigulevich said.

"You are with Volkhov and the neo-Stalinists, hardly friends of mine."

"I was with them until I went to Rome. I have a new mission. I'm to help you stay in power for as long as possible, work to bolster Gorbachev as your next-generation successor, and finally support the revival of Christianity."

Khrushchev scratched his bald head. He knew Grigulevich was a murderer. He didn't think a brief sojourn to Rome would have changed him.

"What happened to you in Rome?" Khrushchev asked.

"I don't blame you for being skeptical," Grigulevich said, "but look at the results. The pope and Miller were slated to be killed, yet both are living.

"I will give you sound advice to outsmart the neo-Stalinists. I only ask that you not betray me to the Kobaists. After this crisis passes, I will use my position in the KGB to ease you into a soft retirement."

"I think you met Miller in Rome, which raises my opinion of you.," Khrushchev said. "I will think about what you have advised. I will be watching and checking up on you. Keep in touch."

§

ONCE GRIGULEVICH HAD departed, Khrushchev called Miller. It was late afternoon on October 24.

"Good afternoon, General Secretary," Kelly said. "Thank you for endorsing the pope's draft of a peace plea."

"It's good, but I called for a different reason," Khrushchev said. "Grigulevich came to see me. He seems to be a different person. What happened in Rome?"

Kelly told him Grigulevich revealed a KGB plot to assassinate the pope and Miller, enabling the local authorities to stop it. He filled the Soviet leader in on what had happened to the sniper and the four KGB agents.

Khrushchev said he was pleased by the failure of the assassination attempts but surprised by Grigulevich's conversion. "He confessed to you?" Khrushchev asked.

"To me and others," Kelly said.

"Why?"

Kelly said he didn't know why Grigulevich turned but maybe he realized the insanity of nuclear war and the inanity of murdering the pope.

"Do you think he's trustworthy?"

"He moves with the changing wind," Kelly said, "but I think he'll support you in the short term, and he was helpful in Rome."

"I'll watch for an agenda," Khrushchev said, "but if it's a real change, it would mean that I have a critical ally in the Kobaist camp."

Khrushchev then changed subjects. He told Kelly he was sending, under pressure from the Kobaists, a confrontational letter to JFK. He also said Washington must allow the Soviet-leased oil tanker *Bucharest*, which carried no armaments, to pass through the US Navy quarantine and proceed to Cuba. It would prove to the military that he was a skillful leader, willing to challenge the quarantine with a nuanced assertion of the Soviet Union's right to freely navigate the high seas while simultaneously denying the US a legitimate reason to block the ship. It would also signal him that JFK understood the sensitivity of his position.

Kelly warned him that pushing the US was not a good idea. Khrushchev said that it was necessary to keep the military with him but that he would follow with concessions.

Kelly said Kennedy was under maximum pressure to remove the missiles immediately. There was neither time nor leeway for posturing. But if Khrushchev balanced the tough approach with concessions, there might be a way out of the crisis. In a tight voice, he told Khrushchev that he would convey his mixed message to the American government. But Khrushchev should not delay taking positive steps.

Khrushchev thanked Kelly and said he appreciated his playing the referee role. Then he said, "Miller, I need you in Moscow."

The Sheriff tensed. He didn't reply to Khrushchev's plea at first. He'd be in danger in Moscow without a backup plan. "Why?"

"Volkhov is up to something, and I'm not sure about Grigulevich," Khrushchev said. "If you were here, I'd have a credible line of communication to Washington to prevent missteps and unintended consequences."

Khrushchev was right. "The ambassador's jet returns to Moscow tomorrow morning. I'll be on it."

Khrushchev told him to go to Monino airbase east of Moscow instead of landing at Sheremetyevo. He said Monino functioned mainly as a museum, but it had a usable runway. He gave him the radio number of the Western Military District and told Kelly to radio the commander it if he had any trouble at Monino. Troops from his elite security regiment would meet the plane and slip him into the Kremlin without the KGB's knowledge, but he underestimated Volkhov.

Chapter 24
A Solution

Moscow, October 25–26, 1962

AFTER KELLY HUNG up the phone, he told the Posse he was going to Moscow in the morning. Khrushchev had asked him to come to make sure there were no mistakes. Margo wanted him to stay in Rome and work with the Soviet leader by telephone. He told her that Khrushchev needed help to contain the growing Volkhov problem. She wanted a backup, but there was no time. He told her he'd be careful and work from the safety of Spaso House, where US marines offered protection, and Khrushchev's Kremlin office, where the Red Army would provide security.

He told the Posse he'd do what he could from Moscow to keep Khrushchev on track to resolve the crisis, but he counted on them to manage the moving parts of the Cuban missile crisis. Any accident could trigger nuclear war. He told them that everyone believed that the doctrine of mutually assured destruction or MAD would prevent such an unwinnable war. The flaw in the MAD doctrine, he said, was that human beings were also irrational. Sometimes visceral emotion blotted out reason.

The Sheriff stressed that the Posse had to be prepared for confusing moves by Khrushchev. They'd need to offer interpretations and insight on what should be overlooked and what was worth pursuing. They had to persuade Washington that it should focus on Khrushchev's positive behavior—which might seem jerky, screwy, or conflicted—rather than public threats emanating from Moscow that were likely driven by Volkhov. At the same time, they had to advise the American government to remain steady and take appropriate, public measures to demonstrate that the US was firm in its demand that the missiles be removed.

Kelly asked the Posse at the US embassy in Rome to maintain a twenty-four-hour watch on events related to the crisis. He wanted them to respond to any development instantaneously. He told them to establish an open channel between the war room in Rome, the situation room in the west wing of the White House, and Khrushchev's office in the Kremlin, where he'd be when he wasn't at Spaso House. He asked Ana and Ed to manage the open channel and Margo to liaise with the Posse around the world.

Before he went to bed, the Sheriff briefed Washington and asked for patience. He told the ExCom that Volkhov was pushing Khrushchev to challenge the Americans because he wanted confrontation. Khrushchev would have to appease the hardliners to maintain the perception of Soviet strength, but he would simultaneously indicate a willingness to compromise. Kelly was worried about the letter that Khrushchev was sending to JFK but reiterated his firm belief that Khrushchev wanted to end the crisis. He'd be in Moscow the next day and didn't know what Volkhov had up his sleeve, but he was worried.

§

THE NEXT MORNING as the Lockheed JetStar made its approach to Moscow, Fill told Kelly that air traffic control said the Monino runway was closed for repairs and he had to land at Sheremetyevo. Kelly sensed that Volkhov was responsible. He knew he was in danger. He told Fill to radio the Russian military commander and explain the problem. The commander told him to follow the directive of the air traffic controller and land at Moscow's main airport but then remain on the plane until the soldiers arrived to escort them to the Kremlin.

Once the plane landed, Kelly borrowed Fill's personal British S-Radio Phone, which had a range of up to thirty miles and called Khrushchev on his private line.. The Soviet leader told him he had just found out from military intelligence that Volkhov had an agent watching the ambassador's plane in Italy and knew he was coming. He said Volkhov had ordered the KGB to land the plane at Sheremetyevo and to bring Miller to his office.

Khrushchev's voice was grave. "He planned not only to prevent you from reaching the Kremlin, but to personally beat the daylights out of you and then throw your body parts into the Moscow River." The Soviet leader reinforced what the military commander had said—remain at the airport. He'd have soldiers there in twenty minutes to escort him to the Kremlin. "Stay put, Miller. Troops are on the way."

Kelly and Fill planned to stay on the plane to await Khrushchev's troops, but Soviet airport officials demanded they get off and go through customs and immigration. Kelly passed through customs and immigration without incident. Fill was suspiciously delayed. Kelly again saw Volkhov's hand. Then two MVD soldiers from the KGB's military wing started to walk toward him. They were less than 200 feet away.

He couldn't wait for Fill or Khrushchev's soldiers. He was on his own. He left the terminal and jumped in a taxi. A light snow had fallen but had melted into rivulets of brownish slush. He told the driver to take him to the Kremlin. Said he'd give him $100 if he could get there quickly without using the main highways and without stopping at any police checkpoints.

The driver looked at him suspiciously. "Why avoid the police?"

"Because they want to kill me," Kelly said. Kelly heard the driver openly debate his options: "Guards with guns but no money. Or a passenger with no guns but $100 and perhaps more."

Kelly smiled. "Okay, my friend. Hurry but don't attract the police, and you'll earn $200."

The taxi driver took off. He stayed away from the main roads where police cars had gathered and went into villages and small towns, sometimes taking single-lane streets and dirt roads. He was a superb driver. He boasted that he'd driven a T-34 tank in the Great Patriotic War. He had large-tread snow tires and bolt-on equipment on his engine to increase horsepower.

As the taxi drew closer to Moscow, the traffic became heavy. In a suburb, when the driver stopped at a crosswalk in a school zone, Kelly saw two police cars approach, one from the north and the other from the west. Other police were coming at the car on foot. Suddenly, the police seemed to be everywhere. There was no hope for escape.

The taxi driver, however, was undaunted. He turned east, away from the police cars and floored the accelerator, which spooked the police on foot. The engine of the car sounded like it exploded, and the car took off. Gunshots rang out and hit the trunk but didn't slow it. Dead ahead was a wide but shallow river, a tributary of the Moscow. Kelly knew Moscow well from when he lived there researching his dissertation. He said there was a bridge four miles to the south. Then he saw police cars head that way.

"I can beat them to the bridge," the driver said. "But if they started shooting again—"

Kelly encouraged him to go for the bridge. There didn't seem to be any alternative. A bullet whizzed by Kelly's head and pierced the front windshield without shattering it.

The driver told Kelly he didn't think he could make the bridge. He slammed on the brakes. Escape again seemed hopeless. Kelly remembered a low-water crossing that wagons used in a small village to the north. He doubted the city police knew of it. The driver swung the car north. The police kept to the south, apparently thinking the taxi's maneuver was a trick to lure them away from the bridge.

The taxi reached the village, crossed the low-water bridge, and headed south toward Moscow. They never saw another police car. Kelly then told the driver to take him to Lubyanka. The driver protested. That place crawled with police. Kelly told him not to worry and promised him a bonus. Both the Kremlin and Spaso House had KGB guards he could not pass without an army escort, but Volkhov would never expect him at KGB headquarters.

The driver was incredulous but dropped him off thirty minutes later outside Lubyanka. Kelly thanked him with five hundred-dollar bills. "To help pay for car repairs."

"I could buy a new used car with that!" The driver sped away grinning.

Kelly walked into the sacristy of St. Louis Church and called Khrushchev. The Kremlin leader was pleased that Miller was safe and sent an army patrol to fetch him. Fifteen minutes later, the Sheriff shook hands with Khrushchev in his office.

§

KELLY SAT ACROSS from Khrushchev, who was seated behind his desk. The Russian leader's forehead glistened with sweat despite the cold breeze from an open window near his desk. It was afternoon on October 25.

"A gift from my grandson," Khrushchev said, pointing to a large pinecone on his desk.

Kelly smiled. He liked Khrushchev's warmth and humanity. "You keep the office cold, but you have a sunny heart."

Khrushchev leaned forward and told "Miller" he was sorry about his harrowing experience to get to the Kremlin.

The Sheriff dismissed the ordeal with a shrug. He was more concerned about Cuba. In his right hand he held a TASS press release reporting that Khrushchev and Kennedy had endorsed the pope's plea for peace after its broadcast that very morning. In his left hand, he had a copy of the confrontational letter that Khrushchev had sent to

Kennedy and a Reuters report that claimed Khrushchev had told an American businessman visiting Moscow that the Soviet navy would attack the quarantine if the US Navy interfered with Soviet ships.

Kelly fastened his eyes on Khrushchev. He told the Soviet leader that he'd agreed to play referee but needed more evidence of a stepdown from confrontation.

"It's a way to a solution," Khrushchev said in a raspy voice. "One step forward, then two steps back. You must explain the dance to Washington."

Kelly said he was there to help but the steps had to be visible and logical. He asked for a secure line and said he wanted Khrushchev to listen in.

Kelly called the Department of State and asked for Secretary David Dean Rusk. The name signaled Dean Rusk that Khrushchev was listening. He informed the secretary that Volkhov was behind the threatening letter and that JFK should not respond to it. It was bait. He strongly advised the secretary to allow the *Bucharest* to pass through the US quarantine. He also said to pay no attention to the Kremlin leader's threats to an American businessman. Khrushchev was just strutting for his military supporters.

The secretary told Kelly that the president would not take the bait, cared not at all what Khrushchev said to a businessman, and was working on the *Bucharest* issue but wanted the missiles removed. Accordingly, he said JFK had ordered Adlai Stevenson to present photographic evidence of Soviet missiles in Cuba at the UN, deliver a tongue-lashing to Soviet UN representative Valerian Zorin, and reject UN Secretary General U Thant's call for a cooling-off period. The secretary also informed him that JFK had ordered plans to invade Cuba, to intensify the campaign to force Soviet submarines to surface and be identified, and to rally world opinion behind the US.

When Kelly hung up, Khrushchev's lips were thin and firm. Kelly told him to relax and explained that JFK aimed to resolve the crisis peacefully but had to maintain an uncompromisingly hard position. Khrushchev said he needed time to think. They agreed to meet again the next morning.

Kelly left the Kremlin and went to Spaso House for dinner and sleep. Red Army troops accompanied him and provided security. At Spaso House, he talked about Khrushchev's meandering letter with the ambassador and then called Margo. He told her that it looked like Khrushchev and Kennedy were on a path toward a peaceful resolution. She said she was happy that the crisis seemed to be heading toward a resolution, but a zany idea about the submarines had come to her in a dream. It might be frivolous, she said, but the more she thought about it, the more it appealed to her. Kelly asked her about the idea.

During World War II Julia Child, who worked for the Office of Strategic Services, had devised a way to keep sharks away from submerged explosives and mines. Their curiosity frequently ended up detonating the explosives and killing the sharks. Julia had developed a shark-repellent substance for the US Navy. Margo's plan was to reverse Julia's idea. She had conceived of a shark lure— immersible, elastic nets composed of multiple, long strings of shiny, magnetic trinkets that looked like fish scales—to be attached to the metal hulls of the submarines by US destroyers hovering above slow-moving or buoyantly stationary Soviet subs.

She thought the sub crews would at least be annoyed at being swarmed by sharks, and the irritation might make them surface. He told her he'd relay the idea to Washington.

On the morning of October 26 Kelly was back at the Kremlin. Khrushchev greeted him with hot coffee, scrambled eggs, pork sausage, and sweet rolls. They ate together around Khrushchev's desk. The Soviet leader beamed. Kelly sensed that he had taken positive steps overnight.

After breakfast, Khrushchev showed him a copy of *Pravda*, which had published the pope's plea. Kelly smiled. "This is wonderful,

General Secretary. It's a strong indication that you want peace. It's also a resounding defeat for Volkhov."

"That's not all," Khrushchev said. "I also recalled more Soviet ships and sent JFK a second letter last night." He handed it to Kelly, who had already been briefed on it and on JFK's response at Spaso House.

Kelly read it in silence as if he had not seen it. It was full of meandering thoughts and non sequiturs, but embedded in the maze was a concrete offer: the missiles would be removed in return for a guarantee that the US would not invade Cuba. Kelly emphasized the central message that was of supreme importance to the American government. "You made a concrete offer."

"Yes," Khrushchev said, "and I had Alexander Fromin from the Soviet embassy in Washington repeat and reinforce the proposal in an interview with John Scali, an ABC correspondent. I want the American people to know that I'm a peacemaker."

Kelly lauded him. Then he brought up JFK's supporting and reciprocal moves. "President Kennedy allowed the *Bucharest* to sail on to Cuba after it was determined that it held no military contraband. In addition, I saw a cable at Spaso House that signaled he is interested in your second letter, which I just read."

"Da," Khrushchev said enthusiastically. "He has accepted my proposal of a quid pro quo solution—missile removal in exchange for a no invasion guarantee."

Kelly reinforced the solution with praise. "I think you and Kennedy are statesmen of the first order and will go down in history as true leaders."

Khrushchev beamed. "Thank you, Miller." Kelly stood up and so did Khrushchev. They embraced. "I think we'll get out of this mess with our lives and dignity restored," Khrushchev said. He walked Kelly to the door and told the army guards to escort him to Spaso House.

The Sheriff thought it looked like clear sailing ahead. He nearly forgot about Volkhov, who still had the means to disrupt the delicate dance between Kennedy and Khrushchev. Volkhov wanted a nuclear catastrophe.

Chapter 25
Volkhov's Two Reprisals

Moscow, October 27–28

VOLKHOV FUMED OVER the publication of the pope's plea in *Pravda*, the central news organ of the Soviet Communist Party, with its blaring headline: "We beg all governments not to remain deaf to this cry of humanity." He also seethed over the recalling of Soviet ships and Khrushchev's second, concessionary letter. He was beside himself with anger that Miller was in Moscow, advising Khrushchev. He decided to wreck the peace train. The wind scattered snow flurries against the window of his office. It was early afternoon on October 27.

The acting director of the KGB sat in his office at Lubyanka staring at the pope's plea on the front page of *Pravda*.

Grigulevich perched in front of him on the torture chair. His long hair was combed back. The faint shadow of a beard outlined his jaw.

"Khrushchev thinks he's outfoxing me," Volkhov said. "I will teach that Ukrainian interloper not to toy with me."

"He's a Russian, just born in Ukraine." Grigulevich shifted his weight and smirked.

Volkhov bit his lip and gave his subordinate a sharp look. "I don't care what he is. And watch your step."

"I apologize." Grigulevich looked remorseful. "But I thought you wanted to be exact."

Volkhov stared at Grigulevich. "Stop annoying me. We cannot allow this crisis to die. It's our chance to push the revolution or get rid of Khrushchev. He's playing footsie with Kennedy and the pope. We're going to give them a hot foot!"

"What do you have in mind?" Grigulevich said.

"I ordered the agents in one of the SAM batteries in Cuba to shoot down an American U-2, no matter what Khrushchev does or says. That should stop the bonhomie and lead to a strong American reaction. Then we will be in the thick of it."

"Are you going to inform Khrushchev?" Grigulevich said.

"Nyet," Volkhov said. "Let him find out when everyone else gets the news." Volkhov looked at his watch and smiled. "It has already happened."

§

THE SHERIFF STARED without focus at the library in Spaso House. A Soviet SAM battery had shot down a U2, killing the pilot and destroying the plane. The Cuban missile crisis was spiraling out of control. Global news outlets reported President Kennedy's words: "We are now in an entirely new ball game." Assistant Secretary of Defense Paul Nitze added, "They've fired the first shot." Radio and television stations broadcasted that US military leaders were pushing for a massive retaliatory attack on Cuba and that Castro had urged the Soviet Union to move forward with a missile strike on the US. The world held its collective breath, waiting to see Kennedy's reaction. October 27, dubbed Black Saturday, opened the door to hell.

Kelly telephoned Khrushchev. In a nervous voice, the Soviet leader claimed he didn't order the attack and pleaded with Kelly to come to his office.

He then called the White House. The president's chief of staff picked up the phone. Kelly told him he doubted Khrushchev had ordered the downing of the U2. He thought it was an accident or a push by the hardliners in the Soviet government.

The chief said JFK was on the phone with the widow of the pilot, Major Rudolf Anderson. He asked him to hold the line because the president wanted to talk to him.

Kelly held the phone receiver tightly. Beads of sweat appeared on his forehead. Ten minutes passed.

"What's going on?" JFK said, as he came on the line.

Kelly knew his answer could stop or start a nuclear war. "Khrushchev maintains he didn't order the strike on the U-2. It was a mistake, or an accident, but it wasn't authorized by the Kremlin."

Kelly heard muffled talking. He pursed his lips and waited.

JFK was on the line again. "I'm giving Khrushchev the benefit of the doubt because of his second letter, but inform him our invasion plans are continuing. Minuteman missiles are on alert, bombers are in the air, U2 reconnaissance flights will continue unabated, and the US Navy will force all Soviet submarines around Cuba to surface and be identified without exception."

The Sheriff told JFK that in his opinion the response was measured and consistent with American security. It didn't clash with Khrushchev's proposal to solve the crisis. Above all, it avoided unintended nuclear war.

Kelly said he hoped there'd be no confrontation between the Soviet subs and the US Navy. Kennedy joined him in that hope and said just before he hung up, "by the way, our naval engineers are going to try Margo's crazy idea." Kelly grinned. He appreciated that JFK's light touch after his litany of forceful steps showed incredible calmness and control. Margo would be pleased. He'd let her know later. His priority now was to help Khrushchev navigate the emergency.

§

VOLKHOV WAITED, PULLING his hair, for an explosive reaction from Kennedy over the downing of the U2. He was perplexed by Kennedy's inaction. Grigulevich sat in front of him on the balanced torture chair. He looked relaxed, which further irritated the acting KGB director. It was mid-afternoon.

"Why isn't the US retaliating over the U2?" Volkhov said.

"I don't think Kennedy wants to go to war." Grigulevich twisted a lock of hair. "He has responded to Khrushchev's proposal to remove the missiles in return for an American pledge not to invade Cuba. He's waiting for Khrushchev to confirm his offer."

Volkhov was flummoxed. "Kennedy's weak, but our roly-poly leader is weaker."

"Perhaps," Grigulevich said, "but both have gone to the brink, looked into the abyss, and pulled back."

Volkhov's eyes bulged. "It's no time to retreat. It's time to squeeze till they squeal."

Grigulevich took a deep breath and let out a sigh. "What are you contemplating?"

Volkhov's eyes were fixed on the steel bars of the window. He turned and looked at Grigulevich. He smiled and pulled out a sheet of stained, smelly paper, scribbling a note. "Take this to Khrushchev and tell him to send it pronto!"

"It stinks. It's disrespectful."

"I don't respect him. He's weak. We must push the revolution."

Grigulevich shrugged.

Volkhov told him the note demanded that the US remove its missiles from Turkey. The Americans had insisted on no reciprocal concessions for removing the missiles from Cuba. This letter would force them to either reject the demand, which would upset the Red Army leadership, or comply, which would be a victory for the USSR. In either case, he said with a wry smile, the pressure intensifies.

Grigulevich asked why Khrushchev would make an additional demand after he had already made his offer for a resolution.

Volkhov said it restored Soviet dignity and was more equivalent.

If Khrushchev refused?

"We will rally the whole Presidium against him. I think we could get the military leaders on board. The Americans are weak. This is our opportunity."

Grigulevich stood up. "Of course I will take him the letter. But it's not enough to block a solution." It produced an explosive reaction.

"I want war!" Volkhov pounded the desk. "Now get the hell out of here."

Grigulevich backed up. "I will take the letter to Khrushchev and urge him to send it right now."

"Do that," Volkhov said sharply. "It's time for the revolution."

Grigulevich left Volkhov in a rage.

§

KHRUSHCHEV RECEIVED GRIGULEVICH warmly. He gestured to the sofa. "Pour yourself a cup of tea and have a seat." The Soviet leader sipped his own cup from an armchair opposite the sofa, gazing at the Soviet hitman. He wanted to trust him, but he was wary.

"I wasn't expecting to see you again so soon. Is there a problem? Miller is on his way."

Grigulevich said the meeting would not take long. He explained that Volkhov had sent him. "It's not good news. Volkhov wants you to send a third note. If you don't, he will call for a vote of the Presidium and some of the military leaders to pressure you to send it."

The Soviet leader glowered. "What does it say?"

Grigulevich passed him a handwritten note. "I'm sorry."

Grigulevich told him it demanded that Kennedy remove Jupiter missiles from Incirlik Air Base in Turkey before the Soviet missiles would be removed from Cuba.

Khrushchev hesitated. He said he had discussed that concession with Miller, and Miller had claimed that JFK would not agree to it. "What do you think?"

Grigulevich told him he didn't see a problem with sending the request. It was clear that the new demand was a way to keep the hardliners at bay. JFK would either disregard it the way he had the first letter, or he might be open to withdrawing missiles from Turkey later. "There's no harm in putting the request out there."

Khrushchev smiled and nodded. "I will send it."

Grigulevich thanked the general secretary for his hospitality. He told him he would be at his service if he needed him. Then he departed. He was glad Miller was in Moscow. He was smart and well connected and was helping solve this crisis. In his pocket he had a telegram from the Soviet embassy in Washington. It confirmed that the picture he had sent to Petrov was Miller, an academic in the DC area who did some consulting work for the State Department. The telegram also reported the sad news that Petrov had died of pneumonia on October 23.

§

KELLY ENTERED KHRUSHCHEV's office about thirty minutes after Grigulevich had left. The Soviet chief shook his hand and offered him tea before they sat down. He said he had a problem.

Kelly sat forward, waiting for the bad news.

"I sent Kennedy a third letter demanding that the US remove its missiles from Turkey."

Kelly rubbed his head with both hands. Would this crisis ever be resolved? The US planned to remove the missiles soon anyway. "Is this pressure from Volkhov?"

Khrushchev nodded. "And from the hardline ideologists and some military leaders."

Kelly grimaced. The Jupiter missiles were not a major issue. They could be removed to help Khrushchev save face, but the deal would have to be private.

Kelly told Khrushchev he'd suggest Washington support the Turkish missile withdrawal providing it was not a simultaneous quid pro quo. It would have to happen later and not be claimed by the USSR as a victory. Most important, Khrushchev must announce publicly his complete withdrawal of the missiles in Cuba in return for a US pledge not to invade.

Khrushchev said that would work. He was ready to move forward.

Kelly locked eyes with the Soviet dictator. "Let's settle it right now. You draft a letter outlining the terms of the resolution of the crisis. I'll review it and if we both approve it, you'll cable it to Kennedy. I'll call Washington, someone of JFK's choosing will visit the Soviet embassy and make the promise about the Turkish missiles. Before I leave your office, you'll send the letter to Kennedy and broadcast it to the world."

Khrushchev nodded. "I want to get off the warpath." He then penned a letter describing the agreement—removal of the missiles for a promise not to invade. He added a separate and private note stipulating that it was his understanding that the US would eventually remove its obsolete missiles from Turkey.

Kelly called the White House and told the chief of staff of the new arrangement. The chief told him to have Khrushchev send the letter and to wait with Khrushchev while he briefed the president. He said he'd call back in two or three hours. Khrushchev would also hear from Soviet Ambassador Anatoly Dobrynin if everything were copacetic.

Three hours later the Soviet ambassador called Khrushchev with the news. It was early morning, October 28, in Moscow. Kennedy's younger brother, Attorney General Robert Kennedy, had met with him at the Soviet embassy in Washington. The younger Kennedy told him that the United States was planning to remove its missiles from Turkey but would not say so publicly. They would do so only after Soviet missiles had been removed from Cuba. And they would put the missiles back in Turkey if the USSR publicized the US action. The US did not want to appear to be gutting the defense and security of NATO or Turkey. It needed time to explain the obsolescence of Jupiter missiles and take other measures to guarantee its commitment to Article 5 of the NATO alliance. He said the NATO states, including Turkey, backed the US position.

Fifteen minutes later the chief of staff called Kelly, still in the Kremlin, and said Kennedy had received Premier Khrushchev's letter, had accepted the deal, and had sent Khrushchev both a confirmation of his acceptance and a thank you note. He added that the President looked to seeing it released to the world.

Later that day, Khrushchev made a formal public statement to Kennedy that the USSR would remove its missiles and bombers from Cuba under UN supervision in return for a US pledge not to invade Cuba. He also sent a private note to Kennedy, stating that he understood that the US would remove its Jupiter missiles from Turkey. With those concessions and understandings, the process to remove the Soviet missiles commenced. The world breathed easier. Kelly thought the crisis was finally over. He thanked the Soviet leader and went to Spaso House to rest and relax. He and Khrushchev failed to understand Volkhov's strength and determination.

Chapter 26
Volkhov's Third Blow

Moscow, October 28, 1962

VOLKHOV'S FRENZIED PACING did nothing to ease his anger. Grigulevich looked on from the torture chair. The room was dank, stuffy. It reeked of body odor and cigarette smoke.

"Why don't Khrushchev and Kennedy fight?" Volkhov cried. "The U-2 and now the Jupiter missiles. No hostilities. A total collapse by our ponderous leader."

Grigulevich scowled.

Volkhov looked for a reason his tactics had failed. "What is Miller doing here?" The man traipsed between Khrushchev's office and Spaso House under the protection of the Red Army.

Grigulevich rubbed his eyes and said he didn't know, but Khrushchev and Kennedy seemed to be using him as some sort of liaison.

Volkhov sat down. He reflected on the sequence of events. Every time he had Khrushchev leveraged, Miller appeared. First in Rome, now in Moscow. He thought the shooting down of the U-2 would lead to war. It didn't. Who could have calmed the roiled waters between Moscow and Washington? Only Miller. Then the problem of missiles in Turkey looked promising for conflict. Again, Miller seemed to solve it.

The KGB leader decided Miller was the problem in his push for war. The American must not be allowed to screw up Volkhov's final plan. As soon as he reached that conclusion, he determined that Miller had to die. Right now, right here. Relying on others to kill Miller had failed. It was up to Volkhov himself.

A plan quickly formed in his mind. He'd send Grigulevich back to Khrushchev to reveal the secret he'd hidden until now. That would overwhelm Khrushchev, ripping open the healing wound of the Cuban crisis. Khrushchev would call Miller for help. Volkhov would intercept Miller, fatally, before he could meet with Khrushchev. The Soviet leader would then be putty in his hands, the revolution back on track.

Volkhov turned to Grigulevich. He didn't share his plan for Miller. He told Grigulevich he had a surefire weapon that would torpedo the peace and guarantee war. He explained it in detail and carefully observed his reaction.

"Very dangerous indeed." Grigulevich's voice wavered.

"I'll worry about that. Tell Khrushchev and watch him squirm."

Grigulevich's stood. "I'll go to Khrushchev and inform him of your plan."

"Do that!" Volkhov laughed. He saw his deputy tremble. He finally had the weapon that would bring on conflict.

Ten minutes after Grigulevich left, Volkhov got into his car and drove to the Kremlin. He thought ten minutes plus driving time of ten minutes was just about enough time for Grigulevich to inform Khrushchev of what was coming, for the Kremlin leader to tell Miller to come to his office immediately, and for him to hide in a janitorial closet outside of Khrushchev's office and wait for Miller to appear. His timing was perfect.

§

GRIGULEVICH LEFT LUBYANKA and drove to Khrushchev's office. It was late afternoon on October 28. Gusts of wind picked up and twirled snowflakes, dropping them into small drifts. The snow made it difficult to see and to navigate traffic, but he focused on reaching Khrushchev, oblivious to the cold. For the first time in his life, he whispered a prayer for the end of warmongering, greed, stupidity, and intolerant ideologies that were divorced from tradition, common sense, and natural law. Before entering Khrushchev's office, he decided to call Miller at Spaso House and tell him to come to the Soviet leader's office quickly because a serious problem had developed. He didn't say what it was but stressed that Khrushchev would want and need him. He hoped his action would persuade Khrushchev that he was trustworthy and, more importantly, prevent a nuclear catastrophe.

"Here again and so soon," Khrushchev said when Grigulevich appeared at his Kremlin office.

Grigulevich smiled. He thanked the Soviet leader for receiving him on such short notice. Khrushchev nodded and told the deputy KGB leader to have a seat in front of his desk. He poured him a cup of hot black tea and handed it to him. Then he sat behind the desk. He already had a cup of tea and picked it up and sipped it.

"What's on your mind?"

Grigulevich grimaced. He didn't touch his tea. He moved to the edge of his chair. "There's something I must tell you. It's extremely serious and dangerous."

Khrushchev looked surprised. He placed his teacup on the desk. "What?"

"Volkhov put four diesel-powered submarines in Cuban waters before the quarantine was imposed," Grigulevich said. "B-4, B-36, B-59, and B-130. Each one is armed with a nuclear-tipped torpedo and the officers are empowered to fire the torpedo if threatened. They are out of communication range and don't know that the crisis has been resolved." He saw Khrushchev's jaw drop.

"Nyet!" Khrushchev shook his head. "How did that happen? Who gave the order?"

"It was a KGB operation that was totally secret," Grigulevich said. "The sub captains were told that their mission was fully approved by you and the Defense Ministry but was so clandestine that there would be no communication between them and the government."

"Who on the submarines decides on whether a nuclear-tipped torpedo will be fired?" Khrushchev asked, his voice sounding shaken.

"Normal protocol is followed, which means the captain and the chief political officer must agree to fire the nuclear weapon. The only check on this arrangement is the chief of staff who oversees the flotilla of four subs and is on B-59. He can veto any decision to launch, providing he can be reached."

"Who is the chief of staff?"

"Commander Vasili Arkhipov," Grigulevich said. "Volkhov thinks Arkhipov will launch the torpedo if the US Navy threatens his subs. In fact, he sent him such an order a little while ago and backed it up by threatening the lives of his wife and children if he fails to comply."

"Volkhov has no authority over the military," Khrushchev said. "I'll have Defense Minister Malinovsky contact Arkhipov and the sub captains and order them not to fire nuclear weapons under any circumstances. The Defense Ministry will place his family in protective custody."

Grigulevich let out his breath.

Khrushchev continued. "I have broken bread with Arkhipov. He came from a peasant family and worked his way to the top on merit. He knows that firing one nuclear torpedo will not only harm the US Navy, but will also destroy his subs. He knows too that the US has massive nuclear weapons and will retaliate. The USSR would be vaporized."

Grigulevich relaxed. The situation was alarming, Khrushchev could handle the crisis. "I hope you can reach Arkhipov before Volkhov does."

"Volkhov is a bedlamite," Khrushchev said. "He's trying to get us into a thermonuclear war. Enough of this death dance. I have already announced the agreement to end the Cuban missile crisis. I will pull out all stops to reach Commander Arkhipov and then I'll deal with Volkhov. I have to call Miller."

Grigulevich smiled. "I thought that you'd want him to know as soon as possible, so I called him before I came to your office. He's on he's way."

"I appreciate that.," Khrushchev said with relief in his voice. "Thank you!"

"What is that noise in the corridor?" Grigulevich said.

§

FOUR RED ARMY soldiers escorted Kelly to the door of Khrushchev's office and departed per their usual routine. He wore a wool-lined raincoat and stood in the corridor for a moment, debating whether to take off his coat. Khrushchev's office was usually cold.

About to knock on the door, Kelly saw Volkhov step into the corridor.

"Miller, come here!" Volkhov said. He held a revolver.

Kelly examined his surroundings. On earlier visits to Khrushchev, he hadn't paid much attention to the corridor. Now he saw that it was dark, with a dreary carpet that stretched its length. The walls held faded pictures of past Soviet leaders murdered by Stalin during the purges who had been rehabilitated by Khrushchev. His best tactic was to distract Volkhov, who was there to kill him.

"Are you here to hang a picture of Stalin?" Kelly said.

Volkhov frowned. "I'll hang a picture of Stalin and hang you right next to it."

"You're a brave man with a gun," Kelly said.

"I'm going to kill you with my bare hands," Volkhov said.

Kelly nodded. He slowly took off his raincoat. "So, it's a fight you want."

"I call it a burial." Volkhov seemed confident but Kelly sensed fear. A fearful man would use the gun. Kelly decided to build up his confidence.

"I'm an academic. You're a skilled fighter who has killed many men with your fists. I'm only here because I have a meeting with Khrushchev. I don't want to fight you."

"You're a coward," Volkhov said. He placed the gun on the floor. "Come, I'll give you an advantage. You strike the first blow. Then I'll whip you into a bloody pulp."

Volkhov stood erect with a confident smirk and no gun. Kelly ran toward Volkhov, catching him by surprise. Volkhov tried to back up but hit the frame of the open door of the closet. Kelly kicked the gun down the corridor and then hit Volkhov hard on the chin. He reeled, backpedaled, and slammed into the wall. He tried to retreat, but Kelly was all over him, giving him no opportunity to regain his balance. Kelly jabbed him left and right. Volkhov staggered but started swinging wildly and charged Kelly.

A right hook stunned Kelly, and he realized that Volkhov was no pushover. He could take a punch and give one in return. Volkhov hit Kelly with three hard blows, and Kelly retaliated with two to Volkhov's midsection and one to his heart. Volkhov kept coming and hit Kelly with a punch that knocked him against the wall, shaking it noisily. Then he tried to knee Kelly in the groin, but Kelly grabbed the knee and flung Volkhov down on his back. He jumped up quickly.

"You are more than a teacher," Volkhov said, breathing heavily. Then he shoved Kelly against the wall and hit him with a solid uppercut. Kelly slipped down, feigning weakness. Volkhov took out a switchblade. Kelly knew what was coming. He spread his legs apart, as if giving up.

His actions made Volkhov reckless. He apparently thought Kelly was exhausted. He stepped forward with a leg between Kelly's outstretched legs and thrust the knife toward Kelly's gut. Kelly twisted his legs and brought Volkhov crashing down, hitting his head with a thud. Volkhov lay there unconscious.

A door opened, and Khrushchev and Grigulevich stood in the corridor. Volkhov didn't move.

Khrushchev strode up to Kelly. "Are you okay, Miller?"

"Yes," Kelly said.

"Where are the soldiers?" the Soviet leader asked.

"They dropped me off and left. I was about to knock on your door when Volkhov appeared. He wanted me out of the way, I think permanently."

"We have a serious problem," Khrushchev said. "It has to be addressed now."

Grigulevich stepped in. "I'll handle Volkhov. It looks like he's fatally hurt."

Kelly didn't think he'd hurt Volkhov mortally, but he had no time to investigate. He wondered at Grigulevich's narrow eyes. Khrushchev stood at the doorway of his office, beckoning Kelly. Kelly picked up his raincoat, saw that Volkhov was still lying on the floor in a small pool of blood, and walked into Khrushchev's office. That's when he learned there was an armed nuclear torpedo aimed at the US Navy.

Chapter 27
Commander Vasili Arkhipov

Moscow and the Caribbean, October 28–29, 1962

KHRUSHCHEV LED KELLY through a door in his office into an adjoining room that was the command-and-control center for Soviet forces around the globe. One wall had huge monitors pinpointing the location of Soviet ships, including submarines in the waters inside the US-imposed quarantine of Cuba. Kelly was surprised. He knew the Russians had such a center, but he'd had no idea it was right next to where he had been meeting the Soviet leader.

The Kremlin chief and the Sheriff sat down behind the technicians who were monitoring the location of Soviet naval ships. Khrushchev rubbed his hands together. He fidgeted in his chair.

Kelly felt a sudden shudder of fear. He had been in a brutal fight, and that was part of the reason for his nervous energy. But most related to the fact that the Soviets had again shifted the goalposts. He'd thought the Cuban missile crisis had been resolved. He sensed that the solution was slipping away. "What's wrong?"

Khrushchev grimaced. He told him about four Soviet submarines near Mariel Bay, Cuba, each carrying a nuclear torpedo with the explosive power of the bomb dropped on Hiroshima. He said Volkhov had directed the sub captains to fire their torpedoes, without any clearance from Moscow, if they felt threatened by the US Navy. The situation was dire because the US Navy was tracking the submarines and demanding that they surface and be identified. To escape the US destroyers, they'd gone deep, out of communication range. "I can't reach them to inform them the crisis is resolved and order them not to fire a torpedo under any circumstance."

Kelly's body went cold with dread, then he ran his hands through his hair. The recklessness. The lack of a unified command. An acting KGB director could secretly order nuclear-armed submarines to Cuba and direct them to fire a nuclear weapon if they decided they were under threat—all without Kremlin oversight. He sat in stunned silence for a moment.

The Sheriff's first inclination was to urge the US government, which had a unified command, to sink the Soviet subs before they could fire the torpedoes. Margo would counsel him to stop, reflect, and check his impatience. But there was no time. One nuclear-tipped torpedo would wipe out a good part of the US Navy—aircraft carriers, cruisers, destroyers, and guided-missile frigates. The Cuban crisis had reached a new, dangerous phase. The world lurched again toward nuclear war.

Kelly asked Khrushchev who commanded the submarine fleet. The Soviet head told him the brigade chief of staff of submarine B-59 was in charge. His name: Commander Captain Vasili Arkhipov. Kelly breathed a sigh of relief and smiled broadly.

§

COMMANDER VASILI ARKHIPOV's four-submarine flotilla had set out from Sayda Bay near Murmansk for Muriel Bay, Cuba, on October 1. His sailors were issued tropical uniforms and anticipated surfacing in warm waters and alighting on the sunny beaches of Cuba.

But the push south was secretive. The submarines stayed submerged except for periodic refueling by Soviet tankers. The officers and sailors had cabin fever by the time they reached the Caribbean on October 23. They wanted to breathe fresh air and exercise, perhaps even anchor at Muriel Bay where they planned to establish a Soviet submarine base.

To Commander Arkhipov's dismay, the US Navy had moved to impose a quarantine around Cuba. The operation included Anti-Submarine Warfare Forces Atlantic, including four aircraft carriers, destroyers, cruisers, missile-guided frigates, and submarines. ASW detection technology, including sonobuoys, magnetic anomaly detection, and spotter planes, had been employed across the seas from Newfoundland to Argentina.

Arkhipov's subs had reached waters inside the quarantine zone before the quarantine was imposed but stayed submerged. He learned on October 24 that the US government had announced a submarine surfacing and identification procedure. It would signal a submarine to surface and identify itself by dropping a few hand grenades on the submerged boat. He didn't like the news.

He craved fresh air, but he stayed submerged. There had been no transmissions between him and the Soviet Ministry of Defense or the Kremlin. He and his fellow submariners had little knowledge of what was happening.

On October 27, life changed. Suddenly, US naval destroyers started intense tracking of three subs in Arkhipov's flotilla, but not his. Arkhipov ordered the subs to disperse, zigzag, and go deep to make tracking more difficult. He ordered the officers to stay in contact with him. He wondered if the intense tracking signaled that war had commenced between the USSR and the US.

He knew the captain and chief political officer on each sub had the power to fire a nuclear torpedo if they agreed that their sub was in jeopardy and had no other recourse. He didn't expect that outcome and assumed, because of the military chain of command, that they would check with him for approval before resorting to a nuclear strike.

A game of cat and mouse played out on October 27. The Soviet submarines turned, twisted, and went deep to avoid American trackers. The American destroyers, however, were persistent and able to lock onto the submarines with tracking devices. They periodically dropped practice depth charges the size of hand grenades. They didn't damage the sub but were more like a knock on the door asking it to surface and identify itself. The sub officers refused and continued to try to lose the American trackers.

Arkhipov's B-59 eluded tracking until late on October 27, when two US destroyers contacted it. One of the destroyers dropped five practice depth charges. Arkhipov decided to go even deeper, cutting him off from his fellow captains and from Moscow. By October 29 the air in the B-59 was stale and the level of carbon dioxide increased. Signaling depth charges indicated that the US Navy was above him and wanted him to surface for purposes of identification. Adding to the disturbance, sharks kept surrounding the sub, occasionally bumping it.

The captain and political officer on B-59 agreed that their sub was in danger from the American pressure and wanted to fire the nuclear torpedo. Commander Arkhipov disagreed.

Over the course of almost two days, the Soviet naval officers argued. During the back and forth, Commander Arkhipov saw fear in the eyes of the sub captain and political officer. He knew he must deescalate the fear before he could reason with them. On October 29, he tried acknowledging and sharing their feelings. "We're justifiably concerned about the American pursuit of B-59. We've been stuck in this confined space for weeks and now we're being harassed to the breaking point."

The captain and political officer nodded vigorously, happy that Arkhipov saw their point of view. "The Americans are forcing us to surrender," the captain said, sitting in the captain's chair near the periscope assembly. "We're likely at war."

The political officer, standing behind the captain, joined in. "They're exploding depth charges around us and somehow have persuaded shivers of big sharks to follow us. We must fire the nuclear torpedo or we'll be forced to surrender or die down here."

"I don't think so." Arkhipov shook his head slowly. He tried to create an atmosphere of calm. He went on to say that none of them knew if war had broken out. He doubted it because the US Navy was not trying to damage the sub. It was simply dropping PDCs around the boat. They were annoying but no more harmful than firecrackers. The Americans were signaling the sub to surface and identify itself. "If we were at war," he said, "the US would be trying to sink us, and we'd be bouncing off the walls of our submarine with the explosions."

The commander watched his subordinates. His words reduced the tension in the bridge. He pushed on. "If you listen carefully, our passive sonar is picking up the sound of lively jazz music playing on the deck of a US destroyer. It would never expose itself in such a nonchalant way if we were at war. We'd put a torpedo down its throat. It's further proof that they simply want us to surface and identify ourselves. Nothing more. As for the sharks, I think some inventive mind has dropped a magnetic lure on our sub that attracts them."

Just then he heard static. The sub's radioman brought him a radio message from the US destroyer above the submarine. He read it and smiled.

§

KHRUSHCHEV LOOKED AT Kelly's smiling face, somewhat puzzled. "We must wait until Commander Arkhipov is within communication range. There's nothing to do but pray."

Kelly turned to Khrushchev. "I think my prayers have been answered. The US destroyer hovering over B-29 can reach Arkhipov using very low frequency radio transmissions."

"It's possible if the ship is right above him," Khrushchev said, "but he won't listen to it."

"He will," Kelly said. "I know something about him that will reassure him that the US Navy doesn't intend any harm to him and his ships."

"What?"

"It's not what, but who," Kelly said. "It's Julia Child and the joy of eating great food *together* and enjoying life."

Khrushchev smiled. He knew Arkhipov would respond to that. "How do you know that?"

Kelly grinned. "I read about him in *Soviet Life.*"

Khrushchev nodded. He knew the article. He eyeballed Kelly, with a curious look. "You read widely. Try it and tell him I want to have dinner with him and his family and that his family is protected."

Kelly called the White House, briefed the chief of staff on the problem, and told him the issue might be resolved if the following message were sent on VLF radio by a US destroyer to the commander of Soviet submarine B-59:

> "*Commander Arkhipov, Julia Child once wrote, 'I enjoy cooking with wine. Sometimes I even put it in the food.' Like you, we want peace and have not declared war on you or your country. General Secretary Khrushchev, who is out of communication range, asked us to tell you on his behalf that he wants to break bread again with you and your family, who are under the protective care of the Soviet military. No tricks, just plain surfacing and identification, and you are free to go. The Cuban missile crisis is being resolved and is not a reason for war.*"

§

ARKHIPOV SMILED WHEN he read the radio transmission from the US destroyer. He now was confident that there was no war and no downside to surfacing. He didn't share the communication with his two fellow officers. It was personal and would not make much sense to them. Instead, he proceeded as he had been doing, reducing tension and being reasonable.

One of the officers, who had been softening because of Arkhipov's logical approach to the harassment of the US destroyers, said it'd be shameful to surrender and surface.

"It is not," Arkhipov said evenly. "We're not surrendering, but simply identifying ourselves. On the other hand, if we launch a nuclear weapon, we would be committing suicide and probably condemning the world to a fiery end. Do you enjoy a delicious meal and a fine glass of wine?"

"Yes," the captain and political officer said simultaneously.

"We can agree on that," Arkhipov said. "I, too, enjoy sumptuous food and good wine. If a nuclear torpedo is launched, we will die, never again to taste any savory dishes."

The captain and political officer seemed confused. Arkhipov knew they worried about their reputations but were warming to his approach. He brought his argument home.

"I know you want to do the right thing," Arkhipov said. "We might all be dead tomorrow. Let's live in the moment and give life a chance. If I'm wrong and this is a trick, I will take full responsibility. I will inform headquarters that you wanted to make a stand and that I overruled you. If I'm right, I will not criticize you and will cook a delectable meal that we can all enjoy and celebrate."

With those incentives, the captain and political officer agreed with Arkhipov. The B-59 surfaced on October 29. Captain Arkhipov soon had confirmed that no war had been declared and that his submarines were not in danger. He also received a delayed communication from Volkhov. The Kobaist leader encouraged him to use the nuclear torpedo and implied that his family was in danger if he did not do so. At the same time, he saw teletypes from Field Marshal Malinovsky and Khrushchev, who ordered him and the other sub captains not to fire any torpedo and to return to the USSR. Khrushchev informed him that his family was safe and would remain secure. Armageddon had been avoided.

Commander Arkhipov invited the captain and chief political officer to the officer's dining room, where he used a unique blend of spices to prepare a tasty meal of smoked fish, sausages, cheeses, and chocolates, topped off by a smooth Georgian cognac. He then told them that the meal was only an appetizer and that they and their wives were invited to dinner at his home in Leningrad where he would cook a French meal of vichyssoise, salad niçoise, and boeuf bourguignon, paired with a fine French burgundy. They poured another glass of cognac and toasted their families, life, and Julia Child.

Before sailing for the USSR, Arkhipov had a minor ripple that he had to straighten out on October 30. The chief political officer of the still-submerged and tracked B-130 informed him the sub captain had placed a nuclear-tipped torpedo into a firing tube. The captain was frustrated over his inability to shake the American destroyers and the breakdown of B-130's diesel engine. Arkhipov ordered the captain to remove the torpedo, surface, fix the engine, and sail with the rest of the flotilla of subs back to Murmansk. The captain replied that the torpedo was out before Arkhipov had ordered him to remove it.

"It's already gone. Just a joke to scare the political officer. He fainted."

Arkhipov replied tersely, "Damn the jokes and the torpedoes. Move out."

Chapter 28
The Aftermath

Washington, November 2, 1962

A CARROT-COLORED LINE appeared across the horizon. The sun was rising, piercing a lowering sky of gray and purple clouds. It had looked like snow might fall, but the scattering clouds revealed a clear, blue-sky day.

Kelly stood with Khrushchev on the tarmac of Sheremetyevo airport. Khrushchev thanked him for his help in winding down the Cuban missile crisis. He added that Volkhov was in critical condition in the hospital and that Grigulevich had turned into an important ally as he continued with his reform policies. And the Soviet chief was planning dinner for Captain Arkhipov and his family, using recipes from Julia Child's cookbook.

Kelly told Khrushchev he'd stay in touch. The two men shook hands and said goodbye.

In Rome, Kelly joined the American Posse members on a US Air Force flight to Washington. They landed late on November 2. They stayed that evening at the Cloister and enjoyed a fabulous meal of moussaka with feta cheese, Greek salad, and baklava that Margo, Ana, and Bone had prepared. They slept soundly. The next day they gave after-action reports to the State Department, the National Security Agency, CIA, Defense Department, and ExCom.

Late on the morning of November 3, Kelly walked to the White House from the State Department. The wind scattered orange, red, and brown leaves along the sidewall. The flute-like song of a red and brown coated wood thrush relaxed Kelly. He was glad to be back in the United States, but he was concerned about the American experiment in democracy. His time abroad and during the Cuban missile crisis had reminded him that freedom and democracy were precious and rare and under constant threat by autocrats, barbarians, and people who had lost touch with or were ignorant of the roots of the American order.

JFK had invited Kelly to come to the Oval Office to get the US top spy's perspective on what had transpired. When Kelly was ushered into the Oval Office by a secretary, he saw JFK sitting in a comfortable rocking chair near his desk. He wore glasses and had a cup of green tea.

The president invited Kelly to pull up a chair. Kelly took a cold glass of water and sat down on a black leather armchair near a small coffee table. JFK looked at him and smiled.

Kelly caught the mood and grinned back. They both were happy that the crisis had been resolved with diplomacy, intelligence, and luck. Kennedy asked the Sheriff for his take on the significance of the near catastrophe and his recommendations going forward.

"Yikes," Kelly sighed. The thought of summing up the crisis was daunting.

Kennedy gently laughed. He said he had confidence in Kelly because of his experience and broad perspective drawn from history.

Kelly thanked Kennedy and said he had two recommendations. He advised that the US and Soviet governments set up a hot line to avoid misunderstandings and to prevent accidents from getting out of hand.

Kennedy sipped his tea. "A very good idea. ExCom and I had discussed that very idea. I think the Soviets would be open to it. We'll establish a red phone system that will allow for instant communication between Washington and Moscow."

Kelly gestured with his head. He then told JFK about the pope's idea. Pope John XXIII wondered about limiting the testing of nuclear weapons."

Kennedy put down his tea on the desk. "Another brilliant suggestion. We will work to complete a nuclear test ban treaty. Khrushchev mentioned it in his note of October 28, so he's on board."

Kennedy sat back in his chair. His dog noticed and moved closer to Kennedy to be petted. Kelly waited. JFK seemed to have something more to say. Eventually he said the pope had played a very positive role in defusing the crisis.

Kelly nodded. He said he had heard Pope John XXIII was on the short list of nominees for *Time* magazine's man of the year and had been nominated for the Balzan peace prize. He added that Khrushchev had showed his appreciation of the pope's effort by moving Ukrainian Catholic Archbishop Josyf Slipyj from prison to house arrest.

Kennedy smiled. If Pope John was given the *Time* honor, he'd be the first pope to win it. He added he was enormously pleased to hear about Archbishop Slipyj. He was a good man who symbolized Ukraine's Western values.

Kelly sipped his water. "If the Ukrainian or Russian democrats ruled, rather than the dictators, we'd be well on our way to a world order that respected the rule of law, human rights, and representative government."

Kennedy nodded. "What about Khrushchev's position?"

Kelly said the Cuban missile crisis was a major defeat for the Soviet Union and the world communist movement. Khrushchev would be held personally responsible. He'd be replaced before long, probably when Beijing obtained nuclear weapons.

"Do you know Gorbachev?" Kennedy said.

"I know of him," Kelly said. "He's a reformer and competent. But communism needs to be jettisoned, not reformed. If Gorbachev comes to power, he'll have to overcome not only its ideological fallacies, but also the police hardliners who want to keep power. The transition would pit Russia's authoritarian tradition, which the security police tap into, against Judeo-Christian values, which work against dictators and autocrats."

Kennedy wanted to know Kelly's perspective on the big geopolitical picture.

Kelly sipped his water again. He said the Cuban missile crisis showed communism's weakness as a development model and the Soviet Union's incoherence as a multinational empire that had no roots. But it had nuclear weapons and leaders with no moral compass. They would lie, steal, murder, and incite war without blinking an eye, simply to retain power and wealth. The USSR was not a happy place. In the end, Kelly predicted that the Soviet Union would collapse. It was, he said, the new sick man of Europe, a role that the Ottoman Empire had played in the nineteenth century before it imploded.

Kennedy took off his glasses. "Is there anything else?" he asked.

Kelly looked directly at JFK. "Mr. President, the KGB has been embarrassed and will seek vengeance. It is a state-sponsored organized crime syndicate with ties to the Russian mafia and organized crime families in Asia, Europe, and the US. Leaders of the democracies must be careful. Our leaders must increase their security details. The FBI should run thorough background checks and keep tabs on any replacements or additions to the Soviet embassy and consulates in the US. Also on any Americans who defect to the Soviet Union and return to the US. And I'd urge you not to publicize your itineraries or routes for public appearances."

"That's impossible." Kennedy shook his head. "My job is to be in public. But I get what you're saying. I'll be careful." He checked his watch.

Kelly realized the meeting was over. He stood. Kelly admired JFK's maturity, wisdom, and calmness in resolving the Cuban missile crisis and told him so.

Kennedy thanked him for his insights and service, escorted him to the door, and said goodbye.

Kelly left the Oval Office with a heavy heart. The hardliners in the USSR had been severely wounded but would not be deterred from pushing authoritarianism. He worried about the stability of the US if the hardliners should try to bait the US again in other parts of the world.

Chapter 29
The Posse Celebrates

San Marcos, Texas, November 20, 1962

ON NOVEMBER 20, Kelly and Margo sat at the breakfast table in their home in San Marcos listening to the radio. The window to the patio was open, allowing fresh air to permeate the breakfast nook.

An announcer interrupted the regular programming and President Kennedy came on the air. He announced that UN inspectors reported that the Soviets had removed all missiles, nuclear warheads, and bombers from Cuba and had returned the offensive weapons to the USSR. The US Air Force had confirmed the UN report. Kennedy also reported that the US had lifted its naval quarantine of Cuba. The Cuban missile crisis was over. Kelly and Margo turned on the television to watch the world celebrate.

Kelly was grateful too, but the authoritarian government that had pushed the world to the edge of mutual destruction still held power.

Late that afternoon, the Sheriff, Posse members in Central Texas, and Meg and Jesse headed to Las Guitarras Cocina Mexicana in Boerne. The larger struggle between authoritarian and democratic orders was not over, but they wanted to celebrate winning a battle.

When they reached Las Guitarras, white-throated sparrows and yellow warblers greeted them with a sweet song of high-note whistles. Sweet autumn clematis with waxy white flowers, stock flowers, and pansies with their colorful faces scented the air from curvy flower beds and flower boxes attached to the building. It was warm, and the late afternoon sun backlit the oak trees, blue agave, and bluestem grass near the restaurant. A small stream that fed into Cibolo Creek, which flowed into Boerne City Lake Park, gurgled.

The group entered the restaurant and sat in a private room at a varnished, rough-hewn red cedar table. White carnations and early blooming Christmas cacti filled the room with sweet scents and radiant color. A mariachi band could be heard softly playing "La Adelita" in the main dining room. Fernando, the owner and head chef, rolled a cart tableside: cold beer and soft drinks, carafes of red and white wine, margaritas, and pitchers of iced tea and water. He knew what the Posse liked after a successful mission.

Soon the table was covered with platters of Margo-endorsed fajitas, chalupas, and blackened corn; bowls of charro beans and chile con queso, and piles of cilantro, sour cream, guacamole, tomatoes, salsa, and tortilla chips. Fernando's famous Chile rellenos with his uniquely seasoned roasted poblano peppers followed. The fresh, spicy smell of homemade Mexican food made the air dance. Knives, forks, and napkins were in a big bucket at both ends of the table. Everyone dug in with gusto.

The Posse had played a key role in getting the missiles out of Cuba. Kelly read aloud a special note of gratitude to the Posse from President Kennedy, and then a note of thanks to "Miller" from General Secretary Khrushchev. The Soviet leader recounted that he had hosted Grigulevich and Commander Captain Arkhipov and their wives at his dacha, and that MasterChef Arkhipov had prepared a sumptuous French meal in the best tradition of Julia Child. He wrote that Grigulevich looked like an Orthodox monk except for the bun that he sported. He sent greetings to Jesse and Meg Byrnes. He also mentioned that Catholic Ukrainian Archbishop Josyf Slypyj would be sent to live in Rome in a few months. Finally, he noted that Volkhov had died of a head injury. Kelly added a footnote. He said that the FBI had turned a Soviet sleeper agent in Dallas into a double agent.

The Posse erupted in wild applause. The Sheriff thanked the Posse for its work. He asked them to take a deep breath and unwind by describing something, even if it seemed frivolous, that gave them hope.

Margo started. "Food played a central role in the successful resolution of the crisis."

Everyone laughed but agreed. They appreciated how food shaped life and happiness. They knew of her role in developing the shark lure, feeding the Posse, and sharing Arkhipov's appreciation of life and food.

Bone followed up: "I hear from Russian sources that some Cuban soldiers are still searching the woods around San Cristóbal for 'El Toro' to get his autograph."

Ed said he thought Bone could be elected president of Cuba if free elections were ever restored. Everyone smiled.

The Warbler put in a word for music. She said it was a unifying force that could breach the Iron Curtain, bring people together, and change lived. The group nodded. They knew her melodious voice had helped put Grigulevich in touch with his spiritual roots.

Ana said the crisis had showed that there should be more women in the top posts of government, the churches, and the military-industrial complex. In her opinion, women were more balanced, tolerant, patient, nurturing, and inclusive than men. Margo and the Warbler readily agreed, and the men didn't disagree.

On another note, Ana thought that some members of the Catholic clergy might be catalysts of change in communist East Europe. She mentioned the bishop of Cracow, Karol Wojtyla, whom she said was so inspiring that he might singlehandedly bring down the Iron Curtain.

Jesse said he agreed with his mother and saw signs of positive change in Soviet satellites, including Mongolia. He thought that the youth in the western part of the USSR and in communist East Europe would topple the Berlin Wall and lead the resistance movement against communism.

Axelrod said that the buds of change were sprouting across Soviet Russia, but that there was still overwhelming support for authoritarianism. He was not enthusiastic about the Russian Orthodox Church. Some of its leaders had become a branch of the communist regime. On the other hand, he was high on Soviet dissidents who pointed out the injustice and inanity of the communist system. He had high praise for Alexander Solzhenitsyn, the novelist, and Andrei Sakharov, the Soviet physicist.

Ed added that he thought the Sino-Soviet feud had intensified and would likely impact the communist movement across Asia. He said communism had splintered in Vietnam, Cambodia, and Indonesia, and nationalism had grown.

Meg reported she had heard from Batu Khulan's kids that Putin and Bobkin had moved up in the KGB in Leningrad. They'd replaced Oleg Smirnov and Sergei Brodsky, who were in a labor camp in Siberia, and now reported to Grigulevich, who had given Bobkin the additional job of improving Orthodox-Catholic relations. The Posse broke out in boisterous laughter and applause.

Kelly had the final word. He said that the US had been lucky to have Kennedy at the helm. His leadership and calm in the face of grave threats, particularly after the U-2 was shot down, was brilliant and awe-inspiring. He thought that with anyone else in the White House, nuclear war would have likely broken out. He also praised Pope John XXIII but reported that he was in failing health. Finally, he lauded IRONBARK. "He gave up his freedom and likely his life to save lives." There was a moment of silence and then a prayer of thanksgiving for the Russian's courage and fortitude.

The Sheriff, the Posse, and Jesse and Meg left Casey's with a renewed hope for a democratic world. But Kelly knew the Cuban missile crisis was a Pyrrhic victory. He saw it as a premonition. It revealed that the enemies of constitutional democracy were strong and influential and willing to risk global annihilation to set up dictatorships and overturn the rule of law. The struggle between authoritarianism and ordered democracy not only continued but had reached a new stage where the stakes were clear and rational behavior was no longer a given.

Don't miss out!

Visit the website below and you can sign up to receive emails whenever Dennis J. Dunn publishes a new book. There's no charge and no obligation.

https://books2read.com/r/B-A-ALZBB-QTWRC

BOOKS 2 READ

Connecting independent readers to independent writers.

Did you love *Red Missiles in Cuba*? Then you should read *The Russian Riddle: Stalin's Date With Destiny* by Dennis J. Dunn!

Read more at https://dennisjdunn.com.

Also by Dennis J. Dunn

Posse Series
Red Missiles in Cuba

Watch for more at https://dennisjdunn.com.

About the Author

Dennis J. Dunn graduated from John Carroll University and received a PhD in history from Kent State University. He taught at Texas State University where he was named a Regents and University Distinguished Professor of History. His research interests include books on the Catholic Church in Soviet Russia, American-Soviet relations, and the relationship between politics and religion in the twentieth and twenty-first centuries.. In 2021 he turned to writing historical fiction in the thriller genre, inaugurating the Posse Series with the publication of *The Russian Riddle: Stalin's Deadly Date with Destiny*. It drew upon his deep interest in the history of World War II, the Cold War, the rich Anglo-Hispanic culture of Central Texas, the Catholic Church, and Russia. *Red Missiles in Cuba* is Book 2 in the Posse Series, and it tells the largely overlooked story of the most dangerous time ever in the history of the world when nuclear annihilation was barely avoided. fHe lives in Texas with his family.

Read more at https://dennisjdunn.com.

About the Publisher

Global Connections, Inc. is the imprint under which the author published *Red Missiles in Cuba* and *The Russian Riddle: Stalin's Deadly Date with Destiny*.

Read more at https://dennisjdunn.com.

www.ingramcontent.com/pod-product-compliance
Lightning Source LLC
Chambersburg PA
CBHW022005170626
46808CB00001B/292